SLAP SHOT

LAUDERDALE KNIGHTS, BOOK ONE

KAT MIZERA

Editing: Tera Cuskaden, Anja Pfister

Cover Design: Dar Albert, Wicked Smart Designs

Cover Photographer: Wander Aguilar

Cover Model: Andrew Biernat

❃ Created with Vellum

1

Ninety degrees on the first day of hockey season. It was either a bad omen or going to bring good luck. I just didn't know which, and I took a deep breath as I walked into Baldwin Arena for the first time before a game. I was starting a whole new era of my life, both personally and professionally, and it was stressful.

Okay, maybe stressful wasn't the right word.

It was *different*.

Everything about tonight's game was different, and I wasn't sure how I felt about it. One minute I'd been on vacation; the next I'd been traded to an expansion team in Fort Lauderdale, Florida. It happened so fast I hadn't had time to wrap my head around it, and six weeks later I was getting ready for our first game.

"Hey." Zakk Marcus-Cloutier, one of my teammates, fell into step beside me as we walked through the player parking lot.

"Hey." I looked up. Zakk was a six-foot-seven-inch defenseman from North Dakota who'd been traded from the Las Vegas Sidewinders. He was a veteran in the league and badass on the ice, but I didn't know him that well.

"You ready?" he asked, grinning at me.

"I was," I quipped. "Until I got outside and momentarily forgot it was hockey season because it's like two thousand degrees."

He chuckled. "Yeah, the humidity down here is a shit show. We had warm days like this in Vegas, but the humidity is a game changer."

We stepped inside the building and were immediately assaulted by the frigid air conditioning.

"I will have the pneumonia in this weather." Felix Lessard, a French-Canadian forward, shook his head as he blazed past us, power walking like someone was chasing him. "Hot, cold, hot, cold…" He was still muttering as he disappeared around the corner.

"Is he still bitching about the weather?" Zakk asked, laughing. "I swear, he whined all through training camp."

"He's young," I said, chuckling. "He's probably never lived south of Detroit."

"Probably not."

We grinned at each other as we got into the main hallway that led to the dressing rooms where we would lock up our stuff and change. I put my bag down just as a soccer ball soared past my head. I snaked out a hand, catching it in midair and arched my brows at the two rookies who came skidding in after it.

"Sorry, man." The one who looked like he still didn't have enough facial hair to shave gave me a lopsided grin.

"Soccer in the hallway!" The other one called out, grabbing the ball, and heading out again.

"They're like toddlers," Zakk said as we entered the dressing room. "Wound up like Energizer bunnies until they crash."

"Hopefully that won't be until after the game," I replied, putting my stuff away and sliding on a pair of running shoes. "But for now, let's show them how it's done."

"You got that right." Zakk fist-bumped me, and we wandered into the hallway where a handful of our teammates had already gathered.

"What's up, boys?" Our head coach, Anatoli Petrov, came around the corner in shorts and a Lauderdale Knights T-shirt, apparently prepared to play with us. "Think you can keep up with your coach?" Coach had only been retired from playing two years, so he was in great shape, and I gave him a fist bump as I stood next to him.

"Think we stand a chance?" I whispered to him.

He grimaced. "These kids are fast," he muttered. "But I'm ready."

"As am I."

We all turned to stare at the team's owner, Remington Knight, and for a moment no one moved.

"You, uh, wanna play, Mr. Knight?" The youngest of the rookies, an eighteen-year-old from Philadelphia named Palmer something, nervously met his gaze.

"If you'll have me." Remy grinned and held out a hand. Palmer snapped the ball in his direction. Mr. Knight wasn't what I'd been expecting in a team owner. He was somewhere in his mid to late thirties and had played pro hockey until an on-ice heart attack forced him into retirement. But he seemed completely at ease with an impromptu pre-game soccer warm-up.

"Let's do it!" Coach made his way over to a couple of the younger guys, while Zakk and I stood next to Palmer and Mr. Knight as one of the rookies kicked the ball to Zakk.

Zakk took it down the hall, kicking toward an imaginary goal where another one of our teammates, who'd just arrived, kicked it back down in our direction.

It was a lighthearted and fun but competitive game with both teams trying to best the other with impossible shots between imaginary goal posts, but it was a great warm-up and a good way to ease pre-game nerves. Coach Petrov had done stuff like this all through training camp to help the younger guys feel more at home and to give those of us who didn't know each other a chance to bond.

There was always a learning curve when you got to a new team, but an expansion team meant *everyone* was new. From the arena staff to the coaches to the players and support staff. We were all learning our way around and trying to memorize dozens of names and faces, while simultaneously figuring out a new coaching and playing system. Not to mention earning our places on the team.

At twenty-seven, this was my third pro team, and I felt pretty good about my ability to fit in, both in the locker room and on the ice, but there was still this feeling of newness. All of us had to learn our way around—there were no shortcuts for that kind of thing—and there wasn't really anyone who could show us the ropes because the ropes were brand new.

Coach Petrov had started training camp with a tour of the whole facility and then did a fun scavenger hunt to force us to work together to find our way around. There had been gift certificates and a couple of highly coveted "day off from practice" passes available, so it had been a great way to get used to the arena. And each other.

And now it was opening night.

The first-ever Knights game.

The first game of the season.

The first professional hockey game in South Florida.

· · ·

The excitement coming from the crowd was as infectious as it was loud. I kept my head down as we skated out for the official warm-up, but it was hard to ignore the exhilaration in the building. The guys on the team were all over the place, so I stood off to the side, chatting with Zakk and one of our goalies, Camden Locke. He was starting tonight so our back-up was in net warming up with the guys, leaving the three of us to watch with an almost detached involvement.

"You nervous?" Zakk asked Camden, cocking his head slightly.

He shook his head. "No. Just a little off. New arena, new teammates, lots of different stimuli that make it hard to center myself. I have a routine, and there's no way to stick to it on a night like tonight."

"How many games have you played since they pulled you out of college?" I asked him, squinting.

He met my gaze. "Not counting pre-season? Twelve."

"So tonight will be lucky thirteen." I clapped him on the back. "You got this."

"Damn straight I do." He said the words, but I'd been around long enough to know when someone was faking it. And Locke was one hundred percent faking it right now.

"Parents here?" I asked him, since I knew he was only twenty-two.

He nodded. "Along with all three of my brothers, my grandfather, and my girlfriend."

"You had a date at the mixer?" I asked, referring to the big party Mr. Knight had thrown the night before training camp started so all of us, along with any significant others and kids, could meet.

He shook his head. "No. She's in college. She plays too, and this is hockey season. She couldn't get away."

"What school?" I asked.

"North Dakota."

Zakk arched his brows. "That's where I went. My sister too. They have an amazing program, especially for women."

"She a goalie too?" I asked curiously.

Locke nodded, a smile lighting his face. "Yup."

"I don't think I've ever known two goalies who dated," I said.

"Is she a senior?" Zakk asked.

He nodded, giving us an update on her stats and a few other things we didn't care about, but our tactic had worked because he was a lot more relaxed. Talking about family or girlfriends didn't always have the intended results, but it had this time. Zakk and I exchanged knowing looks as we all filed back into the locker room.

"All right, boys." Coach Petrov came into the room and shut the door behind him. "This is it. We never get another first time like this, so think about it for a few minutes, and then let it go. There's always so much pressure for an expansion team to win the first-ever home game." He rolled his eyes and motioned with his hands impatiently. "Fuck that. Okay? You hear me. This is the one and only game where you will hear me say I don't give a fuck about winning. Tonight is about pageantry. The fans. Our families. Even the fucking city. So for us, this is like glorified practice. Finding how we gel. We've had enough pre-season games for you to know your lines, your linemates, and the routine. But those didn't count, which means it's all new again. Let's call tonight pre-season 2.0." He looked around. "This is also my first coaching job, not counting my daughter's team"—everyone laughed—"but I don't want you to play for me, for the fans, or even for yourselves tonight. I want you to play for the Cup." He smiled as most of the room stared at him in confusion. "That's right. I want you to play like the Cup is on the line—because win or lose, we've come a long way in a short time. There is no shame in losing in the Stanley Cup Final. There just isn't. Only two teams get there, and it takes about a hundred games, give or take, but you can't both win. There's no shame in losing that championship game unless you didn't even try. And there is no shame in losing your first-ever game as the Lauderdale Knights. Combined, you all have thousands, probably tens of thousands, games' worth of experience. Combined, you've played hundreds of other firsts. All I want tonight is camaraderie and effort. Now go do it."

He stood at the door and raised his hand, nodding his head at Cam who would lead the team down the tunnel. Cam high-fived him, and then we all followed suit. They would introduce the starting lineup, which included me and Zakk, and then the rest of the team since it was our first-ever game.

I skated out when they called my name, letting the cheers and flashing lights and all the pomp and circumstance roll off my back. I'd never been comfortable in the spotlight, but it didn't look like I had a choice in Fort Lauderdale. I was probably the most well-known name on the team, other than Coach himself, which meant there were going to be a lot of eyes on me. Hell, during pre-season I'd been the first one reporters wanted to interview. I was going to have to be seriously on guard, all the time, and make sure I watched every word that came out of my mouth. Not to mention keeping a lid on who I was sleeping with, what I did on my days off, etc.

Mr. Knight's brother was the lead singer of one of the biggest rock bands in the world, Onyx Knight, and Kingston Knight had just been introduced to sing the national anthem. We'd met him earlier, and he was a pretty cool guy, laughing and hanging out with us while we ate our pre-game meal, but now he was all business. He took the microphone and, Jesus, the guy could sing. Onyx Knight was a hard rock band with a metal edge, lots of screaming guitars, and pounding basslines, but this was something else. His voice was rich velvet, like a soul singer, with incredible range and a finish that gave me chills.

The crowd was on its feet, screaming and cheering, and then we were off and running.

I looked up into the crowd, searching.

Was my dad here?

I shook it off.

Head in the game, Vaughn, I told myself, skating to the bench.

Head in the fucking game.

2

I glanced at the time on my phone half a dozen times as I waited for traffic to let up. I was beyond excited to be attending the inaugural season opener for the new professional hockey team in my hometown of Ft. Lauderdale. But I'd been late leaving work, and now I was going to miss the warm-up. Two of my brothers, Mario and Tony, who also worked at our family pizzeria, had left early, of course, leaving me to handle all the last-minute details to make sure the staff was ready for the dinner shift.

What else was new?

I loved my big, loud Italian family, but they drove me crazy sometimes.

Traffic finally moved, I found a parking spot and hurried through the lot to the entrance. My family and I had bought four season tickets, and though there were technically nine of us who'd shared the cost, I'd paid a quarter of it myself, so I had a seat at every game if I wanted it. Which I did. I loved hockey and getting a team here in South Florida was the most exciting thing to happen to me in a long time.

Which was kind of sad, but I really did love hockey.

I grabbed a glass of wine and a bag of popcorn and found our seats. My brothers, Mario and Tony, and Tony's wife Desi, were already in the seats and they looked up as I sat down.

"You're late," Desi said, grinning at me.

I sank down. "Apparently, I'm the only one who cares about whether or not the dinner shift is prepared."

Tony turned to me, eyes wide as if he had no idea what I was talking about, but there was a grin playing on his lips. "What'd we forget to do?"

"Oh, I don't know…count out the register from the day shift cashier? Make sure everyone on the schedule showed up so we wouldn't leave them short with no manager on duty. Shit like that?"

Tony just laughed. "That's why we have you. We cook, you do business stuff."

"We were just excited for the first game," Mario added.

"Me too," I said, sipping my wine. Normally, stuff like this didn't bother me, but tonight I was in a terrible mood for some reason.

"But you always take care of this kind of stuff," Tony continued in confusion. "You never like the cooking stuff. Remember when you tried baking cupcakes and selling them? You hated it."

That wasn't true at all, but I didn't want to fight. The reason I hadn't been able to continue with my cupcake business was because the pizzeria took all my time. It had been that way since I was about fifteen. It wasn't always fair, but there was no point in ruining the first Knights game by arguing with my brothers. Especially when it wouldn't change anything.

"Hey, did you have your dress fitting?" Desi asked me, changing the course of the conversation.

Dress fitting?

I took a sip of wine and stared out at the ice, wracking my brain to figure out what she was talking about.

Crap.

The *dress*.

I'd forgotten about the fitting for my wedding dress.

"Juliet?" Desi was looking at me funny.

"They postponed it," I lied, mentally grimacing. How had I forgotten about that?

"Oh, well, then maybe I can go with you when they reschedule," Desi said happily. "I love the dress you picked."

"Thanks." Ironically, I hadn't picked the damn dress; my mother had.

We had to stand for the national anthem, so conversation died and then the game started. I was on my feet immediately, cheering and whistling. Though I'd grown up in South Florida, we still considered ourselves New Yorkers. I'd been ten when we moved here from Long Island, so I remembered Mario and another one of my brothers, Roberto, playing hockey when I was little.

There were six of us kids, all two years apart. I was the only girl and the youngest, which was another reason I was annoyed. Older brothers were supposed to look out for their little sister, not treat her like an afterthought. Especially after we'd lost our father two years ago to cancer. Mario was the oldest at thirty-five, and twice divorced with no kids. Then came Roberto who was thirty-three and married but no kids yet. Anthony, who went by Tony, was thirty-one and had been with Desi since high school. They'd gotten married right after graduation and had three kids. Salvatore was twenty-nine and engaged, and Peter was twenty-seven and as single as ever.

Then there was me. Twenty-five, engaged, and struggling to figure out what I wanted to be when I grew up. The only thing I knew for sure was that I didn't want to work in our family pizzeria for the rest of my life. I was so tired of being questioned about everything I did, but it was just easier not to push back against my family. No matter how much I loved them—and I knew they loved me—it usually felt like it was me against them. In everything.

For now, I lost myself in the game.

This new team, the Lauderdale Knights, had a lot of talent, and I'd been the one to propose we buy season tickets for the family. Everyone had hemmed and hawed but finally decided to go in on them with me. The boys all loved hockey too, but I was the biggest fan, so they were happy to alternate going to a game now and then while I planned to be at every damn one.

During the first intermission, Desi and I escaped to the ladies' room, and she met my eye in the mirror as we washed our hands.

"You okay?" she asked, cocking her head. "Something's off with you tonight."

"Just a little stressed about the wedding," I admitted. "Carlo and I had a fight about the food, and I'm frustrated."

"You fought about the food?" She took a lip pencil out of her bag and lined her lips.

We'd fought about more than the food, but I couldn't tell Desi I'd been thinking about postponing the whole thing. That would cause a shit storm I didn't need right now.

"I want something elegant; he wants the family to cater it. Italian food."

"Well, we're Italian and most of our guests will be too."

"We eat Italian, like, five days a week," I protested. "It's boring."

"Sometimes, but still delicious. Especially when you have to feed three hundred people."

"But doesn't filet mignon and salmon sound exotic and lovely?" I countered. "With wild rice and—"

"Can you picture any of your brothers, except maybe Peter, eating salmon?" Desi laughed. "And it'll cost a fortune if everyone picks the filet."

I blew out a breath. This was so typical of my family. I'd just explained how unhappy I was about an element of one of the most important days of my life, and all she cared about was how much it was going to cost. Granted, filet mignon and salmon would come to about fifty percent more, but I only planned to get married once, and my family could afford it.

"It's my wedding too," I said softly, meeting her gaze in the mirror. "And so far, I've been outvoted on the date, the food, the cake—"

"The cake? I didn't know you picked cake flavors."

"We went last week. I loved the white chocolate raspberry, but he wanted the chocolate ganache."

"Oh, chocolate!" Desi's eyes lit up. "Too bad I'm not marrying him—I hated that stupid white cake we had at our wedding. But Tony wanted all the traditional shit."

"So you gave in to what he wanted?"

"Of course."

"But what about what you wanted?" I asked, frowning. "I haven't gotten my way on a single thing. It doesn't seem fair."

"Look, wedding planning is always a shit show, so just breathe. Remember how much you love Carlo, and how it's just one day out of your whole life. Just think, this time next year you'll probably be pregnant, and we'll be planning your baby shower."

I couldn't describe the sadness that washed over me at the thought of being pregnant a year from now. Carlo and I wanted kids, but there were dozens of other things I wanted to do first.

"Oh, did I tell you about the shoes I got for the wedding?" Desi slid her arm through mine as we walked back into the concourse, carrying on the conversation as if I wasn't having a mini-panic attack over the thought of getting pregnant.

What the hell was wrong with me?

The Knights were playing the Alaska Blizzard, who'd won the championship last year, so the guys from Lauderdale had something to prove, and you could tell. They were playing hard, fighting to win every face-off, and practically flying up and down the ice. Maybe it was because I was so excited to have a hometown team, or maybe it was because I was trying to stop thinking about all the things stressing me out, but I was on my feet for most of it, cheering for the Knights and chirping at the Blizzard.

When a player named Vaughn Elliott scored the first goal of the game, the season, and the franchise, I was yelling like a lunatic. The whole arena seemed to be on their feet, a sea of orange and blue jerseys, and I forgot all about my personal life, my professional life, and even my annoying family.

"Way to put one on the board," I yelled, clapping as Elliott skated along the bench, high fiving his teammates.

There was one minute left in the second period and most of the fans stayed on their feet as the Knights won the next face-off. A defenseman named Zakk Marcus-Cloutier took the puck down the ice and passed it to Elliott. They went back and forth a few times, skating in and around the Blizzard. Elliott skated up the middle, close to our seats, and wound up, taking a slap shot that sent the puck flying.

It went high, up over the glass and in our general direction. Between the lights and everyone around me standing up, I lost sight of the puck. I heard my brother yell my name and turned just as pain exploded through my head.

3

VAUGHN

The day after a big win tended to be mellow, but not with Coach Petrov. He'd essentially given us permission to lose last night—reverse psychology in my opinion, not that anyone was asking—but now we had eighty-one games to go and a lot of eyes on us both individually and as a team. Last night's win would be forgotten before we got to Halloween if we didn't continue to show the hockey world what we could do, and that was probably a bigger reason why Coach had pushed us to have fun last night instead of focusing on the scoreboard.

"A few announcements," Coach called out, gathering us around him. "First, Sunday is family skate day. Bring your significant others and kids to practice, and let's have some fun. Afterward, there will be pizza and cake in the locker room." He paused. "And yes, practice is mandatory even if you're single and don't have kids. There are going to be a lot of team-building events throughout the season, and they're all mandatory unless we've discussed it privately. Now, we're going to run some drills…except you, Vaughn. I need a moment." He motioned to me, and I frowned in confusion.

I was never a team troublemaker, and I'd had a good night last night, so I had no idea what was going on. I skated over to him and stepped behind the bench. "Coach?"

"Listen, you're not in any trouble, but something happened last night."

"Was it the fan who got hit in the head?" I asked slowly. I knew my shot had gone into the crowd and hit someone, but the press hadn't asked me anything in the post-game interviews, so I'd forgotten about it. "He okay?"

"She." He hesitated. "Is in the hospital. Concussion, stitches, I'm not sure what else. Apparently, they had to take her out on a stretcher."

"Damn." I felt bad. It happened on occasion, but it had never happened to me, and I hated the idea that I'd hurt someone. "What do I need to do?"

"Technically, nothing, but this is a new team, and we don't want to start off with bad press. I was thinking you could go up to the hospital and visit. The PR team put together a care package with a jersey and such, so after practice, maybe have it signed by everyone and then go up to Dane Nicholls' office and find out the woman's name and which hospital she's at." Dane was the head of Media Relations, which was another way of saying PR.

"Yeah, of course." I shook my head. "Sorry, Coach. I didn't—"

"Of course you didn't." He shook his head. "It's not a problem, but we want to get in front of it. Just in case. So after practice try to go see her? If she, or the family, push back about a visit, just leave the gift, and go home. I'll get both PR and the legal department on it if there are any issues."

"Consider it done."

"Thank you. Now get to work." He clapped me on the shoulder, and I skated out to find my line.

"What'd you do?" Zakk asked as I skated past him.

"You didn't beat up his son or something, did you?" One of the rookies called out, laughing.

I rolled my eyes. "You mean his son who plays for the Sidewinders?" Coach's oldest son, Anton, played for his old team in Las Vegas. It was amazing to me this guy didn't know that.

The kid turned red, a bunch of guys laughed, and I slowed to a stop next to Zakk, waiting for the next drill to start.

One of the assistant coaches yelled for us to move, and we hit the ice hard. I was a little distracted, though, thinking about the woman I'd hit with the puck and wondering if she was okay. Though most shots lost a lot of steam once they got up and into the stands, they could still pack quite a punch.

"Remember that shot I hit into the stands last night?" I asked Zakk when we had another break between drills.

"Oh, hell. They okay?"

"Don't know. All Coach told me was that it was a woman, and she's in the hospital."

"He wants you to go visit?"

I nodded. "I don't mind doing it, but what the hell do I say? I mean, do I apologize?"

"I think a generic apology is okay, since it was obviously an accident, and it happens now and then in hockey. I would stay lighthearted, try to be friendly and not focus too much on the negative. Unless she's in a coma or something, but I'm thinking they wouldn't send you if that was the case."

"I really fucking hope not."

The PR team had put together a huge gift bag for the woman I'd hit with the puck, and I picked it up as we got back to the locker room after practice. There was a jersey, two T-shirts, a hoodie, pucks, socks, and what seemed like one of every single thing in the merchandise shop.

"Damn, hope you got a discount on all that," Camden said as he sank down next to me and peered into the large shopping bag.

"It's for the fan I hit with a puck last night," I muttered, pulling out the jersey. "You want to sign this for me?"

He took the sharpie from me. "Holy shit. I knew someone had gotten hit, but I didn't realize she was in the hospital."

"I know."

Zakk sank down on my other side and took the jersey from Cam, signing his name and passing it on.

"Hey, did you guys hear about the trade?" Palmer came over and grabbed the jersey, signing it absently.

Before he could say anything else, another one of our teammates, Jude LeBlanc, came in with a player I recognized from the Alaska Blizzard—Ryder Kingston.

"Hey, guys. Say hi to Ryder. He was just traded last night. Since we played together in Anchorage, I thought I'd introduce him to everyone."

"Holy hell, you got traded last night while you were here?" Cam asked, standing up and extending his hand. "That's nuts."

"I had a feeling it was coming," Ryder said, nodding and shaking hands with the group of us standing around. "I'm more worried about my fiancée. She hasn't been through a trade before so it's kind of new for her, even though we've talked about it."

"Give me her name and number," Zakk said. "I'll have my wife call her. She can probably answer all her questions and help her with the logistics."

"That would be great. I appreciate it." Ryder nodded, pulling out his phone.

They exchanged numbers, and I mentally wrote him off. Not because I didn't like him or wanted to be an ass, but there was always a divide between the single guys and the married guys on every team. Even the guys who had serious girlfriends fell into the married category. It was just different. On the ice was one thing, we were a unit, but the guys I'd probably be spending my time with when we were off was different.

The single guys tended to party. A lot. And we stuck together in our shenanigans. The married guys usually went home to their families, and while I wanted that for myself someday, that day wasn't today. I was having way too much fun, and now I was in South Florida where I'd heard the weather was hot and the women were hotter. So my plan was to get friendly with the single guys, start figuring out where the ladies hung out, and begin hitting up those places.

From what I could see, the single guys were me, Jude, and the rookies. I wasn't sure about Felix, and Palmer wasn't old enough to get into a bar, but there had to be some guys interested in going out. Cam might go since his girlfriend was away at college.

"Drinks tonight?" Cam was asking, snapping me back to the present.

"I'm in. I have to go to the hospital, but I probably won't be there long."

"Anyone know their way around?" Jude asked. "Should we Google bars and pubs?"

"I've found a few sports bars I like," Zakk said. "I've been here two months already. We can start at Derby's, and if you don't like it, we can go elsewhere."

"You going out with us?" I asked him in surprise.

He laughed. "I'm married, not a monk. Tiff and I go out with our friends whenever we want. First thing we looked for was reliable babysitters because with four kids, we need breaks now and then."

"Sounds legit."

We all started talking about when and where we were meeting up, with more and more guys joining in, so I told Zakk to text me when they had a definitive time and place.

I didn't have a suit with me since this had just been practice, and I mentally debated going home to put one on. I couldn't show up at the hospital dressed in shorts and a T-shirt, so it was probably best to detour toward home before I went anywhere.

I grabbed the bag of goodies and headed to my new Corvette. I'd traded in my SUV the minute I'd heard I was going to Florida. With no real winters to speak of, I didn't need a big truck, and I'd always wanted a Vette. I slid behind the wheel, still in love with the leather and all the gadgets, and headed for the house I'd rented two months ago. I lived about fifteen minutes from the arena in a quiet area that had a good school district, consisted mostly of single-family homes, and was upper middle-class. I'd considered an apartment somewhere near the intracoastal but opted for quiet and quicker access to the arena over proximity to nightlife.

I had to focus on my game, and when I had time off, it wasn't like it was that far. Fort Lauderdale wasn't that kind of big city where traffic could make a short trip seem interminable. At least not for someone who'd lived in places like L.A., where traffic was a game changer. I'd been drafted by L.A. and played there four years before being traded to Minnesota. I loved living in L.A., but even on a professional athlete's salary it had been expensive as fuck. Minnesota had been a lot more affordable, but for some reason I'd been bored there.

I hadn't been here long, but it felt like Florida might be the best of both worlds, with plenty to do, a reasonable cost of living, and of course, hockey.

Looking forward to hanging out with the guys tonight, I wanted to get this hospital visit over with. So after I changed, I grabbed my keys, wallet, and phone, and headed back out to my car. I backed onto my street and had just gotten to the stop sign at the top of the development when I noticed that big black pickup with big tires and completely opaque windows.

I glanced into my rearview mirror, frowning.

Dammit.

I didn't know whether the truck belonged to my father, but it sure looked like it. Why the hell was he sitting in my neighborhood watching me?

Annoyance ripped through me.

Maybe it was nothing.

But on the off chance it was something, I planned to get to the bottom of it.

4

I had the mack daddy of all headaches, and I hadn't even opened my eyes yet. I rarely woke up with headaches, and the TV was on, which made no sense. I found myself struggling to open my eyes, but the bright lights in the room made me immediately squeeze them shut again.

As I grew more aware, I realized people were arguing.

"Why on earth would you let her get seats so close to the ice?" someone was saying.

"How was I supposed to stop her?" a man demanded. "She paid for them, and those are the seats she chose."

"You're the older brother—you're supposed to let her know when she does something dangerous."

I wanted to tell them to shut the fuck up, I was trying to sleep, but it seemed like so much work to force my lids apart.

"Juliet? Are you awake? Can you open your eyes?" This was a different voice. Softer. Much more soothing.

Except…who was Juliet?

Inexplicable fear shot through me with such ferocity, I immediately tried to sit up.

"Oh, hey, it's okay." A gentle but firm hand on my shoulder kept me from getting up, but my heart was racing, and my eyes popped open wide as I looked around.

"You hit your head in an accident." The woman talking to me was dressed like a nurse, and now that my eyes were open, I saw I was in a hospital room. "You've been asleep since last night. Can you tell me your name? I'm Jackie."

I stared at her in confusion. "M-my name?"

"Yes."

"It's..." My voice trailed off. Why didn't I know my name? "Is it...Juliet?"

"I don't know. You tell me."

Panic rushed through me once again, and I turned to stare at the people in the room. Two men who looked to be in their late twenties or early thirties, a middle-aged woman probably in her fifties, and a woman who was possibly in her mid-twenties.

They looked a little familiar, but I couldn't place them.

"I don't know." I met the nurse's gaze worriedly. "How can I not know my name? What's wrong with me?" Tears came in a rush, and the nurse quickly started to talk, brushing my hair away from my face and fluffing up my pillow.

"You had a little accident. Do you remember?"

"No!" I looked around and despite some familiarity, it was like looking into the faces of strangers. Suddenly my chest felt tight, my heart started to race, and I didn't know what to do.

"Everything is going to be fine," Jackie said quietly. "Try to relax. You took a hockey puck to the head and have a concussion. You have ten stitches in your head, and some swelling, but Dr. Montrose will be in soon to talk to you. Would you like some water?"

"I..." I had stitches? I raised my hand to my head and touched a bandage that covered my right temple and went back into my hair. Everything was sore, making me wince.

Jackie put a plastic water bottle with a straw in front of me. "It's right there if you need water. Do you want ice?"

"Yes, please," I replied automatically, as if that was something I liked. Did I like ice water? I was pretty sure I did.

Jackie followed my gaze as I continued to look around. "Do you recognize your family?"

I cleared my throat, anxiety coursing through me. "I don't know any of you."

"It's me. Mom." The middle-aged woman came forward and cocked her head slightly. She had warm, thick-lashed hazel eyes filled with concern, shoulder-length dark hair that was a little unkempt, and bright pink lipstick. "Maria Penelope Calavope Cicero."

Somehow, hearing her whole name made me smile, as though this was something I was familiar with. Except I wasn't particularly familiar with her, and tears filled my eyes again.

"I'm sorry," I whispered. "You look familiar, but I can't place you."

"It's all right, love." She put a cool hand on the side of my face. "It will all come back."

"I'm, uh, your brother, Tony." One of the guys stepped forward, frowning a little. "You don't recognize any of us?"

"I'm sorry," I said again.

The young woman came forward. "I'm Desi, Tony's wife. We were with you at the game when you got hit."

"Game?"

"The Lauderdale Knights. It was opening night."

"Oh. Hockey." That sounded familiar. Something I enjoyed.

Mom—I didn't know what else to call her—smiled. "You remember!"

"Well, I…know it's hockey." I was grateful Jackie was here, putting ice in my water bottle and then making some notes in the computer.

"Are you hungry?" Jackie asked.

"No."

"I have chicken soup." Mom immediately pulled out a Tupperware container from a bag on the floor. "This will make you feel better."

"Give us a few minutes," Jackie said firmly before turning back to me. "How do you feel other than the headache and anything related to your memory?"

I hesitated and closed my eyes. I was okay. My head was pounding and the area where the bandage was throbbed a little, but my body felt fine overall. "I have to go to the bathroom," I said, abruptly opening my eyes.

"We'll wait outside." Tony and the other guy stepped into the hallway, and I sat up.

Jackie disconnected the IV I hadn't noticed until now, helped me up and held my arm as we made our way to the bathroom.

"You okay on your own?" she asked. "Just call if you need anything."

"I'm fine. Thank you." I quickly closed the door behind me and then stared in the mirror.

Fuck.

The woman looking back at me was familiar, as if looking at a friend I hadn't seen in a long time, but it was disconcerting to realize I didn't know my name, age, or anything else. I had hazel eyes, much like my mother's, with long, dark hair and a smattering of freckles across my nose. I was pretty enough, but my face was currently a mess, with smudged makeup and a few flecks of dried blood. The bandage covered the injury itself, but there was enough bruising on my forehead and just below my eye to tell me it was significant. I didn't want to know if they'd had to shave any of my hair to do the stitches.

I was a freakin' mess and didn't want to think about the possibility of a scar across my temple or cheek. I had too many other things to worry about right now.

I quickly used the toilet and then got up to wash my hands and face.

That's when I noticed the diamond ring on my left hand.

Holy shit.

Was I engaged?

Not knowing anything about myself was fucking exhausting.

I also used a lot of curse words in my head.

Did I curse a lot out loud?

I hated not knowing the answers to anything and had to take a few deep breaths to keep from going back into panic mode. I didn't understand any of this, which made it easy to get anxious. My memory would come back, though. Right?

I opened the door and found the room full of even more people.

"There you are." A guy I didn't know but who had a warm, friendly face, was grinning at me. "I'm Peter—your favorite brother."

I didn't know the guy from Adam, but somehow, I believed him. I managed to smile back as Jackie helped me back into bed.

"Hello." A man in a white lab coat came in smiling. "I'm Dr. Montrose. How are you feeling, Juliet?"

"Not so great," I murmured. "Is Juliet my name?"

"Indeed it is. Juliet Cicero." He paused. "Doesn't ring any bells?"

I shook my head.

"Do you recognize your family?"

"A little familiarity, but not names or anything specific."

"Okay, I need everyone to step into the hall so I can evaluate the level of Juliet's amnesia. You can all come back in a few minutes."

"She needs us here," Mom cried dramatically.

"We need to know what's going on," Tony added.

"She has to eat," Mom continued. "And I think the bandage has to come off. The stitches need to breathe."

"I don't—" I began, but my family was on a roll, talking over both me and the doctor.

"All right, everyone out." Dr. Montrose knitted his brows together. "And no more than three visitors at a time. This is a lot of chaos for her right now. Thank you."

"You can't kick me out!" Mom drew herself up to her full height.

"Mrs. Cicero." Dr. Montrose fixed her with a look. "Please. Five minutes."

"Ma, come on." Tony finally took her arm, and they all reluctantly filed out with Jackie closing the door behind them.

It was a relief to have some peace and quiet, but then Dr. Montrose started asking me all sorts of questions, and while I knew the year, I didn't know the month or day. I had no idea how old I was, where I lived, or what I did for work, but I loved the color red.

"I don't want you to worry," Dr. Montrose said after he'd asked me a few dozen questions. "This is more common than you think. Most likely, your memories will come back a little at a time, within a couple of days, maybe a little longer. Sometimes they come back in a rush, though, so be prepared for that also."

"But…what do I do?" I asked, bewildered.

"You're going to stay here for another few days because there's some swelling on the brain. We're giving you medication that should reduce it, and I think that's when your memories will come back."

"Why am I so scared?"

"That's fairly common. You have what we call post-traumatic amnesia, which happens after a significant head injury. It seems to have manifested as retrograde amnesia, where you remember things from a long time ago, but everything leading up to the accident is gone. The puck that hit you knocked you out cold and while the swelling is a little concerning, let's give it a few days. I'm sure it's going to be much better." He got up. "Would you like me to call your family back in?"

"I guess?" What else could I say?

They came in en masse, talking over each other once again as Mom tried to make me eat soup I didn't want. They seemed intent on telling me about themselves as they tried to jog my memory.

"Pizza," I said suddenly. "Why does pizza feel important?"

Mom smiled. "We own a pizzeria. Cicero's of Sicily."

"That sounds familiar."

"Where is Carlo?" Mom demanded suddenly, looking at Mario. "Why isn't he here?"

"He had an emergency at work," Mario said. "He was here most of last night, and he'll be back as soon as he can, but the issue was with a big customer and he had to deal with it."

"Who's Carlo?" I asked curiously.

Mom looked at me in confusion. "Your fiancé."

I remembered the ring and looked down at it. It was a simple white gold or platinum band with a small diamond, but it didn't look familiar at all.

"When are we getting married?" I asked.

"January first."

"New Year's Day?"

"That's the day you went on your first date," Mom said, smiling. "Don't worry too much, okay? Have some soup."

I wrinkled my nose. Did I not like chicken soup? I had no idea.

Dad loved chicken soup.

I didn't know where the thought came from, but I felt a wave of emotion as the memory of a funeral whipped through me. It was such a strong reaction, I had to close my eyes for a second.

"Dad died," I said quietly, looking around. "We had a big funeral. There were hundreds of people…right?"

Mom nodded; her face suddenly tight. "Yes. Two years ago." She crossed herself, murmuring, "God rest his soul."

Shit. Why did I remember stuff like this instead of my freakin' name?

"Excuse me. May I come in?"

The most beautiful man I'd ever had the pleasure of laying eyes on was standing in the doorway and excitement fluttered through me.

Was this *Carlo*? Maybe being engaged wasn't such a bad thing after all.

This guy looked like he could be a Carlo. Tall with broad shoulders that filled the doorway, and the most amazing eyes. I couldn't tell what color they were from here, but they were deep and gorgeous. And fixed on me.

"Hi." I smiled at him because I couldn't seem to help myself.

"Hello." He smiled back. "I'm—" He was cut off as a tech brushed past him, coming over to the bed.

"Hello, Juliet. I'm Nita. I need to draw some blood."

"Blood?" My eyes widened. I didn't know much, but I knew I didn't like needles. "Oh, no, I don't do needles."

"It's hospital policy, ma'am. Dr. Montrose said—"

"No." I shook my head.

"It's okay." Carlo was still smiling at me. "They're really good here. It won't hurt."

Looking up into his gorgeous brown eyes, I was momentarily mesmerized. Was I really engaged to this gorgeous hunk of man?

"It'll be over before you know it," Jackie said. "Just close your eyes."

Without thinking I reached for Carlo's hand. "Will you stay with me?"

"Jules—" Tony started to say something.

"It's fine." Carlo said, looking over at him. "And yes, I'll stay with you. Close your eyes and think of something wonderful."

"Ice cream," I replied, letting my eyes fall shut. His strong, lightly callused hand was warm in mine and for the first time since I'd woken up, I relaxed a little.

"Make a fist," the tech said.

I complied without opening my eyes, even though my breath hitched a little.

I absolutely hated needles.

Oh, wow. Something else I knew about myself.

"All done." The tech was smiling as I opened my eyes, and she bustled out.

"Hello, there." Another woman came in, this one in scrubs, with a notepad. "You were asleep this morning when we filled out the menus for dinner tonight. Do you want to do that real quick so I can make sure you get fed?"

"Oh." I swallowed, trying to get my bearings back.

"She has soup," Mom said. "She doesn't need that."

"Yes, I do." Carlo was still holding my hand, and when he started to loosen his grip, I tightened mine. I wasn't ready to let go. This was the first thing today that felt completely right. Comfortable. Like we'd been holding hands forever.

"Jules—" Tony called to me but the nurse had put the menu in front of me.

It was basic stuff, so I just picked the simplest choice. "A cheeseburger and fries, please."

"Salad?"

"Sure."

She typed something into an iPad, picked up the menu, and hustled out.

"So, hello again." Carlo smiled, his eyes crinkling a little. "I'm Vaughn Elliott."

Oh, shit.

Who the fuck was Vaughn Elliott, and why did his name sound familiar?

5

VAUGHN

I'd had no idea what to expect when I got to Juliet Cicero's hospital room. But the adorable brunette with sparkling eyes and a needle phobia wasn't it. Holding her hand while the tech took blood hadn't been in the plans either, yet here I was. I'd tried to pull away twice, but she'd held on for dear life, and it was kind of cute. Well, despite the messy hair, bandage covering one side of her head, and the hospital gown, *she* was cute.

Now she was staring at me in obvious dismay, as if she'd thought I was someone else. Which made no sense. I'd assumed she recognized me, since I'd been told she was a season ticket holder, but now that I'd officially introduced myself, her cheeks had turned pink and there was a little bit of both horror and embarrassment in her eyes.

"Who are you?" she asked, a line forming between her brows as she looked up at me.

"I'm Vaughn. From the Lauderdale Knights. Sadly, it was my slap shot that put you here."

"Slap shot?" she echoed. "Wait, this happened at a hockey game, right?" She looked toward one of the guys standing around the bed.

"Holy shit, you're really Vaughn Elliott." One of the guys came toward me with an extended hand. "I'm Tony Cicero, one of Juliet's brothers."

"Nice to meet you." I smiled, shook his hand and those of the others in the room, losing track of their names.

"Juliet has amnesia," Tony said. "She doesn't remember the accident."

"I'm really sorry about all of this." I turned my attention back to Juliet. "I didn't plan to stay very long, but I wanted to see how you were. I've never hit anyone with a puck before."

"Well, I can't remember any of it, so from my perspective, you have nothing to apologize for."

I chuckled. "So, uh, how many stitches?"

"Ten, they tell me."

"I'm hungry," Tony said to no one in particular.

"You're always hungry," his wife replied, shaking her head.

"Can I have some of the chicken soup since Jules doesn't want it?"

"Go get something from the cafeteria," Juliet's mother said. "The soup is for her."

"Why don't you all go get something to eat?" The nurse suggested. "That way, Juliet can talk to one person at a time."

"We can't leave her with a stranger," Juliet's mother protested, her eyes wide.

"I'm staying," the nurse said. "So she won't be alone."

"It's fine, Mom," Juliet said. "Go eat something."

There was some grumbling, but food won out and Juliet turned back to me once everyone but the nurse had left. "Your name sounded vaguely familiar, and I remember thinking the Knights had gotten extremely lucky you were available in the draft."

"Well, it's not really luck since I volunteered to be left unprotected."

"Why?" she asked. "Didn't you like playing in Minnesota?"

I noted the nurse's head jerking up before we all froze for a beat. "You remember that my old team was Minnesota?" I asked slowly.

Her eyes widened. "I guess I do."

"Anything else?"

She seemed to be thinking hard but then let out a long, sad sigh. "No. That's it."

The nurse smiled. "It's okay. Small steps."

"Ugh. This sucks." Juliet rubbed the bridge of her nose. "The family I don't recognize is looking at me like I've sprouted wings, my head hurts like a motherfucker, and I just held the hand of a complete stranger. I'd like a do-over. Can I get a fucking do-over for this day?"

"Hey, don't be so hard on yourself." Impulsively, I pulled up a chair next to her bedside and sat down. She looked sad and mad at the same time, and I felt the unexplainable need to make her feel better. "You've had a head injury. They can be serious. Give yourself a break."

"Part of me wants to scream 'let me out of here' and get away from everyone." She paused, turning a pair of gorgeous hazel eyes to me. "But I don't know where I'd go. I don't remember where I live."

"What do the doctors say?" I asked, leaning forward.

"That there's some swelling, but my memory should come back as the swelling goes down."

"But in the meantime, it's scary."

She nodded. "Very."

"I'm sorry. And I'm even sorrier I'm the reason you're here."

"It was an accident."

Our eyes locked, and I had the strangest urge to hold her hand again. She looked small and afraid in the hospital bed, bringing out that weird need to protect her. I didn't even know her, but she was in this situation because of me, and if holding her hand or sitting here instead of going out drinking with my teammates might help in any way, it felt right to do it.

"I, uh, brought some presents," I said after a moment, lifting the bag. I placed it on the bed beside her, and her eyes lit up when she pulled out the jersey.

"Oh, wow. This is…signed by the whole team?" She looked excited. "I love this. Thank you."

"Are you a big hockey fan?"

"I am." She grinned at me and then glanced at Jackie. "Something else I seem to know about myself."

"Are you a native?" I asked curiously.

"Yes and no. I've been here most of my life, but I was born in New York —Long Island—and I remember my brothers playing hockey when I was a kid."

"Did you play?"

"No. We moved to Florida when I was ten, so all that fell to the wayside." She paused and glanced at Jackie. "Is it weird I know this kind of stuff but not my name?"

"Brain injuries are as different as they are interesting," she replied.

Juliet was thoughtful for a minute but then dug back into the bag, pulling out the socks next. "These are cute." She met my gaze. "But not signed."

I laughed. "You want me to sign the socks? There's a Sharpie in my pocket."

"Yes, please."

I was surprised but amused and obligingly took out the Sharpie and signed her socks. "What else?"

"I don't know yet." She dug everything out of the bag and smiled at each new item like a kid on Christmas morning. She rested the baseball cap on her head without actually putting it on—after I signed it—and set the notebook and pen set we'd included on her tray table.

"What do you think?" I asked when she was done going through everything.

"No hockey stick?" she asked, arching her brows, though there was no doubt mischief danced in her eyes.

"If you want a hockey stick, I can bring you one tomorrow," I said.

"Cool. Make sure it's signed." The grin on her face told me she was teasing, and I couldn't remember the last time I'd had so much fun with a woman I wasn't out on a date with.

"Deal." I reached for her notebook and flipped to the front page. "I'm going to give you my cell number, so we can keep in touch. Call or text me tomorrow and let me know if you're still here or if you've gone home. I can have the stick delivered to your house if you're not here anymore."

She smiled. "I was kidding about the stick."

"I'm not. I'll be happy to get you one." I put the notebook back on the tray table.

"You're nice, Vaughn. Thank you. And thank you for coming by. You didn't have to." She paused. "Or did the team make you?"

I shook my head. "They didn't *make* me. They asked me if I would, and I didn't hesitate. I feel really bad that I hit you hard enough to knock you out, even though I obviously didn't mean to shoot the puck into the stands. We get penalized for that."

"I don't think I've ever seen it happen in person," she said thoughtfully.

"Was this your first hockey game?" I asked suddenly.

"As an adult, yes. I know we went to them when I was a kid, but I don't remember going as an adult, though it seems like the last few years of my life are gone from my memories and—oh!" Her eyes widened. "Holy shit, that was weird."

"What happened?" Jackie asked quickly, getting to her feet.

"I'm okay, I just had a memory pop into my head, and it was like a flash of pictures… the first pre-season game you guys played. I guess *that* was my first live game."

I squeezed her arm. "See? Everything is going to be fine. Your memories are already starting to come back."

"I hope so." She took a deep breath. "By the way, I'm sorry I grabbed your hand the way I did. I thought you were my…fiancé. I don't know why I assumed that."

"Hasn't he been here since you woke up?" I asked confused. If she were my fiancée, I wouldn't have left her side.

She shook her head. "No. His name is Carlo, and we're getting married in January, but I literally have no idea what he looks like. Is that weird?"

I hesitated because I honestly had no advice for her. "I don't know," I admitted. "You have a head injury. I don't think anything qualifies as weird right now."

"Maybe not." She put everything back in the bag. "Thank you for all this stuff. It's really great. I can't wait to hang the poster somewhere. As soon as I figure out where I live." She frowned suddenly, wincing.

"You okay?" I asked.

"I don't know anything about myself, and I keep waffling between talking and asking questions that make me feel better and going into a complete panic mode when I think about all the things I don't know."

"Don't stress the unanswered questions," I said softly. "I've never had amnesia, but I know head injuries are serious, so don't tax your brain. Try to rest and let the memories come back naturally."

"I'm trying," she whispered. "It's so scary, though. My family is familiar, like people you recognize but you're not sure from where? And I'm starting to remember little things, like the fact that I love hockey, but everything is so…blank."

"You have my number. If you need anything at all, please don't hesitate to call. I feel responsible so just reach out, okay?"

"I'd give you my number if I knew what it was." She snickered and Jackie chuckled too.

"That's why I gave you mine."

"I'm sure your family knows where your things are," Jackie said. "I believe your purse is in the closet, but I haven't gone through it."

"Oh, may I have it?" she asked.

Jackie got a small, black purse with a long strap out of one of the drawers and handed it to Juliet. She immediately started pulling out everything and triumphantly held up her phone.

"Sonofabitch," she muttered. "Battery is dead."

"I'm sure we can find you a charger," Jackie said.

"Or I can bring you one in the morning," I offered.

"That sounds wonderful." Juliet smiled at me, and for the second a tiny spark ignited. It disappeared almost as quickly as it had come, but it was there, and I felt a physical response to something intangible that barely had time to register.

"I should probably get going," I said after a moment. I got to my feet just as someone came into the room.

"Jules! You're awake." The guy was short but fit, and he glanced at me curiously. "Hi. I'm Carlo."

I extended my hand. "Vaughn Elliott from the Lauderdale Knights."

"Oh. Was it your shot that hit Juliet?"

I nodded. "Yeah, I'm really sorry about that."

"It was nice of you to stop by. Thank you." He turned to Juliet. "How are you feeling, love?"

"Tired," she said softly.

"I'm sorry." He reached for her hand. "You really don't recognize me? I can't believe this happened. Tony texted me that you don't remember anything."

"It's a little disconcerting."

"You'll feel more like yourself once you get home and relax in familiar surroundings.

"Yeah. I suppose so." She seemed at a loss, and I wished her family would come back in.

This wasn't my problem, though.

"Anyway." I cleared my throat. "Take care, Juliet. It was nice to meet you. Carlo."

"Are you leaving?" Her eyes all but pleaded with me to stay, but I couldn't.

For reasons I didn't understand I was incredibly attracted to her, but that was a dead-end because she was engaged and would undoubtedly get her memory back any time now. The last thing I needed was to hook up with someone who was engaged. That wasn't the kind of man I was.

"Yes, but I'll swing by with a stick for you tomorrow after practice if that's okay."

"Yes. Thank you." Her smile was tremulous now, and I felt like shit for leaving her.

"You're very welcome." I nodded at Jackie and turned and walked out of the room even though a tiny voice inside of me was screaming at me to stay.

6

C arlo never stopped talking. He was sweet, asking how I was and being incredibly attentive, but when he realized I didn't recognize him, not even a little, he started to try and fill in all the blanks. The wedding plans. The house we'd been thinking about putting an offer on. His job as an IT something-or-other. His family's plans to come for Thanksgiving. I wanted to remember something—anything—about our relationship, but I didn't.

Thankfully, my family came back in right around the time my dinner arrived, and they seemed to enjoy listening to his stories, which allowed me a little peace.

My family seemed to adore him, and they stood around talking about work and football and someone named Tito, the whole group essentially ignoring me. Except for my mother, who kept insisting I eat a little of her chicken soup. Carlo would occasionally smile over at me but seemed much happier hanging out with my brothers than with me, and it was almost a relief.

This was the most surreal situation to be in. While my mother and brother Tony were vaguely familiar, like acquaintances you hadn't seen in years who you run into on the street, Carlo, Desi and the others were complete strangers. It was so fucking weird. And worse than that, the only person who'd made me feel comfortable and at ease other than Jackie was Vaughn, the one person who was literally a stranger to me.

None of it made sense and at some point, I must have dozed off because the next time I opened my eyes the room was empty, and it was dark outside the window. I looked around and saw that someone had thoughtfully plugged in my cell phone and left it on the tray table, so I tugged it closer and picked it up. Maybe my phone would have some answers my brain didn't.

Luckily, I had face recognition enabled so I didn't have to think about a passcode, and I stared at the home page curiously. I had fourteen missed phone calls, twenty-two texts, and 427 emails. That was a little overwhelming, so I started with the texts.

Someone named Chloe had texted me seven times.

CHLOE: Hey, I have access to decent Wi-fi for the next couple of hours. What are you doing?

CHLOE: Are you there? Geez, this is the first time in weeks we can talk and you're ignoring me.

CHLOE: Hello? What are you doing that you're not looking at your phone?

CHLOE: OMG, are you and Carlo having sex??? Ew. Hurry up already!

CHLOE: Well, we're going to be heading back to camp in about twenty minutes, so this is our last chance to chat. I'm kind of worried. Are you okay?

CHLOE: Okay, we're leaving in five so I'll give you an overview of what's going on with me and then I guess you'll answer when you can. First, I met someone. One of the doctors here. He's twenty-nine and has the best abs I've ever seen in person. If you know what I mean. Dark hair, blue eyes, super smile. Since you're not answering me, I guess you'll have to wait to find out the rest.

CHLOE: Bonus: He lives in Miami!

I scrolled up to read our older texts and got the feeling we were close. Lots of fun chatter about anything and everything. I finally figured out she was abroad on some kind of Doctors Without Borders thing, but the text from the day she was leaving said she'd see me in six weeks. Based on the date, that was next week, and part of me was relieved that someone I was close to might be able to answer questions for me. I had my family, of course, but I had a feeling they would tell me the things they thought were best for me instead of the things that were important to me. I wasn't sure why I felt that way, but it was a strong feeling in my gut I couldn't ignore.

I had one text from Carlo, obviously from last night.

CARLO: What time are you getting home from the game? I think we need to talk about the wedding.

Obviously, after what happened at the game, I hadn't answered.

I had eight messages from people I assumed worked for me, all about either switching shifts with someone or taking a day off in the future. I'd have to remember to tell Tony or Desi about it so they could handle it because I didn't know who these people were or what to do about their requests.

There was a text from someone named Michelle asking if she needed to dye her shoes to match her bridesmaid dress, one that came from a random number with nothing but a URL I figured was spam, and then a handful from my mother that had been sent before I got hurt, all regarding my upcoming wedding.

I paused to stare down at my engagement ring.

I didn't *feel* engaged.

That was silly, of course, because I didn't know anything about my life right now.

The overload of information was overwhelming to me, so I closed my phone and put it back on the tray table. My biggest wish was that I'd sleep tonight, and when I woke up in the morning, I'd find out this had all been a nightmare.

———

Luckily, Carlo and my family were busy with their jobs and lives, so they didn't spend as much time at the hospital as I'd feared they would. I was by myself most of the next day, which was peaceful, but a little lonely. Carlo and my mother came by before work, and though they both offered to stay, I'd told them to go because there was nothing they could do for me. The swelling on my brain had to go down, and until then I was okay with the nurses taking care of me. Sadly, I hadn't woken up with my memory back, but I was a lot more self-aware and there were things I knew instinctively, like how much I loved hockey and that I drove a red Dodge Charger.

I spent more time on my phone, perusing my social media and trying to get a feel for who I was, but mostly I napped. Pictures, texts, and social media posts only gave me a snapshot of what my life was like, and it was frustrating. Dr. Montrose had come by and told me to be patient.

That was easy for him to say—he wasn't the one who couldn't remember much.

Tony, Desi, Mom, Peter, and Carlo stopped in around dinnertime, filling me in on people and events I didn't care about. I knew they meant well, but all I felt right now was lost. They were trying to pretend everything was okay, and I wished I could make them understand I wasn't the Juliet they knew. In fact, right now, I didn't exist at all. A few details of my persona had come back to me—like the fact that my birthday was the sixteenth of June—but overall, I was a big, blank slate of irritation, anxiety, and frustration.

I sighed with relief when they finally left, but it was strange to be alone in my current state because I enjoyed the quiet but not the ever-present anxiety. I'd tried to read up on amnesia, but the screen of my phone was small, and I'd gotten a headache, so I'd given up. Which left me with more questions than answers and a tightness in my chest that didn't go away. I'd mentioned it to the doctor, and he'd said it was normal to be out of sorts, so I shouldn't worry.

Like not worrying was even possible.

I'd just reached for the remote to the TV when there was a light knock on the door and a familiar face peered in.

"Hey. You feel like a visitor?"

"Vaughn, hi." For some reason, seeing him made me smile.

"Hey." He came in holding a hockey stick and immediately held it out to me. "As promised."

"How did you get in?" I asked, taking it from him. "Visiting hours are over."

He put a finger to his lips. "Shh. I may have taken a few selfies with the nurses."

I laughed. "I'm sure that made their night."

"Knight or night?" He teased, sitting in the chair next to me.

"Both."

We laughed, and I held up the stick. "Is it signed?"

"It sure is. It's one of mine from opening night, signed by me."

"A game-used stick? You're the best." Our eyes locked, and for a few seconds my anxiety lifted. I forgot all about the chaos of my life.

"So, how are you feeling?" he asked, leaning forward, his deep, caramel-colored eyes meeting mine.

I gave a little half-shrug. "I don't know. Okay, I guess."

"Memory still hasn't come back?"

"No. I mean, some things, like I remember my car and how excited I was about Lauderdale getting a pro hockey team, but it seems like I've blocked out all the big stuff. My family, my fiancé…all of it."

He cocked his head. "So you don't remember him at all?"

"Nothing." I made a face. "And then I feel guilty for not remembering, which is dumb, because it's not like this is my fault."

"I guess technically it's mine." His eyes met mine again, and I quickly shook my head.

"Oh, gosh, no! Don't feel bad. It was an accident. You didn't know this would happen. They're going to do a bunch of tests tomorrow to see if the swelling on my brain has gone down and whatever else. I kind of tuned it out because it seems to make me anxious."

"Is there anything I can do?" he asked quietly.

"You could…hang out and talk to me," I responded slowly. "It's nice to talk to someone who doesn't know everything about my life and just wants to chat. No expectations."

"I can do that." He smiled. "Wanna hear about the team?"

"Yes!" I grinned. "Tell me all the things."

He chuckled. "Well, let's see. We have a game tomorrow before we head to Tampa for a game on Sunday. The in-state rivalry is supposed to be a big deal, even though it's not since we technically don't have any rivals yet, but I think it's good for marketing, so they encourage us to hate the other team in Florida."

"I guess that makes sense. So the rivalries around the league aren't real?"

"Yes and no. Like the two New York teams—of course they're rivals. That's been going on for ages, and it makes sense because there aren't any other cities that could handle two pro teams so close together like that. But in other cases, it's more about player rivalries. Guys who've never liked each other, or certain games got brutal and then the rivalry continued going forward."

"Do you have rivals?"

He smiled. "Not really. There are a couple of guys I think are douchebags, but that would be the same anywhere, you know? Some people you like, some people you don't."

"I can't think of anyone I like or dislike right now," I admitted, chuckling. "I guess except you."

"Hopefully I fall into the like category."

"For sure." I smiled. "So, do you have a family? Wife? Girlfriend? Boyfriend?"

He shook his head. "I am free and clear of any type of significant other."

"How come? Are you one of those guys who's anti-commitment?"

"Honestly, I haven't had time. I know that sounds dumb, but I've been laser-focused on hockey since day one, and while there have been some girlfriends now and then, none of those relationships felt right. I guess what it boils down to is that I refuse to settle. I don't know exactly what I'm looking for, but I know I haven't found it yet."

"That makes perfect sense. I just wish I knew whether or not I've found what I'm looking for."

"Your memory will come back soon, and you'll get all the answers," he said gently.

For some reason, that's what I was afraid of.

7

———

VAUGHN

I was up early most days. When I wasn't on the road, and it wasn't a game day, practice was usually at ten, so I liked to get up, stretch, eat something, and check my email. It was a nice, leisurely way to start my days, so getting up early was a worthwhile tradeoff. I kept the same routine on game days for the most part and did the best I could when we were on the road. I was regimented when it came to hockey, but that was why I could play at this level. I was a lot more relaxed in the off-season, so I didn't mind the sacrifice. Especially considering I made a fuck-ton of money.

Since there was a game tonight, we had a mandatory morning skate today, and afterward I planned to stop by the hospital for a quick visit with Juliet. I'd stayed way too long last night, but it was easy to talk to her, and she seemed so lost right now. Initially I'd gone to visit her out of a sense of responsibility, and because Coach had asked me to, but today I *wanted* to go back.

Shit.

She's engaged.

I repeated that to myself as I drove to the arena.

She's taken.

I tried to focus on putting on my equipment.

"Hey, how's the woman you hit with the puck?" Ryder asked me as he laced up his skates.

"She's okay, but her memory hasn't come back yet."

"Shit. That sucks."

"Yeah, I'm going to stop by after practice to see how she's doing." I hadn't meant to tell him that, but I noted several of the guys around us stop and look over at me.

"Is she hot?" Cam asked slowly.

Fuck. This was not what I needed right now.

"She's got stitches, bandages, and a big bruise on her face," I replied. "But yeah, I think she's pretty. What does that have to do with anything?"

Several of the guys burst out laughing.

"Come on, man." Ryder grinned. "Isn't this your…third visit?"

"She asked for a stick," I said defensively. "That's why I went by last night."

"And today?" Cam asked.

"I'm just being nice. I thought she'd be out by now, but she hasn't gotten her memory back. I feel responsible." I wasn't sure why I was aggravated by the line of questioning, but I was.

"Uh huh." Ryder laughed.

"She's engaged," I said, standing up. "So this is just me being nice and doing damage control. That's it."

"Ten bucks says he takes her out," Palmer said to Felix.

Felix shook his head. "This is stupid bet. I will lose."

Then they all laughed.

"You guys suck," I muttered, grabbing my stick and heading for the tunnel.

I didn't know what was wrong with me because I never let my personal life interfere with hockey or filter into locker room talk. And in this case, it wasn't even my personal life since the only reason I knew Juliet was because of the game the other night.

I was still going to stop by today, but I'd make it a quick one, and that was it. This was the last time.

I repeated that to myself during practice, on the drive to the hospital, and even while I was standing in the gift shop paying for flowers. I'd noticed no one had sent her any, and it seemed a shame. I didn't know what kind of flowers she liked or what her favorite color was, so I settled for basic red. Everyone liked red roses, right?

I picked up the roses and headed up to her room, knocking lightly before sticking my head in.

"Juliet—" I froze as I took in her red, puffy eyes and the tissues she held in her hand. "Oh, hey, if this is a bad time, I don't have to stay." I stood in the doorway, unwilling to go any further without her consent.

"Hi." She swiped at her eyes. "Sorry. I'm a wreck. But you can come in. Are those for me?"

"I didn't know what kind of flowers you liked, but these kind of reminded me of you."

She managed a tremulous smile. "They're beautiful. Thank you."

I put them on the table and then turned to her. "Are you okay?"

"No." She shook her head. "I'm trying so hard not to stress, but my memory hasn't come back, and my family is driving me crazy, and tomorrow I have to have a CT scan to find out if my brain is broken…" She burst into tears all over again and my heart lurched painfully because I'd done this to her.

I moved to her side and took one of her hands between both of mine. "If you want, I'll get one of the neurologists who deals with head injuries for the league to consult with your doctor. I can make a call right now."

She lifted tear-filled hazel eyes to me. "C-could you?"

"Sure." I handed her a few more tissues and pulled out my phone, texting our team doctor. We all had his number for medical emergencies, and while this wasn't technically an emergency, I felt like this counted as a team issue. I gave him the pertinent details and asked about a specialist. He responded right away, asking for her doctor's name, and telling me he'd have someone get in touch with him ASAP.

"Okay, I'm getting someone our team doctor knows to consult with your doctor."

"Thank you." She sniffed and blew her nose. "God, I'm a wreck. I'm so sorry to drag you into my drama."

"It's not drama. You have a head injury. It makes sense you'd be emotional."

"And the worst part is, the more my family tries to help, the more I want them to leave me alone. Which makes me feel like an asshole."

"Head injuries are nothing to mess around with," I said. "The loss of memory plus the swelling on the brain has to be impacting you emotionally as well as physically, and probably psychologically as well. Don't be so hard on yourself."

"Dr. Montrose was just here, and when he said they were doing another scan tomorrow because my memory hasn't returned, it freaked me out. I'm sure you want to run screaming from the room."

"It's fine. I don't mind giving you a shoulder to cry on. It's the least I can do considering my part in all this."

"I know you're only here because the team is probably worried about liability, but you don't know how much I've appreciated your presence the last few days."

"The team handles stuff like liability without getting the players involved," I said quietly. "Technically, I didn't even have to come the first time, much less yesterday or today. I'm here because I want to be. Yes, I feel bad that I'm the reason you're here, but also…" My voice trailed off.

Why the fuck did I keep coming back?

I couldn't put it into words without sounding like an idiot.

"Also… we clicked." She swallowed as she vocalized what I hadn't wanted to say.

"Yeah. That."

Shit. This was a dick move. I absolutely couldn't visit again because every damn time we were in the same room I felt like I'd known her forever. Even when she was a crying, emotional wreck, like right now, I just wanted to be there for her. There was also no chance I was leaving her alone while she was so upset. So I'd sit here for a little while and be her friend, and then I had to get as far away from her as possible.

"It's going to be okay, you know," I said, sitting on the chair next to her bed. "Your memory will come back, you'll get back to planning your wedding and the rest of your life just like before the accident, and all of this anxiety and stuff will go away. You'll see."

"I can't shake the feeling that nothing is ever going to be the same," she whispered.

"That's anxiety and head trauma talking," I said. "Promise."

At least that's what I kept telling myself.

She met my gaze. "I can't explain it, but I'm so confused. It seems to me if Carlo was the love of my life, the man I'm supposed to marry in three months, I would feel something. *Anything.* Like, when I'm around my mom, I don't remember any details, but there's a warmth there. I know she loves me. I know there's something special between us. But Carlo? Nothing. Not even a glimmer of recognition, anticipation, excitement, nothing."

I didn't know what to say to that.

"You need to give it time," I said finally. "It's only been two or three days. This stuff takes time. One of my buddies when I was in the juniors took a puck to the head while we were messing around during practice, so he didn't have a helmet on. Knocked him out cold, and he couldn't talk when he woke up. He was a mess. But his memory and talking and everything came back in a few weeks, and he plays for the team in Vegas now."

She swallowed. "That's good to hear."

"Anyway, I can't stay long because we have a game tonight. I need to go home and close my eyes for an hour or so. Game days are intense, and I try not to mess up my routine."

"Oh, of course. Go." She nodded. "I'll be fine. I'm calmer now."

"Will you be watching?"

"The game? If they get the channel here, absolutely."

"You can also watch online on your phone."

"I wish I could go," she said wryly. "But I'm guessing breaking me out of here would cause all kinds of trouble."

I chuckled. "Yeah, I don't think that's the best move."

We were quiet for a few minutes and even though I couldn't read her mind, I knew what she was thinking because it was all I could think about too.

There was this thing between us.

A spark of electricity that had been undeniable since she'd unwittingly held my hand before she knew who I was.

It fucking sizzled when we were in the same room, and we both felt it.

But that engagement ring on her finger meant she was off-limits and that was a line I wouldn't cross. No matter how much I wanted to.

And she was too fragile for something like this anyway.

Whatever there was—whatever there might be—ended now.

"I really have to go," I said softly.

"I know." She looked at me curiously. "Will I see you again?"

I paused, a little surprised at her directness. "Do you want to?"

"I do."

"But—"

"We can be friends, can't we?" The words seemed to tumble out before she could stop them, as if she was struggling with this as much as I was.

"Sure," my traitorous mouth responded. "You have my number. Call or text anytime."

She smiled. "You might regret that."

"Nah." I smiled back. "But I really have to go. If I don't nap, it'll mess up my whole routine."

"I understand. Thank you for stopping by and saving me from my meltdown."

"That's what friends are for, right? Talk to you soon." I squeezed her arm and then turned to walk out of the room, shaking my head.

What self-inflicted let's-be-friends torture had I just brought on myself?

I was a fucking idiot.

8

I woke up to a flood of memories. They whiplashed through my brain with such speed and ferocity, I sat up in alarm. It was still dark out, but I was wide awake and suddenly remembered everything. Mom had brought me my laptop, and I'd done some digging last night, but all I'd managed to find out was that amnesia was different for everyone, there were a few different kinds, and that memories could come back slowly, all in a rush, not at all, or anywhere in between. So I'd been a little discouraged when I fell asleep.

Now I was wide awake, my heart pounding furiously.

I was getting married in three months.

And I fucking hated the wedding dress my mother and I had picked out.

In fact, now that I could remember everything, I was angry.

Why had I allowed my family and my fiancé to walk all over me with regard to the wedding? I hadn't gotten what I wanted on a single element of the wedding or reception, and the day of the accident, Carlo and I had a big fight about it. I'd called him selfish, and he'd called me spoiled. Then I'd told him I was having second thoughts before storming out of the restaurant and heading for the game.

Now my confusion made sense. I hadn't been able to remember any details, but something wasn't right with Carlo and me, and now I knew why.

I'd been hesitant to say anything to anyone other than Chloe because I knew my family would freak, but the argument we'd had right before I got hurt had been intense. Carlo was a good guy, but he could be old-fashioned and a little overbearing sometimes, much like my family. The difference was that I wasn't going to marry my family. Old-fashioned and overbearing didn't work for me in a relationship, and while I'd kept my mouth shut before, something inside of me was hinting that I couldn't do that anymore.

Maybe it was having a near-death experience since a shot to the head could have killed me. Maybe it was the fact that I'd met my family and fiancé for the first time as a stranger and had been spectacularly underwhelmed. Or maybe the hit in the head had knocked some kind of emotional screw loose, but whatever it was, nothing felt the same anymore. Not even now that I had my memory back.

The day was filled with tests and more tests and conversations with doctors, which was a good distraction because I waffled between relief and anxiety. When Mom, Desi, Tony, and Carlo came in around dinnertime, there was a lot of excitement about the return of my memory and the fact that Dr. Montrose had let me take a shower today.

"The flowers are beautiful, Carlo," Mom said, leaning over to smell them.

Carlo blinked. "They're not from me, Mrs. C."

Mom frowned and looked at me. "Where did they come from?"

"Uh, the Knights sent them."

"The hockey team?" She made a face. "Bunch of heathens! I hope they're going to pay your hospital bills."

"That's why we have insurance," I said quietly.

"There will be co-pays and who knows what else," she countered. "You should tell your friend Vaughn you need help paying the bills."

"Let's wait until we see what's covered," I said.

"Hey, so a couple of the waitstaff didn't get paid this week," Desi told me sheepishly. "Do you think you'll be back by Wednesday to help figure out payroll?"

"Seriously?" I looked up at her. "I wind up in the hospital and no one got paid?"

"Well, some people got paid," Tony said. "Just not everyone. Desi doesn't know the program and—"

"I'll be there on Wednesday," I said, irritated. I'd shown Desi how to do payroll at least four or five times. Yet, she never remembered how the program worked. Every single time I went on vacation or had a sick day that prevented me from doing payroll, everything went to hell and it was exhausting.

"All right, Wednesday is three days away," Mom said quickly. "We'll figure it out."

"Do you think you'll be going home tomorrow?" Carlo asked, reaching for my hand.

"It depends on the results of the CT scan," I said. "Dr. Montrose said he'd have them in the morning."

"You'll feel better once you're home," Mom said. "In your own bed with your own things."

"And you've got to reschedule your dress fitting right away," Desi reminded me.

Yeah, that was way up on my list of things to do.

Not.

"I can't even think about the wedding right now," I said quietly.

The room went silent, and everyone turned to look at me.

"You're tired," Mom said after a moment. "You'll feel up to it once you're home."

I opened my mouth, but as usual, no one was listening to me.

"I'll call the shop and explain what happened," Desi said. "I'm sure they'll work with us because they obviously already have the dress and want to get paid for it."

She pulled out her phone and started typing something.

"And we have to finalize the menu," Mom said.

"And the bridesmaids are asking about shoes," Desi added.

"Okay, can we stop, please?" I asked, frowning. "I'm in the hospital. I've had my memory back, like, five minutes! Can I have, say, a day to get my thoughts together before you barrage me with things to do?"

There was another brief, awkward silence, before Mom stepped in. "She's right. What are we doing? She's still in the hospital. There's no reason to overwhelm her." She reached out and cupped the side of my face. "We're just so glad you're going to be okay. We were worried."

"We should get going so we don't get you tired," Mom continued, motioning to Tony and Desi.

"I'm going to stay a while," Carlo said to them. "That's why I drove myself, so I could spend a little time with my girl."

Mom gave him a look. "Not too long."

"I know, Mrs. C." He smiled at her as he sank into the chair next to my bed. When we were alone, he turned and reached for my hand. "So how are you really?" he asked.

"Tired. Stressed. Anxious."

"I'm sorry."

"It's not your fault."

He cleared his throat. "So, uh, you remember everything, huh?"

"You mean the fight we had before I left for the game? Yeah."

"You never seemed that excited about wedding planning," he said after a moment, his dark eyes meeting mine. "So I thought it would just make things easier if I did most of it."

"Not wanting to do all the planning doesn't mean I don't care about the details," I said quietly. "And then you just made decisions without me. Even when I asked you to stop."

He sighed, threading his fingers through mine. "I honestly thought you'd like not having to make those decisions."

"What about the cake?" I demanded. "I told you I didn't want a chocolate wedding cake, but you ordered the ganache anyway."

"I screwed up," he admitted. "I'm sorry. I guess I was mad I'd worked so hard at something you didn't want to do, and you were unhappy anyway."

"Carlo, we've both been unhappy about a lot of things the last few months," I said slowly. "You want to live close to your parents in Coral Springs. I want to live closer to the ocean. I want to go to Hawaii for our honeymoon. You want to go to Italy to see family you don't even know. The list of big things that we disagree on is long. And honestly, I'm beginning to wonder if it wouldn't be best to put everything on hold."

"On hold?" He blinked. "You mean…the wedding?"

"Everything," I said slowly. "The wedding and the engagement too. I feel like I need a break after everything that's happened."

"A break." He was staring at me as if he didn't understand.

"Don't tell me you're happy," I said, meeting his gaze directly.

"I love you," he replied.

"It's not the same thing."

"You need to rest," he said after a long silence, finally releasing my hand.

"Rest isn't going to change the fact that neither of us have been happy for months, Carlo. Me getting hurt just made me realize that life is too short for both of us to make what could potentially be a huge mistake."

"You mean getting married?" He cocked his head. "I've loved you since high school, Jules. I've never loved anyone else, never had sex with anyone else, never even thought of being with anyone else. How can you say this is a mistake?"

"I say it because deep down, you know I'm right. Admit it—you were disappointed I don't want to go to Italy."

"I was, but this is what marriage is—compromise and communication."

"But there is no compromise. The only houses you've been looking at are in Coral Springs, even though I want to look in Pompano and Lighthouse Point. Same thing with the cake. Same with the catering. It's a thing with you. With us. And maybe we need to think about what it means going forward."

"Fine, you want a white cake at the wedding?" He threw up his hands. "I don't care. We can change it."

I hesitated, wondering if he was going to get angry. "You really think this is about the cake?" I asked softly.

He shook his head. "You've been in an accident, Jules, and have a brain injury. I don't want to do this now. I think after you've had some time to think, you'll see everything is okay, and you're just emotional right now."

"Seriously?" I scowled. "Why won't you listen to what I'm really saying? That we should take some time apart to really think things through. To think about why we disagree about so many important things. And how—"

"Fine. You want some time apart? Then gimme back the ring." He held out his hand.

I stared at him in surprise and then slowly pulled the ring off my finger, holding it out to him.

"This is what you want, Jules? Really?"

"I want some time to think, Carlo. To focus on what's important. Both to me and to you."

"Okay, then, you can have all the time you want."

"Carlo, I'm trying to be an adult about this. Why are you acting this way?"

"I've spent my entire adult life loving you, and you're just throwing it away." His back was turned, and I sighed because I hated he was hurt and angry about something we both needed to consider.

"So it's better to not talk things out, go ahead and get married, have a few kids, and then realize that this wasn't meant to be?" I demanded.

"I don't know, but if you don't love me enough to work things out, then what is there to talk about?"

It felt like this conversation was going in circles. "But I'm trying to talk to you. You're the one getting mad and not communicating."

"I asked for the ring, and you didn't even hesitate—you took it off. That told me everything I needed to know."

I didn't know what to say to that because it was true—I hadn't hesitated at all.

"I just want some time to make sure we're doing the right thing."

"And you think being apart is going to help?"

"Well, going forward with the wedding certainly isn't."

"Wedding's off. Engagement is off. Everything is off. You happy?"

I blinked back tears because I didn't know what else to say. "I'm sorry," I whispered as he grabbed his phone off the table where he'd put it.

"Take care, Jules." He strode out of the room, and I closed my eyes.

That hadn't gone at all the way I'd thought it would.

9

We lost to Tampa, which was frustrating, but we were still getting our bearings as a team. We'd just gotten back last night. and Coach Petrov had set up a day at a driving range today. And even though I hated golf with the fiery passion of every sun in the universe, I obligingly did my thing. I was distracted, though, which I tried to avoid when I did anything with the team.

I thought about Juliet a lot more than I'd thought about a woman in a long time, and now I had the growing worry that my father was stalking me or something. I'd suspected the black pick-up I'd seen in the neighborhood belonged to him, but he wasn't the only guy in the world who owned one. If I was a little more mature and a lot less bitter about what a shitty dad he'd been, I could have called him and just asked him what was up. But I was who I was, and he hadn't reached out either. We didn't talk much, but we did have each other's numbers.

"Not a golf fan, eh?" Coach Petrov came to stand beside me as I stared off at nothing, so lost in thought I'd missed my turn.

"No. Not really."

"You might be the only hockey player in the entire league who doesn't play," he said, a faint smile on his face.

"Yeah, I know." I scratched my head. "Sorry, Coach."

"It's all right. You don't have to love these activities I dream up as long as you're polite about them."

"I'm trying."

"Something's on your mind," he said after a moment.

I sighed. I never talked about my dad. With my last two teams, it hadn't mattered because I told them we didn't have a relationship. And we didn't. Well, not much of one, but now my gut told me that black pick-up was his, and I didn't know what that meant. If he was up to something, it could impact not just me, but the team, and I'd never let that happen. I'd get traded or quit hockey completely before I let my father's life hurt anyone else close to me.

"My dad," I said after a moment. "I thought I saw him near my house and… It's never good when he comes around. We don't really speak, and he wasn't around much when I was growing up, so it worries me."

"Does he live here?"

"No. He lives in California. And the weird thing is, I think I've spotted him twice, but he hasn't called or stopped by or anything, so I don't know what that means. And yeah, I know I should just call and ask, but it's hard. Our relationship is fucked up."

"Fucked up or not, if it's impacting you this much, you probably need to do it anyway." He paused. "I've had a very strained relationship with my father as well. He was KGB when I was a kid—you know what that is?"

My eyes widened. "Well, yeah. Holy shit."

"You keep this to yourself, you understand?"

I nodded.

"So believe me, I understand what that's like. I thought my father was a criminal and a terrible human being, but there was a lot more to it than that. Sometimes parents do things we don't necessarily approve of, but it's because we don't know the full story. I'm not saying that's the case with your father, but maybe if you talked, you'd find out more than you think. I know I did."

I looked away. "I know you're right, but it's so hard. He left when I was a baby, and then he'd come around a few times a year, like Christmas, or for a random week in the summer. My mom loved him so much—she never got remarried or even dated anyone else. And then she died. In her forties. Alone and in pain. I couldn't even get there in time to be with her. Her whole life was wasted because of him, and I fucking hate the cold-hearted bastard."

Toli nodded slowly. "I understand. But your hate only hurts *you*. If he's truly the cold-hearted bastard you say he is, you think he gives a shit? He's living his life, and you're sitting here distracted and pissed off, which gets you nothing."

Crap.

He was right.

I knew it, but it was hard as fuck to let go of a lifetime of hurt, resentment, and hate.

"Anyway, think about it. I know it's hard." He patted my shoulder and started to walk away.

"Coach?"

He turned. "Yes?"

"How do I…do that? How do I let go of the memories of my mother crying herself to sleep, all the times I prayed my dad would show up to watch me play when I was little and then cried because he didn't…and then other shit he pulled when I was old enough to understand? How do you let go of all that?"

"Three options. You either say fuck him, I'm done, and put him out of your mind. Or you find a therapist to help you. Pro tip: Zakk's wife, Tiff, is a psychologist with a huge practice in Vegas. Doctor-patient confidentiality applies. And she's amazing." He paused. "And option number three is to call him up, or go see him, and talk it all out in person. That might lead back to option number one, but it also might put you on a totally different path."

"Thanks, Coach."

"You're welcome. Now go hit a few balls."

I ambled over to where Ryder, Jude, and Zakk were shooting the shit.

"You in trouble again?" Ryder asked, arching a brow.

I chuckled. "Nah. Golf just isn't my thing."

"I bet pretty brunettes with puck-shaped dents in their skulls are, though." Jude laughed, and I couldn't help but chuckle.

"You're an asshole, you know that?"

"You gonna take her out or what?" Zakk asked.

"I told you—she's engaged. And she friend-zoned me."

"Ouch." Ryder grimaced. "Sorry."

"No biggie." I looked around. "You guys hungry? I'm about done with golf."

"I could eat," Jude said.

"I need to get home," Ryder said, shaking his head. "Peyton's been alone with the baby all day, and I'm betting she's wiped."

"Same for me," Zakk said. "Tiff runs a pretty tight ship with four kids, but I like to be home for dinner when I'm not traveling."

"I bet Cam and Palmer will come with us," Jude said.

"Let's go."

Maybe a big-ass steak and a few beers with my buddies would take my mind off the situation with my dad. Not to mention keep me from thinking about Juliet. I seriously did not have time for this shit.

I was almost home when I saw a dark pick-up pull into traffic behind me. I glanced in my rearview mirror, squinting, but it was hard to see now that it was dark. Either my fucking dad was following me, or I was a paranoid sonofabitch.

I went past the turn for my development, got to the intersection, turned right, and then pulled into a gas station. The pick-up slowed down, made the right, and moved past me.

Yup. That was my dad in the driver's seat.

Losing my patience, and with Coach Petrov's words in the back of my mind, I yanked out my phone and dialed my dad's number, drumming my fingers on the dashboard as I waited for him to answer.

"Vaughn?" My dad's deep baritone was so familiar it made me a little nostalgic, even as pissed off at him as I was right now.

"Why the fuck are you following me?" I demanded.

"What are you talking about?"

"Shut the fuck up," I snapped. "I literally just watched you drive past the gas station where I pulled over. You're on Nob fucking Hill Road."

There were a few seconds of silence before I continued. "Don't blow smoke up my ass, Dad. Just tell me why you're here, and why you've been following me."

"Can we go somewhere and talk?"

"Yeah. My house. Turn around and meet me there." I disconnected and tossed my phone down on the seat before I made a left toward home.

This was stupid.

My father—the sperm donor I'd spoken to maybe five times in the last nine years—had no business being here. And I definitely didn't want him anywhere near my house. But he already knew where I lived so it was the safest place to have what would undoubtedly be a heated, and personal, conversation.

I parked in the garage and waited for Dad to pull up behind me.

He got out of the truck and approached me slowly.

I hadn't seen him since Mom's funeral, and I'd been too grief-stricken to exchange more than a handful of words with him before I left. He looked a little older, with more gray in his hair, but otherwise the same.

"Hello, son."

"Dad."

We stared at each other.

"You going to invite me in?"

"Sure." I turned and went in through the garage, hitting the button to close the door behind us. "Want a beer?" I asked him.

"No, thank you." He stood in my kitchen looking tired and more than a little awkward. He was a big guy, an inch taller than me and a good fifty pounds heavier, but he stayed in great shape for a man in his late forties.

"So, what's going on?" I leaned against the counter, watching him.

"It's kind of a long story."

"Then maybe you should get started telling me."

"I don't know how much your mom told you."

"About what? You?"

"Me. The club. All of it."

"Club." I snorted. "It's a *gang*, Dad. It's not a fucking club, it's a goddamn motorcycle gang, and you're their criminal leader. Right?"

He didn't say anything.

"Well? Yes? No? Maybe? Are you going to talk, or should I fill in the blanks for you?" I couldn't help but get more and more pissed off. This conversation had been a long time coming, and I had run out of fucks to give.

He nervously ran a hand through his too-long hair and finally nodded. "I have something for you."

"What is it?"

He pulled an envelope out of his pocket. "This is from your mom."

"From mom?"

"She said… Well, I'm sure she explains in the letter."

I took it from him and stared at my mom's familiar handwriting. It made missing her so much more poignant, and it took a few seconds to compose myself.

"I think maybe it's better for you to read it on your own," Dad said. "Then when you're ready, reach out and we'll talk." He patted me on the arm and headed back out the way we'd come in. I stared after him for a second before opening the envelope and unfolding the single sheet of paper.

D*ear Vaughn,*

If you're reading this, it means I'm gone, and you and your father are being stubborn as hell. So it's time to set the record straight. I'm writing this on your twenty-first birthday, because you're old enough to know the truth, and your father has strict orders to only get it to you if he doesn't succeed in rebuilding your relationship on his own...

I read the whole thing. Twice. And swiped at my eyes to make sure I didn't do something stupid like cry in front of my dad. I hadn't been expecting a letter from Mom, and even though it didn't say much other than how much she wanted me to give my dad a chance, they were literally the last words she'd ever communicate to me.

10

Being home at my mom's house was nice. The accident had happened Wednesday, and I got out of the hospital the following Monday afternoon. Mom picked me up, brought me home, and I got right in the shower. Dr. Montrose said it was okay to wash my hair—the soap and water wouldn't hurt anything—and it felt good to be clean. The scar on my temple was healing better than I'd thought it would so I let my curly hair air dry as I pulled on clean pajamas. The only thing I wanted to do today was watch mindless TV, eat something fattening, and sleep through the night with no interruptions.

Though my memory had come back, I had no memory of the accident. The last thing I remembered before waking up in the hospital was that I'd gotten to the arena late and missed the warm-up. After that, most of what I remembered was Vaughn.

The visits to my hospital room.

Me stupidly holding his hand.

The wonderful gifts he'd brought.

I itched to text and tell him I was home, but I decided not to. I needed to rest, recover, and deal with the fallout from the breakup with Carlo first. My family had undoubtedly heard that something was up because I knew for a fact my mother had noticed the ring missing on my finger, but she hadn't said a word. I figured she was waiting for the right time, but it wouldn't be tonight. At least I hoped not.

I turned on the TV in my room, crawled under the covers and the next thing I knew it was morning. I slept almost fourteen hours, and by the time I padded downstairs to make coffee, I felt like a new woman. Mom was in the kitchen doing something on the stove and she turned with a smile.

"Good morning. How are you feeling?"

"Much better, thanks." I leaned over, kissed her cheek, and turned on the coffee machine.

"You want me to make you some eggs?"

"I'd love it, thanks." My mother loved to cook, and I loved her cooking. It also made her happy to fuss over me, so I'd let her since I knew she was going to bring Carlo up, no matter what I said or did.

"What will you do today?" Mom asked. "I'm going to the restaurant for a little while. I think the boys are struggling."

I rolled my eyes. "They've been working there longer than I have, and yet I can do everything in the restaurant except make the pizza dough, but they can't. Why is that?"

She smiled. "Because it's always been you."

"What's always been me?"

"Running the show. From the time you were five years old, you started rolling silverware and seating guests. When you got tall enough to reach the register, you started taking money and credit cards. By the time you got to high school, you helped your father with inventory and ordering, making the schedule, and payroll. And your father always wanted you by his side. At that point, we knew Peter and Sal weren't interested in the business, and Mario and Tony were already helping with the dough and everything in the back, so the rest fell to you."

"How come nobody asked me what I wanted to do?" I asked, leaning against the counter.

She turned to me in surprise. "We didn't have to. You were up with your father every day. No one told you to, you just did it. It was obvious what you wanted."

I took a sip of coffee. "I guess that was my fault, but when I said I wanted to go to college, everyone told me it would be a waste of money."

"Well, the pizzeria is very successful, and you already knew everything you needed to know to run it. Why spend the money?"

I frowned. "I don't think that's the point."

"Anyway, that was a long time ago. Now you're going to get married and have babies."

"Mom." I took another sip of coffee, figuring I'd better get this over with. "We've canceled the wedding and broken off the engagement."

"I know."

"That's it? You know?"

"You're just out of the hospital. You hit your head and had a swollen brain for a few days. I don't want to fight or upset you, so we're going to let it be for a while. You need to relax and not have any stress. In a few days, you'll realize how emotional you were, and you and Carlo will make up."

"No." I shook my head. "Carlo and I had been fighting long before I got hurt."

"About what? The wedding? Leonora told us about the cake and the food. Okay, he was a little selfish, but he realizes now he needs to be more open to what you want since it's your wedding too. It's not a big deal." Leonora was Carlo's mother.

"And the honeymoon. The guest list. The dress—"

"The dress!" Mom whirled around, spatula in her hand. "I picked the dress."

"I know." I met her gaze.

"You don't like it?" Her face fell. "But I thought you loved it."

Crap. I hated disappointing my mother, so I softened my tone. "I loved the one with the lavender embroidered flowers on the train and you ordered the other one before I could tell you."

"Oh." She looked away. "Well, I thought you wanted something traditional. You don't want to look like someone from the 'Real Housewives' on your wedding day."

"No, but I wanted to look like me." I put a hand on her arm. "I'm sorry. I should have said something sooner about the dress, but it doesn't matter. The wedding is off, so we have to make a list of everyone we need to call."

She put a plate of scrambled eggs in front of me. "You just got home from the hospital. You don't need to think about that now. There's plenty of time for all that."

Before I could answer, my phone rang, and the name Lauderdale Knights flashed on the screen.

"Hang on, Mom." I hit the button to take the call. "Hello?"

"Hi, is this Juliet Cicero?"

"Yes."

"This is Dean Nicholls from the Lauderdale Knights. I'm calling at the request of the team owner, Remington Knight. He was wondering if you'd like to join him for practice and a tour of the arena on Wednesday morning."

"Oh." I couldn't help the grin on my face. "I'd love that. Thank you."

"He'll send a car for you at nine thirty if that's okay?"

"Oh, he doesn't have to do that," I said. "I can drive."

"He understands, but he's rolling out the red carpet, so to speak."

"Well, then I'm looking forward to it. Thank you."

"If anything changes, you can reach me at this number."

He verified my address, and I was still grinning when I hung up. "The owner of the Lauderdale Knights just invited me to practice and to tour the arena."

"Nice. See if he'll pick up the bills from the hospital while you're at it." Mom put the frying pan and spatula in the sink.

"Geez, Mom." I sank down and dug into my eggs, ignoring her huff as she left the room.

***

A long, black limousine pulled up to the house at precisely nine thirty on Wednesday morning, and I was shocked to see Remington Knight in the back. He was a former player who looked like he was in his mid to late thirties. He was broad-shouldered and handsome, with a close-cropped beard and short dark hair. His brown eyes were warm and friendly, and his handshake dry and firm.

"Nice to meet you," he said as I slid into the seat across from him. "I'm sorry it was under these circumstances, but I'm glad to hear you're okay."

"Thank you."

"Well, I'm sure everyone has said this already, but if there's anything you need, please don't hesitate to ask."

I smiled. "I already have season tickets, so I think I'm good."

"Would you like to attend a game from my box?" he asked. "The guys leave on a road trip soon, but I'd love for you to be my guest when they get back. And you're welcome to bring someone with you as well."

"That sounds like fun," I said, "but honestly, I'm fine. You don't have to be so nice."

He chuckled. "I try to be nice to everyone, but you're a special case since you got hurt at my arena, by one of my players, on our very first home game."

"Aside from what will probably be a scar I'm doing great."

He paused to study my face. "Is there going to be a scar? If so, I can find you a plastic surgeon."

"Oh." I was startled. I hadn't even considered that. The stitches were rough and ugly right now, but I'd covered them up to come out today since I hadn't wanted Vaughn to see them. "I haven't thought that far ahead. The doctor who stitched me up said my hair will cover most of it, but there might be an inch or so visible on my temple. I'm not real worried about it yet since I don't know what it'll look like once the stitches are removed."

"Just let me know."

"Thank you. I appreciate that." I gazed straight ahead, wondering if I was going to have a chance to talk to Vaughn today.

I really hoped so.

"You okay?" Mr. Knight was watching me intently and I blinked, realizing I'd been so lost in thought I hadn't heard what he'd been saying.

"I'm sorry, I was just thinking about practice. I've never been to one, and I probably never would have if I hadn't gotten hurt."

He grinned back. "Tired of everyone fussing over you? I get it. No worries. We won't bring it up again, and anyway, practice is fun to watch. I'm looking forward to it as well since I'm not always able to get down there in the morning."

"You're going to watch with me?" I asked in surprise.

"I watch whenever I can. I didn't buy my own hockey team for the money."

I chuckled. "Works for me."

We got to the arena, and someone brought me a latte, exactly the way I liked it. Someone else appeared with a basket of muffins and bagels, and Remy—who'd told me to use his first name—grabbed a blueberry muffin as I settled into seats behind the bench. I was too distracted to eat and had to admit to getting a thrill at being so close to the action.

"Now this is where I should have gotten my seats," I murmured, looking around. "I like being a little higher up so I never lose sight of the puck but sitting here would be pretty epic too."

"Put in a request with your sales rep for next season," he replied. "I'm sure he can make it happen."

"These seats are definitely out of my price range," I admitted.

"Well," Mr. Knight stared straight ahead. "I could probably get you a discount. But I don't want to give you any special treatment since it makes you uncomfortable."

It was hard to tell if he was kidding, but the slight twitch of his lips made me laugh. "I can probably tolerate a *little* more special treatment."

He laughed. "When the time comes, reach out to me. Just call my office here at the arena. My assistant will know to put you through."

"I might just take you up on that."

Practice was awesome. I loved seeing the guys running drills, skating, and occasionally goofing around. They had distinct personalities, and it was fun watching them, but mostly I watched Vaughn. He was tall, six-four according to his online profile, and though the equipment he wore hid his body, I knew he had broad shoulders and narrow hips. He was gorgeous too, even with his hair damp with sweat and a helmet on. I could imagine him getting sweaty doing other things, and I momentarily lost myself in a fantasy, wondering what that would be like to be with someone like him.

"Ready to go meet the team?" Remy was asking me.

I realized practice was over, and I stood up, watching as the guys filed into the tunnel that led to the locker room. Vaughn glanced up and met my eye, winking as he passed us, and I couldn't help but smile back at him.

"He's single," Mr. Knight said, watching us.

"What?" My eyes snapped to his, and I was fairly sure my face turned red.

"You heard me." He led me up the stairs toward an elevator. "You two would be cute together."

"Oh, I'm not looking for—"

"Yeah, yeah." He interrupted me laughing. "We all say that. Next thing you know—boom! You're married."

"Is that what happened to you?"

He nodded. "Yup. I went to look at a real estate investment in British Columbia last December, met the most amazing woman, and now we're married."

"Sounds very romantic."

He chuckled. "Yeah, kinda."

We got on the elevator, went down a couple of levels, got out, walked around a couple of corners, and then I was in the locker room. And it was so fucking cool.

The guys were in various stages of undress, though no one was actually naked—thank God—and I immediately sought out Vaughn. Yup, he was even more beautiful in nothing but bike shorts, and it took every ounce of self-control I had to keep my eyes above his chest. The abdominal V was like a beacon calling to me, but I absolutely wouldn't look.

Okay, maybe just a peek.

Jesus, he was gorgeous.

"I'm hungry," Vaughn said to me after I'd met most of the team. "You want to get something to eat?"

Oh, hell yes, I did.

11

VAUGHN

I hadn't meant to ask her out, but it happened so naturally, and I would have been a liar if I'd said I hadn't noticed that there was no longer a ring on her left hand. It might not mean anything, but I figured taking her out to lunch to ask her in person wouldn't hurt anything. If she was still with Carlo, I'd leave it alone, but there was something about her that made me want to know more, see more, talk more.

She looked beautiful today, with her hair a soft bouncy swirl around her head, mascara accentuating long eyelashes, and something on her lips that made me want to taste them. I had to remind myself a thousand times that the ring might just be at the jeweler's being resized or something, but I needed to know sooner rather than later.

"Where to?" I asked as we got into my Corvette.

"The beach," she said after a moment. "Let's go down to Deerfield. We can eat at JB's and maybe take a walk on the pier after."

"I don't know my way around yet," I told her. "Can you guide me?"

She nodded. "Take I-95 to the tenth street exit and then east."

"I can do that." I headed for the highway.

Normally, I played it cool with women, but I needed to know what was going on with Juliet and Carlo before we spent any amount of time together.

"So…you're not wearing your engagement ring," I said once I got on the highway.

"Nope. I gave it back to him."

"How come?"

"We've been together a long time," she said after a moment. "Since senior year of high school. We'd started arguing more, hanging out less often, just living separate lives. I'd mentioned taking a break about eighteen months ago, and he showed up with a ring. He proposed in front of the whole family, and after losing my dad not too long before that, it was like this big, happy occasion after the rough year we'd had. And I kind of had no choice but to say yes. Then everyone, including me, I guess, threw themselves into wedding planning."

"But?"

"But a few weeks ago, we went to do the tasting thing for the cake. We'd been arguing about other aspects of the wedding, but it was mostly stupid stuff. The cake thing blew up, though. I wanted something fun and traditional —big multi-tiered cake with flowers and maybe white chocolate something or other. Carlo decided, for the first time in his entire life, he wanted to buck tradition and get a chocolate ganache wedding cake. I know it sounds stupid, but I wasn't happy about it. I pushed back. He dug his heels in. Then, he literally told the rep from the bakery that we were going with the chocolate ganache, got up, and walked out. So I followed him, and we had a huge fight in the parking lot. In the end, I gave in, but something snapped that day, and I knew I didn't want to marry him anymore."

"This was about a hell of a lot more than cake flavors," I said dryly.

"Exactly. But it's so hard. My family adores him. My mother and his mother have been friends since we lived in Long Island, and they're so excited about officially becoming family. He and my brothers hang out all the time. Carlo is like an extended family member, so it's going to be hard to make the break. My mom already said that I'm not myself because I got hit in the head and in a week or two, I'll come to my senses."

I glanced at her. "Is she right?"

"I don't think so. There have been a lot of problems in the last year or so, and after what happened, I feel like fate is trying to tell me something. Like I'm getting a second chance at something. I'm just not sure what."

"Your family's kind of overbearing, huh?"

"They are." She sighed. "Don't get me wrong—my family is amazing. Loyal and hardworking and generous, but the tradeoff is that everyone is in everyone's business, all the time, and because I'm the youngest, and the only girl, I get treated like an afterthought sometimes. And until now, I've never stood up for myself."

She said that last part slowly, as if it just occurred to her, and I glanced at her curiously. "How come?"

"I don't know. I guess I've always done what was expected of me."

"And now?"

"I'm not sure, but it feels like the real me is buried deep inside, and now she's kicking and clawing to come out. Wow. I can't believe I said all that. You probably think I'm crazy."

"Nah." I shook my head. "You're not the first person to do what your family expects instead of what you want."

"Did you?"

"Did I what? Live up to my family's expectations?" I chuckled. "There were no family expectations, to be honest. Growing up, it was mostly just me and my mom. She wanted whatever I wanted, and all I ever wanted was to play hockey."

"What about your dad?"

"My dad was…" My voice trailed off. How was I supposed to explain my father? A criminal? A deadbeat? An asshole? He was all of those things, but after reading my mother's letter, I now knew he wasn't. Not exactly. It was hard to explain. "I guess my dad wasn't a traditional father. He and my mom split when I was a baby, but he came around a few times a year, and they'd be together. We'd be a family. Like for three weeks in the summer and a couple weeks at Christmas or whatever, and then he'd disappear again. My mom didn't like to talk about their relationship, and she died two years ago. In September."

"My dad died two years ago in September too," she said softly. "Heart attack."

"Cancer."

"When?" she asked after a moment. "What day?"

"September eighteenth."

"Oh, wow. Same day as my dad."

"Really?" I looked over at her. "That's kind of freaky."

"What time?" she asked.

"It was late. I wasn't there. I'd seen her the week before, but when I talked to her that morning, she sounded bad. I had a game that night, so I played and then rented a car and drove out there. She was in New Hampshire, and we'd just played a pre-season game in Boston. I got there about one in the morning, and they told me she'd died at eleven thirty."

"We don't know what time Dad died exactly, but it was between ten and eleven in the evening. He was working late at the restaurant, catching up on orders and stuff, and he was alone. Mom finally got worried about three in the morning and sent Peter to check on him."

"So your brother found him?"

She nodded. "Yeah. It was…rough."

"I can't even imagine. Mom was diagnosed with stage five colon cancer in June and was gone by September. It was quick, and I'm kind of grateful because she didn't want to suffer."

"At least you had a chance to say goodbye, say all the things you might have wanted to say. We had no chance with Dad."

"I'm sorry." I reached across the console and closed my hand around hers. Her fingers threaded with mine, and we sat like that for a few minutes.

"Were you close?" she asked finally.

"Very. She was my biggest fan, my biggest supporter. I miss her every day. Were you close to your dad?"

"Yeah. I was definitely Daddy's girl. Things were different when he was alive because even though my family was the same, Dad was always there as a buffer. He understood me more than anyone else. It's hard to explain."

I got off the highway and headed east since we were going toward the beach.

"JB's has valet parking, which will probably be safer with a car like this."

"I hate letting anyone drive my car," I said, "but you're probably right."

"She's a beauty." Juliet looked around. "She's still new."

"Yeah, I've only had her a month."

"Gorgeous."

"Thanks."

I pulled up to the restaurant's valet, and we walked inside. The doors were open to the back, which led to a patio. Beyond it was the beach, and it was beautiful today. The water was smooth as glass and the weather was perfect. It wasn't too hot, there was a nice breeze, and the sky was as blue as I'd ever seen it.

Something about being out with Juliet made everything feel right in my world, despite all the changes going on in my life. Talking to her was comfortable, and as the waitress seated us outside, I couldn't help but gaze at her across the table.

"What?" she asked softly.

"Just thinking how pretty you are."

She smiled, dipping her head a little, as if that embarrassed her. "Thank you."

We talked all through lunch and after we finished. She told me stories about her family's restaurant, and I told her about life as a professional athlete. It seemed like the afternoon passed in a flash, and I hadn't even realized how late it was until the waitress told us she was going home.

"Want to take a walk on the beach?" I asked Juliet as we got up.

"Sure."

We walked outside, and we took off our shoes. Then I reached for her hand and our fingers curled together naturally.

"I'd like to take you out on a real date," I told her as we walked through the warm sand.

"This wasn't a real date?" She glanced up at me with a playful grin.

"Well, kinda, but it was more an impromptu opportunity to hang out. I'd like to take you to dinner, maybe go dancing or something. Do you like to dance?"

"I do." She leaned closer to me as we walked.

"I travel quite a bit with the team, but I'll do my best to make time for you if you'd like to hang out and get to know each other."

"I'd like that." She paused. "But can I ask you a question first?"

"Sure."

"I guess I'm just wondering why you want to go out with me. Don't professional athletes usually surround themselves with models and cheerleaders and stuff?"

I hesitated because she was right, but she was also wrong.

"I think professional athletes date women they're attracted to, just like anyone else. We usually have opportunities not every guy has because of the money we make and our celebrity, but it still boils down to attraction and there's no doubt you and I have it."

"So it's still there, the attraction between us." She had a soft smile on her face. "I thought maybe I'd imagined it."

"No." We stopped walking and faced each other. I was debating whether I should kiss her when she took the decision out of my hands, lifting to her tiptoes and lightly pressing her lips to mine.

The kiss was soft and sweet, her lips a whisper against mine.

Then she pulled away.

"Why'd you stop?" I asked quietly.

"I wasn't sure you wanted me to keep going." Her eyes met mine.

I slid an arm around her waist and pulled her against me. This time I took the lead, grazing her mouth with mine and savoring the moment. The sun was low in the sky, giving us a magical backdrop. Her lips parted slightly, and I toyed with her tongue, keeping my touch light but my intentions clear since she'd mentioned she wasn't sure I wanted her to kiss me.

We slowly pulled apart, and I moved a lock of hair out of her eyes because the wind had picked up.

"Wanna walk some more?" I asked.

"Yes."

I smiled and took her hand.

12

My date with Vaughn had been wonderful. We hadn't done much of anything but walk, talk, and eventually eat again, yet I'd had such a good time. He was gentle and laid-back—everything my family wasn't—and it seemed like I could talk to him about anything. I could have stayed out with him all night, but he had a trip to pack for, and I was tired, no matter how much I tried to hide it.

Vaughn had said he would call or text while he was gone. Then he'd walked me to my front door, kissed my cheek, and taken off in that incredible car of his. I'd stared after him for a few seconds, wishing I was going with him, and reluctantly walked into the house. Luckily, Mom was asleep, and I got to bed without having to answer any questions. I knew they would be coming in the morning, though, and I tossed and turned all night.

Even though my memories had all come back at this point, it was odd how I felt like someone different now. I still couldn't remember the accident, but most of the gaps had filled in. The weird thing was, instead of making me feel better, it made me feel like I was an imposter because I didn't like the woman I was. Or had been. I wasn't sure how to distinguish between who I'd been before and who I felt like since everything had happened.

The old me had been a pushover, allowing my family to control almost everything about my life, from the guy I'd been engaged to, to where I worked, to who my friends were. Other than Chloe, I didn't have a lot of girl-friends, and it had taken a puck to the head to make me realize how lonely I'd been. In a large family like mine, it was easy to get lost in the shuffle and somehow, I'd become the reliable afterthought. Everyone knew I'd do what needed to get done, even when they didn't pull their weight. And no one batted an eyelash. Meanwhile, I felt like I was relegated to working at the restaurant for the rest of my life, and I hated it. But my family either didn't notice, didn't care, or some combination of both.

For the first time in my life, I realized how much that hurt my feelings.

I didn't have time to dwell on any of my deep thoughts because my mother had left me a note that, once again, payroll had been screwed up and could I please go into the restaurant and make sure it was fixed?

Since I didn't have any physical restrictions, I showered, had a quick breakfast, and headed to the pizzeria. This was my first time driving since the accident, but it felt good to be behind the wheel. I love my Charger, and though I was a careful driver, I took any opportunity I could to go fast. It always freaked Carlo out, one of a million things about him that annoyed me, so he'd always driven when we went places together.

I walked into the pizzeria as the lunch crowd was picking up and a group of regulars called out to me. I smiled and waved, pausing to talk to one of the waitresses, who immediately came running over.

"We've missed you!" A young woman named Shelly said. She was a single mom in her early twenties who worked the lunch shift a few days a week and dinner shifts on the weekends.

"Thanks." I gave her a quick hug, whispering under my breath, "Did you get a paycheck last week?"

She shook her head. "No. But I know you'll fix it."

"I'm going over the books today."

"No problem." She hurried over to a table, and I walked into the back.

We had public restrooms, an office, a small break room, and a storeroom, and I'd taken over the office that had once been my father's. The other room was used more for counting out the cash register and clocking in and out than for breaks, but it was good to have a space to go with a door.

I sank down at my desk and logged into the computer, pulling up the program we used to do payroll.

"Luna called out," Desi said, sticking her head in the door. "Can you help on the floor?"

I looked up. "Doctor said not to lift anything heavy or exert myself for two weeks," replied. "That means not waiting tables."

"But…" Her voice trailed off and she sighed. "Okay, but I have a doctor's appointment at one."

"I don't know what to tell you." I went back to what I was doing and felt a momentary flash of guilt. Desi and I were pretty close, but as the new me stood on the outside looking in at the old me, I realized she often used our closeness as a way of getting me to pick up her slack. Yes, she had three small children, but they weren't my problem. If she and Tony couldn't afford daycare, then she should stay home with them instead of coming in for half a shift here and there.

The payroll was a mess. Someone had tried to input the hours but had instead changed the hourly pay rate to however many hours each waiter had worked, and left the number of hours at zero. Some of the timecards were missing, so I had to pull up credit card receipts to figure out who'd been signed on to the register each shift.

It wound up taking me three hours, which was a lot more than it usually took, but I fixed the previous week's errors and did the current week's numbers even though it was a day late. Sometimes the payroll service we used could get out paychecks in a rush, but sometimes they couldn't, and if that was the case, some of our staff—including me—wouldn't get paid until Monday.

I'd just finished up when my mother stuck her head in.

"Did you get payroll done?"

"Yes. Both last week and this week. But I don't know if we'll get the checks tomorrow. They probably won't come until Monday."

She nodded. "We can give anyone who asks up to a hundred dollars out of petty cash. Just mark it down and then they'll either pay us back in tips or subtract from next week's hours."

"Okay."

"Are you going home?"

"I think so. I've got a little bit of a headache."

"All right. I took a lasagna out of the freezer. You want to put it in the oven around four thirty?"

"Sure." I grabbed my purse.

"Are you leaving?" I ran right into Tony as I stepped into the hallway, and he stared at me.

"I have a headache," I said.

He frowned. "Desi had to leave so it would be great if you could count out the registers and stuff. We had a bunch of issues last week."

"I'll stay and do it," Mom said, nudging him. "Let her go home."

He opened his mouth, but Mom gave him 'the look,' and he closed it again. "Yeah, okay." He turned and went back to the kitchen, and I frowned.

"What did you tell him?" I demanded.

"Nothing." She arched her eyebrows at me. "Why?"

"You gave him that look you always give us when you want us to shut up, and he walked away."

"You need to rest," she said, shrugging. "I told them not to bug you for a week or two. That's all."

"I'll stay and count out the register," I murmured, opening my office door again. "But I'm going to stay in here and close my eyes for ten minutes. Have the staff come in here to count out when they're done, okay?"

"You sure?" She eyed me, but I could see the relief in her face.

"Yeah, I'll be fine."

I sat down behind my desk and leaned back in Dad's old chair. I'd been thinking of buying a new one because it was so uncomfortable, but it had been his and somehow sitting in his chair, at his desk, using his computer, comforted me. It kept him close, especially now when I felt like I needed him more than ever. I didn't know what he would have said about everything that had happened in the last week, but I was positive he would have gotten a kick out of me going out on a date with a professional hockey player.

For the first time since this morning, I thought of Vaughn.

Hanging out with him had been wonderful.

Holding hands and walking on the beach had been romantic.

Kissing him had been mind-blowing.

No one had ever kissed me like that.

And while I was a little embarrassed at how forward I'd been by making the first move, I had no regrets. It had been the most amazing day and we had plans to go out to dinner when he got back to town.

"Knock knock." Someone actually knocked on the door to the office.

I looked up and squealed. "Chloe!"

"I'm back!"

I jumped up and met her halfway as we hugged.

"I've missed you so much," I whispered.

"I missed you too." She looked at me and frowned. "What happened to your head?"

"It's kind of a long story," I sank back into my chair. "You have time to hang out?"

"I do." She perched on the edge of the desk. "The email you sent me was kind of cryptic, so I figured we'd need a few hours to catch up."

I held up my left hand. "Notice anything different?"

Her eyes widened and then she grinned. "You broke off the engagement! Yes!" Then she clapped a hand over her mouth. "I mean, I'm sorry. Are you okay?"

I couldn't help but laugh. "Yes, you bitch. I'm fine. I broke up with him."

"You haven't been in love with him in ages. You never should have said yes when he proposed."

"I know."

"So, how do you feel now that it's done?"

I paused. "Well, yesterday I went out on a date with a professional hockey player."

Her mouth fell open. "Holy shit. I definitely need to hear this story."

"It might take a while."

"Is he hot?"

"Go ahead and google Vaughn Elliott."

"Should I do it now?" she asked, laughing.

I shrugged playfully. "Maybe."

"You're killin' me." She pulled out her phone and started typing. Then her eyes widened, and she stared at me. "*Dude.* You better give me every single detail."

I laughed.

It was so good to have her home.

13

I'd avoided thinking about my conversation with my dad because I still didn't know what to make of it. The gist had been that he was getting out of the MC and wanting to settle down somewhere close to me. Something about promising my mother when she'd been sick that he'd work on our relationship. No one had thought to ask me what I wanted, but that probably wasn't fair because I'd moved out a long time ago and Mom and I had been living different lives.

Hearing my father talk about her as if they'd been close, even after all the years apart, had rubbed me the wrong way, and I'd ended the conversation too soon. Now I kind of regretted it because I wanted to know more. Especially after reading that damn letter. It seemed like there had been a lot about my mom I didn't know, and that annoyed me for some reason.

For the first time in a long time, I missed having someone to talk to, and I thought of Juliet on the way back to the hotel. I got settled in my room after a big win against Washington and decided to text her.

VAUGHN: Hey, how are you?
JULIET: Ugh. I've had a long week.
VAUGHN: You feel like talking about it? I can call you.
JULIET: Sure.

"Hi." She sounded tired when she answered.

"How's things going?"

"It's been a long week."

This was Sunday, and we'd gone out on Thursday, so it had only been three days.

"What happened since I saw you?"

"Well, my family is driving me nuts."

"What did they do?"

"On one hand, they're tiptoeing around me trying to be really nice, but at the same time they have no idea how to run the business part of the restaurant, and I've had to work until eight or nine every night to get caught up on all the things they didn't do in the week I wasn't here."

"Saying no is hard when it comes to family," I said gently.

"You say that like you've been there," she said.

"I'm kind of going through it now," I admitted. "With my dad."

"I thought your dad isn't in your life?"

"He hasn't been." I sighed. "It's a long story."

"I'm happy to listen."

"My parents were high school sweethearts. My dad's dad was in the gang —club—and there was no doubt my dad was going to join too. Mom said the initial plan was for him not to. For them to get married and move away. He was always good with vehicles, mechanic stuff, and they figured they'd get by. She'd always wanted to be a teacher and got a scholarship, so that was the plan. Then my grandfather got arrested and supposedly they needed my dad to do something. What that something was, she never told me, just that he got caught and arrested. The only way he could afford a lawyer and all that was if he agreed to join.

"Mom wasn't happy about it, but they got married, and Dad promised her he'd find a way to pay them back so he could get out. Everything apparently changed when she got pregnant with me. The way she told the story, she didn't want that life for me, so she left him when I was three."

"The way she told it?" Juliet asked quietly. "Is there another version?"

I blew out a breath. "I saw my dad last week. He showed up out of the blue and was sitting in the cul-de-sac of my neighborhood. I called him and asked him what the fuck he was doing. To make a long story short, he wound up coming over and we talked. He made it sound like he and my mom decided it would be best for me if she left, instead of the way she'd told it, that she left on her own."

"Which do you believe?"

"My gut instinct is to believe her, but now that I've been sitting on it for a week, I feel like maybe I jumped to that conclusion too quickly. He has no reason to lie about that part of it. I already know she never got over him because she never so much as went out on a date with another man. And when Dad came around, which was usually only a few times a year, they were together like a regular couple. Holding hands and kissing, sharing a bedroom, all of it. As a kid, I thought it was normal. Now that I'm older, I realize she never moved on. Unfortunately, she died before I thought to ask her about those kinds of things."

"And you're afraid to ask him?"

"It's not that I'm afraid. I don't know him, not as an adult, and that's what's frustrating. He used to come around in the summer and at Christmas, up until I was about thirteen. Then he started coming for long weekends at random times. By the time I went away to the juniors for hockey, I rarely saw him. He came to my first NHL game and has always gone to any games I've played in California, though I didn't usually know he was there or see him. And the last time I saw him before last week was at Mom's funeral."

"If you want my opinion, I think you should ask him everything you want to know," she said after a moment. "I know it's hard, but you'll never forgive yourself if something happens to him and you have to spend the rest of your life with all these unanswered questions. Look how frustrated you are that you never talked to your mom about them."

"I know. I just don't know if he's going to tell me the truth."

"Why lie? Your mom is gone, and you're a grown man."

"I'm a *very rich* grown man."

She sucked in a sharp breath. "Oh. I see. And he's part of a criminal organization, so this might be some sort of ruse to get close to you and your money."

"Exactly."

"You know, I understand why you think that, but you said a minute ago your mom loved him and never got over him. She loved *you* enough to leave him and keep you away from that life, but she never stopped loving him. Do you think she would love a man like that?"

"I want to say no. My mom was smart, sassy, and shrewd. She was as tough as nails on the outside, and she didn't take shit from anyone. Not from him and not from anyone else. But she fell in love with him at fifteen. As far as I know, she was never with anyone else, and it kind of pisses me off that he left her like that. What kind of man does that to the woman he supposedly loves? Not to mention his kid."

"You have to ask him."

"I know." I stretched out on the bed. "You're so easy to talk to, but we're kind of depressing tonight, huh?"

"You're easy to talk to as well. And we can talk about all the depressing stuff while you're gone and then when we're together, we can talk about other stuff."

"Now that sounds like an excellent plan. So, what kind of food do you like?"

"All food," she said, laughing. "But if we're going out, no Italian. I eat enough of that at home and the restaurant."

"Seafood?"

"Love it. There's a place called the Rustic Inn I absolutely love. It has some of the freshest, best seafood in South Florida. And it's casual. Have you been there yet?"

"No, but it sounds awesome. I'll see if I can make us a reservation, but I don't know what day yet. It depends on practice and if Coach decides to add meetings or anything."

"No worries. Just try to give me twenty-four hours so I can make sure everything is taken care of at work."

"Didn't the doctor say not to overdo it for a while?"

She snorted. "Well, that's only if it's convenient for the family."

"You have to take care of yourself, babe. I keep telling you—head injuries aren't anything to mess around with. I know this isn't a regular thing for you, but as an athlete I've seen a lot of damage caused because guys refused to take it easy."

"I know. You're right. I guess they don't consider sitting at a desk doing paperwork the same as physical labor, you know?"

"But it *is* physical when it comes to a brain injury. Your brain is the body part you're working too hard."

She was quiet for a few seconds. "Thank you for pointing that out. I guess it's mostly my fault because I hate seeing things not running smoothly at the pizzeria. Like my dad is watching and would be disappointed."

"If your dad is watching, he also saw you get clocked in the head by a hockey puck that gave you stitches, amnesia, and a concussion. I'd like to think he wants you to heal completely before worrying about the restaurant."

"You're absolutely right. My dad would probably be furious if he saw me at the restaurant right after getting out of the hospital."

"You should get some rest."

"So should you."

"I plan to." I suddenly had a thought. "So I get back to Lauderdale around three a week from today, and there's a very small chance Coach will keep us for a meeting or anything. How about I pick you up about five and we can go to dinner? That way, I'm as sure as I can be that I'll be free since we don't usually do anything when we get back from a longer trip like this."

"That sounds great."

"I don't know how busy I'll be this week, but I'll text when I can."

"Okay."

"We'll talk soon, Juliet."

"Looking forward to it."

So was I.

I put down the phone and stared up at the ceiling.

We'd been on the phone an hour, and it had flown by. Normally I didn't enjoy talking on the phone, but it was nice with Juliet. She was attentive and thoughtful, whether she was talking or listening, and I liked her a lot. I'd never talked about my parents' relationship to anyone before, and it had felt good to get it off my chest. Now if I could just figure out what to do with my dad, I might be able to get a good night's sleep.

Impulsively, I picked up my phone again and dialed his number.

This was probably a dumbass thing to do but it felt important to be open to him. I had to be careful because I still didn't trust his motivations, but at the same time I had the opportunity to have my dad back. Maybe I was a sucker, and probably still struggling from the loss of my mother, but the draw to my father was stronger than I'd thought it would be.

"Vaughn?" Dad sounded confused.

"Yeah. Hey."

"Everything okay?"

"Yeah." I cleared my throat. "I was thinking about maybe, uh, continuing the conversation we started. You caught me off-guard that night. I think I'm ready to hear more."

"Aren't you on the road?"

"I'll be home on Sunday. I have a date Sunday night, a game Monday night, and practice Tuesday morning, but we could maybe have dinner or something Tuesday."

"I'd like that."

"Are you still in Lauderdale?"

"Uh, no. Had to run up to the Carolinas for a bit, but I'll be back down there Monday."

"What's in the Carolinas?"

"Just some friends I wanted to see."

I was suspicious but decided not to push it. I still hadn't decided how much of a relationship we were going to have, so for now, it was none of my business anyway.

"All right. Then I'll see you next week."

"See you then." He paused. "And son?"

"Yeah?"

"I'm glad you called."

14

Despite my good intentions, a leaking pipe in the kitchen of the pizzeria derailed my plans to spend less time working the following week. We'd had to shut down at two o'clock on Tuesday and send everyone home while we waited for the after-hours plumber to arrive. Then most of the family showed up to help clean up the mess because it had been awful. We hadn't finished until three in the morning and by the time we got home, I'd had a terrible headache. I'd slept for nine hours and dragged myself into the restaurant to do payroll, but I'd left by five and went back to bed.

Most of the time I felt fine, but it was abundantly clear I had to take it easy. Dr. Montrose had said to be cognizant of the headaches, and to let him know if they became frequent, so I'd put my foot down on Thursday and didn't go in at all. I'd worked a few hours both Friday and Saturday night because it was just too busy not to be there, but I'd gone in late and left early.

Today was Sunday, and I'd woken up with a smile because I was going to see Vaughn tonight. I had to get through family dinner first, though I wasn't eating, and that would undoubtedly raise all kinds of questions.

I showered and dried my hair, taking a moment to stare at the area on my temple where the puck had hit me. The stitches had been taken out and replaced with little butterfly strips. So far, it didn't look too bad, but there was definitely going to be a scar, and I ran a finger over the area. I'd need to cover it with makeup in the future, but hopefully it wouldn't be too visible when I didn't. I could also part my hair on that side to help hide it. Thank goodness I had a lot of hair.

I put on mascara, bronzer, and a little lip gloss for now, but I'd touch everything up before Vaughn got here. I wasn't sure if I'd invite him in or not, since I was sure my family wouldn't be thrilled I was going out with him. I'd decide closer to the time when he arrived, after seeing how the day went. This would be the first time I saw the whole family at once since the accident, and it was going to be a full house.

The noise alone told me people had already started to arrive and before I even got to the bottom of the stairs, my twin three-year-old nephews, Anthony and Albert, came rushing over to greet me. They were Tony and Desi's boys, and I adored them, so I wrapped my arms around them tightly.

"Do you have a boo-boo?" Anthony asked, staring at my head.

"I do. I got hit with a hockey puck."

He grinned. "That's cool."

I laughed.

"Boys, leave your aunt alone!" Desi called. "Come drink your milk."

The boys took off running, and I turned just as Carlo came in the front door.

Oh, fuck me, I thought in irritation.

"Hey, Jules." He approached me gingerly, as if nervous, which wasn't like him at all.

"What are you doing here?" I asked, clenching my jaw almost painfully.

"It's Sunday dinner, you know?" He gave a little shrug. "Your mom invited us because we're family." Since he said us, I figured Leonora would be coming as well.

"We're not engaged anymore," I said quietly. "We're not even dating anymore."

He winced. "Come on, Jules. I know you've been through a lot, but I thought we could talk, you know?"

"I don't know what there is to say," I said quietly, glancing over at my brothers, who were pretending to be interested in the football game on TV.

"I dunno." He looked sad, and I silently cursed my mother for putting us in this position.

Carlo wasn't a bad guy. He just wasn't the guy for me, and the accident had finally given me the shove I needed to end it. Unfortunately, my family wasn't on board, and they were using his feelings for me to manipulate both of us.

"I'm sorry my mom told you to come over," I said softly. "But I think it's better this way."

"Better for who?" he asked.

"Carlo!" Mom came into the room with a broad smile and leaned over to hug him. "Why don't you watch some football while Jules helps in the kitchen. You two can catch up later."

I turned and blindly followed my mother into the kitchen, my heart thumping uncomfortably.

"What did you do?" I demanded. "Why would you invite him?"

Her eyes widened. "Why would I invite who? Your fiancé?"

"He's not my fiancé!" I threw up my hands. "I gave him back the ring and ended it."

There was a moment of silence as Mom, Desi, Robbie's wife Diana, and Sal's fiancée Michelle, all looked at each other.

"You're confused," Mom said. "You got hit in the head. It's okay. He'll be patient."

"I'm not confused," I said. "I'm finally doing what I want, instead of what everyone else wants. Carlo and I should have broken up years ago. We grew apart. It happens. I just didn't have the balls to say anything until now."

"You're hysterical." Mom was shaking her head and turned back to the stove, stirring the sauce.

"First I'm confused, then I'm hysterical. Which is it?" I looked around at everyone, as if daring them to answer me, though I kept my voice low.

My family had always been loud, busy, and nosy, but I didn't remember them being this manipulative.

"We all go through phases where we think the grass is greener somewhere else," Desi said slowly. "Tony and I did too. But we hung in there and look at us now."

"It's not the same," I said. "I wish you guys would try and understand. This is hard for me too, but all you've done by inviting him over today is embarrassing me and rubbing it in his face that I don't love him that way anymore."

"You woke up from a hit on the hit and decided this," Mom said without turning around. "This is ludicrous. You know whatever this is, it's not permanent. You're going to realize you're making a big mistake, and we're just trying to make sure Carlo is still around when you do."

I stared up at the ceiling, counting to ten.

Part of me momentarily wondered if she was right, but deep down I knew better.

"I'm going to get some air." I walked out to the pool and sat in one of the lounge chairs, staring out at the water and wishing Vaughn was around to calm me.

There was something about him that had soothed my frayed nerves from that first night we met when I'd inadvertently held his hand.

But he was traveling, and today was going to be the longest day ever until he got here.

———

By the time Vaughn texted to tell me he was on his way I was a wreck. Carlo and Leonora had been at the house all afternoon, hanging out with my family and acting like nothing had changed. Peter was the only one of my brothers who had the grace to look a little mortified at the whole thing, but I was grateful to know at least one of them understood how awful this was. I truly didn't want to hurt Carlo, but he was letting my mother manipulate him even more so than I was, and he was going to have to figure it out on his own.

Everyone had been shocked when I'd announced I was leaving, so I'd grabbed my purse and almost flew out the front door. I got into Vaughn's Corvette before he had a chance to get out.

"Hi." I gave him a small smile.

"Hi." He smiled back. "You look tense. You okay?"

"Can we just head to the restaurant? I might need a bottle of champagne or something to tell this story."

"Oh, boy." He pulled out of the driveway, and I told him the easiest way to get to the highway.

"Did you talk to your dad?" I asked, hoping to delay talking about my situation until I'd had a glass of wine or something.

"I did." He nodded. "We're going to have an early dinner on Tuesday."

"That's great. You'll see, it's going to be a good thing for you."

"I hope so."

"Just keep his background, the money stuff, all those things, in the back of your mind. I think your gut will tell you when and if something feels off."

"Everything about my dad and me feels off, but I'm trying. If nothing else, if it blows up, someday I can look back and say I genuinely tried."

"I think it's smart. So you don't have regrets."

"Do you have regrets?" he asked quietly. "To do with your dad, I mean."

"Not really. We were close. I saw him almost every day, we talked all the time, hung out a lot, and spent time as a family. I'm sorry I didn't get to say goodbye, but I told him I loved him all the time, and I knew he loved me."

"That's the only good thing about cancer," he said after a moment. "At least we got to say everything we wanted to say. I didn't ask her some things I should have, but at the time I didn't want to upset her and stuff. But the big stuff, like how much I loved and appreciated her, she knew."

"That's good." I slid my hand over the console and rested it on his, squeezing lightly. "We weren't supposed to talk about depressing stuff tonight."

He smiled, threading his fingers through mine. "Yeah, but it got us holding hands, so win-win."

15

VAUGHN

Once again, Juliet and I had fallen down a rabbit hole talking about our parents. Even after we were seated in the restaurant and had ordered wine, we continued to talk about her dad, my mom, and other various family members. It was a little odd for two people who were only out on their second date, but it was so damn easy. I truly loved talking to her, and the best part was that it felt mutual.

"Oh my god, these are the best crab legs ever. Anywhere." She leaned back in her chair.

"They're pretty damn good," I agreed. I didn't normally eat like this during hockey season, but the food had been amazing.

"I might have to swim laps in the pool after this," she murmured. "I'm stuffed."

"Tell me about it." I chuckled. "I have to be on the ice in the morning and then play a game tomorrow night."

"We could go walk on the beach when we leave here," she suggested. "It's nice out tonight."

"That's sounds like a good idea."

We talked some more, finished a bottle of wine, and then headed out to my car after I paid the check. I felt like I should take her dancing or somewhere other than for a walk on the beach, but I liked that's what she wanted to do.

She didn't seem interested in meeting my friends, going anywhere fancy, or even doing much of anything but talking. It was a nice change from the women I usually dated who wanted to see what there was to see and be seen in the process.

Coming from a big Italian family, I'd expected Juliet to be loud and boisterous as well, but she wasn't.

"Do you want to talk about what happened with your family today?" I asked when we were finally at the beach in Deerfield, where we'd walked last time. I'd taken off my shoes and socks and rolled up my jeans, and she'd taken off her sandals. We'd laced our fingers together and were walking on the shoreline even though it was dark. There were lights on the shore, of course, and we weren't going in the water, but it was equal parts romantic and creepy.

"Not really." She stared off at nothing. "My mom invited Carlo and his mom to Sunday dinner. It's a big deal at our house, and we haven't been doing them as much since Dad died, but Mom's been starting them up again. I came downstairs, and he was already there. It was sad and embarrassing because he's not a bad guy, you know?"

"Do you still care about him?" I asked slowly.

"I do. We've been together since high school. But I'm not in love with him anymore if that's what you're asking."

"But does he understand that? If your mom thinks you're getting back together, does he have the same expectation?"

"I've told all of them that. More than once."

"Well, I'm sure as you start canceling all the wedding stuff, it'll sink in."

She almost stumbled as we walked, and I tightened my grip on her hand. "You okay?" I asked.

"Yeah. But I just realized I left everything for my mom to handle, and I'm willing to bet she hasn't canceled anything. I'll have to make some calls."

"Are you going to wind up paying a lot of cancellation fees?"

"Probably, but that's okay. I have money saved up, so I'll just pay them." She nudged me with her elbow. "Why are we talking about this stuff again?"

"What do you want to talk about?"

"Anything but my family, Carlo, or the wedding."

"Are you coming to the game tomorrow night?"

"Of course."

"Would you like to come back to the family lounge after the game, and then maybe we could go out for a late drink?"

"Yes. I'd love that."

"Cool." I stopped walking and pulled her closer. "I really enjoy spending time with you, Juliet."

"I do too." Her eyes lifted to meet mine.

God, she was pretty. I'd been trying to go slow and be a gentleman, both because of her recent injury and because her personal life seemed pretty chaotic right now. I'd thought about the kiss we'd shared a lot, and I wanted to do it again. I cupped the side of her face with my hand.

"I think about your gorgeous face a lot," I whispered.

"I think about you a lot," she whispered back.

I dipped my head and found her mouth. She opened sweetly, her body moving against mine as I dropped my shoes and wrapped both arms around her. She fit against me perfectly, her full breasts pressed against my chest and making me think about things I didn't want to think about yet.

Our tongues worked in tandem, dancing and twirling, as the wind blew around us. I let one hand slide down along the curve of her back and then let it rest on the swell of her ass. She was lean but curvy, with a flat stomach and a small waist. Her legs were long, and I wanted to see her in shorts. Hell, I wanted to see her in nothing but skin, but we probably weren't there yet.

I pulled away as the wind picked up and whipped her hair around and between us.

"We should probably get going," I said, staring deep into her eyes. "Seems like a storm is coming."

"Yeah, it feels like rain."

I picked up my shoes and took a moment to adjust myself since I was painfully erect after all that kissing. Then I grabbed her hand, and we started heading back toward the car.

The skies opened, and the rain came down like Mother Nature had been waiting for us to finish kissing so she could douse us. We started to run, laughing as the rain and wind pelted us. Juliet pulled away and spun in a circle, her face to the sky and her arms out at her sides.

"This is amazing," she said, shaking her hair and letting it billow out behind her like a wavy cloud of silk.

I looked up at the sky, wondering what she saw that I didn't, but in that moment a feeling of freedom came over me. Not that I was somehow caged or anything. Just a moment that was perfect contentedness. And I couldn't ever remember another time it had happened with a woman.

I grabbed her and kissed her again, our mouths moving together hungrily this time. I wanted her so bad, but I also wanted to wait. She was in the middle of so much drama with her family and the injury that I didn't want to add anything that could complicate her life further. But the way she was kissing me back told me she didn't care.

That she wanted me too.

I deepened the kiss, gripping her ass with one hand and digging the other into the hair at back of her neck. Our tongues were in a fight for dominance, or maybe it was just excitement, and I rocked my groin against hers. A moan escaped her, and she slid her fingers under my shirt, resting her palm flat against my torso. Being skin-on-skin, even with such minimal contact, had my erection straining against my jeans, and I was going to take her right now if we didn't ease up.

"Wanna go back to my place?" I asked, hoping my raspy voice didn't give away how badly I wanted to take her to bed.

"Mmm, yes." She smiled up at me.

I grabbed her hand, and we ran.

W e were both soaked, but luckily I had a couple of beach towels in the back of my car. We sat on them to protect the fancy leather seats, and then held hands the whole way back to my house. I hadn't yet brought a woman home to my place in Florida, and it felt right that it would be Juliet. I wasn't sure why, but everything about her lent a calming presence to the chaos of everything involved with a trade to an expansion team. And the budding new relationship with my dad. And the pressure of making a name for myself professionally in this new city.

When I was with Juliet, even when we talked about our families and stuff, all those pressures seemed far away. It was one of many things I liked about her.

I turned onto my street and groaned.

"Shit."

"What?" she asked in alarm.

"My dad."

"Where?"

"In my driveway."

"Oh." She glanced at me. "That's okay. I don't mind meeting him. Unless you don't want me to?"

"Not at all. I mean, he's kind of gruff, but you'll probably like him."

She looked down. "That sounds great. Except I'm totally drenched, and my nipples are showing."

I grinned. "And I was so looking forward to seeing more nipple."

We chuckled together as I pulled into my garage.

"Wrap the towel around you like you're cold," I told her. "And I've got a bathrobe you can put on."

"Okay."

I parked and then got out of the car, the wet towel draped over my shoulder.

"Hey, Dad."

"Hey." His eyes traveled to Juliet. "I'm sorry. I didn't think…"

"It's all right. Do you want to come in? We were walking on the beach and got drenched so we're going to put on dry clothes and stuff."

"I don't want to intrude." Dad looked super uncomfortable, and while I wanted him to leave, I didn't want to ruin what we'd started to build. It was too new for me to be a dick about him showing up unannounced, so I shook my head.

"Nah. Come on in and meet Juliet." I walked over to her and grabbed her hand. "Babe, this is my father, Adam Elliott. Dad, this is Juliet Cicero. The woman I knocked out with a slap shot to the head on opening night."

Dad's eyes widened, and then he laughed, extending his hand. "Nice to meet you, Juliet. You sure you want to date a guy who tried to kill you?"

She laughed too; the towel draped over her like a cloak. "Don't worry. I'm on to his tricks. I think I'm okay as long as I don't let him near any hockey pucks in my presence."

"That's fair."

We walked into the house, and I told my dad to hang on as I led Juliet to my bedroom and then into the master bath. I pulled a bathrobe out of the closet and handed it to her.

"Here. Change, dry off, whatever you need. There are more towels in the closet. Just make yourself at home. And I'm sorry about this, but I didn't want to be a jerk and tell him to leave."

"It's fine." She put a gentle hand on my arm. "Really. Your relationship with your dad is more important than our raging hormones."

I laughed and leaned down, kissing her firmly, though I kept it chaste. "I will totally make this up to you."

"Don't worry about it."

I grabbed a dry pair of sweats and a T-shirt and changed in the bedroom since it was kind of chilly with the air conditioning on. Then I padded into the kitchen where my dad had made himself at home, boiling some water on the stove.

"I saw you had tea in the cupboard," he said.

"You drink tea?" I frowned. That was so out of character for a badass biker who'd done hard time in prison. But maybe I was stereotyping since I didn't know anyone *else* who'd been in prison.

"Your mom loved it and made me like it too." He gave a lopsided grin. "It's the little things that make them happy, you know?"

I opened my mouth, but I didn't know how to respond to that because it had been a long time since I'd had a serious girlfriend, and I'd been a lot younger then.

"Uh, yeah, tea is fine. Mom got me drinking it too. A cup of chamomile at night helps me wind down."

"Exactly." He got some mugs out of the cabinet like he lived here. "Juliet seems sweet. This thing between you serious?"

"This is our second date," I said, getting sugar and honey out of the pantry. "Way too soon to know."

"I knew the first time I kissed your mom," Dad said.

I met his gaze and made a face. "You were, what? Fifteen? All it takes is a kiss at that age. It's a little different at twenty-six."

"It's not." He shook his head. "Not at sixteen, not at twenty-six, and not at forty-six. You still know."

I shrugged. "Well, maybe it's different for me." His words had some truth to them, but I wasn't going there. Not now anyway. And definitely not with him.

"Your robe is so warm and comfy." Juliet came into the room, dwarfed in the massive bathrobe I'd never used, a big smile on her face.

"I'm glad." I nodded. "Do you like tea?"

"I love tea. Especially at night. There's nothing like a good cup of chamomile."

Dad chuckled. "Girl after my own heart."

"How long are you in town, Mr. Elliott?" Juliet asked, leaning against the counter.

"Just call me Buzz," he said. "And I don't know. I have some unfinished business back in California, but I'd like to move here permanently."

Thank god the kettle boiled just then so we were distracted steeping tea bags and then settling in the living room.

To my surprise, Dad and Juliet started talking about her family's pizzeria, her Charger, and a mutual love of Formula One racing, which I hadn't known about either of them. Dad was charming and funny, telling interesting stories that made Juliet and me both laugh, and I couldn't help but think of my mom.

This was the man she'd been in love with. The man she'd stayed faithful to even after what I now knew had been a fake divorce. The man behind the biker façade.

And for the second time in a matter of hours, I was truly content again.

Juliet, I thought to myself, *centered m*e.

It was a little disconcerting considering how we'd met and how little time we'd known each other.

When you know, you know.

Dammit.

16

JULIET

I got to the arena early on Tuesday. I was going to watch the whole warm-up from right up near the glass, and I was already loving it. Part of me was a little embarrassed at the idea of being a fangirl while simultaneously dating someone on the team, but why was that a thing anyway? If we weren't fans, why were we even here? And my relationship with Vaughn outside the rink had nothing to do with my love of hockey or this team. I could have both, and I refused to be embarrassed by any of it.

A light tapping on the glass startled me, but I smiled at Vaughn who looked sexier than ever, his tousled dark hair curling just a little around his face as he skated to a stop. Our eyes met, he winked, and then he was gone.

I was freakin' crazy about him and despite the drama going on at home and at the restaurant, I was happy. My mother hadn't spoken to me since I'd left to go out with Vaugh on Sunday, and Tony and Mario were giving me the cold shoulder at work. Desi told me they all assumed I was sowing some oats before the wedding, which reminded me that I needed to make some calls to the different vendors. I kept forgetting to do that, but I pulled out my phone and made a reminder for tomorrow.

I made my way up to our seats and found Peter there eating a hot dog. He looked up with a grin. "Hey."

"Hi." I sank down next to him.

"Did you really go out on a date with one of the Knights on Sunday?" he asked.

I dipped my head to hide my grin. "I did. It was actually our second date."

"Is he a good guy?"

"He's...a *really* good guy. So far anyway." It was nice to hang out with Peter for the first time since my accident. All of us were relatively close, but as the two youngest, Peter and I had a special bond.

"Are you gonna see him again?"

"We're going out after the game tonight."

"What about Carlo?"

I met his gaze directly. "Come on, not you too. That's done."

"Does *he* know that?"

"He should."

"Should know and does know are two different things."

"I formally broke up with him at the hospital," I said. "Then I reiterated it on Sunday when he was at the house. I don't know what else to do. Everyone seems to think I just got a wild hair up my ass, and I'll get over it."

"Will you?"

"I wasn't totally happy before, but I just went along with what everyone wanted." I paused. "You realize that puck could have killed me, right?"

He grimaced. "Jesus, don't even say that."

"It didn't, but it could have, and the more I think about it, the more I realize I settled with Carlo. And no one should settle, least of all me."

He was quiet for a moment before nodding. "God, no. I hate the thought of you settling. I won't, and you shouldn't either. But be prepared for the backlash."

I sighed. "Why can't you guys just accept what I want? I'm so tired of feeling guilty."

"Welcome to being Italian and Catholic."

"I'm agnostic and you're an atheist. Mom hasn't been to church since last Christmas."

"Yeah, well, you probably shouldn't remind her of that."

We both chuckled.

"Hey, guys." Mario and Tony joined us, sinking into the other two seats.

"You owe me," Mario said to me.

"For what?" I asked suspiciously.

"Mom invited Carlo to the game with me tonight, but I got Tony to say he'd already called dibs, and he wanted to be here because we wanted to see New York play."

"And Desi's pissed," Tony added.

"She has to stop," I muttered. "I'm dating someone. Carlo and I are done."

"Mom just went to the dress shop and changed the dress you'd ordered," Mario said quietly. "You need to talk to her because this is going to get really expensive."

"Why is she so determined for me to marry Carlo?" I asked in frustration. "We honestly have nothing in common anymore, and he was miserable too. He just hasn't realized how much better off he's going to be. I drove him crazy."

"Italian. Catholic. Guilt." Peter said with a little shrug.

I rolled my eyes. "Well, it's stupid. Mom and Dad were lucky that they fell in love in high school and never looked back. But I'm different."

"Trust me," Mario said. "I've been divorced three times. I'm not doing that shit again until I meet the perfect woman. Perfect for me, I mean."

"Then why don't you guys ever have my back on this when Mom is around?" I demanded.

"Italian. Catholic. Guilt." All three of them spoke in unison and then burst out laughing.

I didn't think it was funny, though.

Luckily, we had to standup for the national anthem, and I was glad because I was furious. Taking it out on my brothers, who'd done me a solid tonight, wouldn't solve anything, though. I was going to have to talk to my mother, and I wasn't looking forward to that at all.

I lost myself in the game because it was exciting. Vaughn scored in the second period, and I screamed so loud I was afraid I'd lose my voice. The Knights were so good, so exciting to watch, it lit me up from the inside out. Knowing Vaughn, having kissed him and held hands and talked for hours and hours, made it that much better. I'd only broken up with Carlo two weeks ago, but I'd checked out emotionally months ago. I was ready for something new, and Vaughn was more than I'd ever imagined I'd find. It probably wouldn't go anywhere, and I might have been setting myself up for heartbreak, but I was having too much fun to worry about it.

I hugged my brothers when the game was over and then hurried to the elevator that would take me down to the family lounge. I was a little nervous at the idea of hanging out with the wives and girlfriends, but I wanted to see Vaughn.

I stepped out of the elevator and looked around in confusion. You had to show a special pass to even be allowed on the elevator, and though Vaughn had told me to turn left and go down a long hallway, I felt like a fish out of water.

"Hi. Are you Juliet?" A tall, gorgeous redhead came up to me with a friendly smile.

"Yes."

"I'm Tiffany Marcus-Cloutier, Zakk's wife. Vaughn said you'd be coming down and might get lost, so I came to escort you to the lounge."

"Oh! Thank you. I was a little overwhelmed when I got down here."

"No worries. So, did you enjoy the game?"

"Of course. I was a season ticket holder before I met Vaughn. I'm a huge fan of both the sport and the team."

"Good to know. It's exciting when they win. Less so when they lose. I don't know how long you've been dating, but the vibe tonight will be totally different than it would be after a loss."

"We've only been together a couple of weeks," I admitted. "It's all new to me."

"Well, hang on to your hat, because dating a professional athlete is going to be a wild ride."

"How come?"

"They travel a lot, there are women throwing themselves at them constantly, and even when they're home sometimes they're so focused on the game they forget everything else. It changes a little when you have kids, but obviously you're too new for that so it could be frustrating when he doesn't call for days because they're playing and working so hard."

"How long have you been married?" I asked her.

"Just a couple of years," she said with a grin. "We had the kids first and then decided to make it legal. My first husband died of a heart attack and left me with two little boys, and I had no idea what to do with myself. I wanted to be a thousand percent sure I was okay on my own before I married Zakk. I know that probably doesn't make sense to you, since we were together, just not married, but in my head, I needed time."

"It totally makes sense."

"Here we are." She let me walk into a large, brightly lit room. "Come meet some of my inner circle." She waved to a pretty blond with curly hair. "Tessa! Come meet Juliet. This is Vaughn's new girlfriend."

"Hi!" Tessa smiled, holding out a hand. "It's so nice to meet you."

"I'm not really his girlfriend," I said, shaking her hand. "We've only been dating a few weeks."

Tessa winked. "No casual hook-ups or women a guy isn't fairly serious about gets invited to the family lounge. Trust me."

"Tessa is married to Coach Petrov."

I may have gaped a little. "You're Toli Petrov's wife? Oh my gosh. I was such a big fan of his when he played."

Tessa grinned. "He will be super excited to hear that. I think he misses being in the spotlight."

"He's the head coach of a hot new team," I protested. "He's still in the spotlight."

"Hi, sorry I'm late. Stella wouldn't go home with the nanny." A pretty brunette joined us, looking around. "Please tell me there's wine."

"I'll get you a glass," Tiff said. "Say hello to Juliet."

"Hi. I'm Peyton, Ryder Kingston's fiancée. Who are you dating?"

"Vaughn Elliott." This was all so matter-of-fact, as if it were a foregone conclusion that I was going to be Vaughn's girlfriend. We hadn't even slept together yet.

"Nice to meet you! Welcome. Our one-year-old had a fit when she found out she was going to leave before she saw daddy." Peyton rolled her eyes. "She is such a daddy's girl."

I met a few more wives and girlfriends before the guys started coming in to join us. I tried not to watch the door, but I couldn't help it.

"It's okay to be excited," Peyton whispered to me. "Ryder and I are engaged, living together, and have a baby, and I'm still excited when I see him."

"It's so new," I whispered back. "This is our third date."

Her eyes rounded. "And he brought you to meet us? Wow. He must *really* like you."

"I'm the one he hit in the head with the puck on opening night."

She stared at me. "Oh wow. That was *you*." She giggled. "That's awesome. And now this is your third date. I love this."

I grinned back. I couldn't help it. Everyone was nice and friendly and not at all what I'd been expecting. I wasn't sure exactly what I'd been expecting, but the women I'd met were sweet and down to earth, not the divas I'd read about some of the professional athletes dated.

"Hey." Vaughn's deep voice warmed me, and I turned to him just as he lowered his head to press a light kiss on my lips.

"Hi." Just that little peck was all it took to leave me breathless.

"Did Tiff meet you at the elevators?"

"She did. Thank you for that. I was a little overwhelmed."

"I figured. I still get lost sometimes." He slid an arm around me. "A group of us were talking about going out for drinks. You in?"

"Whatever you want to do. I came in an Uber so I wouldn't have to leave my car here when we went out."

"I didn't even think of that." He shook his head. "Next time, maybe you can ride with one of the other wives."

"It's no big deal. Where are we going?"

"I don't know yet. You have any ideas?"

I chuckled. "About a hundred. Depends on what we want. Sports bar where we can drink and have snacks? Somewhere that's still serving real food this late? Close to the arena or closer to the beach? You need to narrow it down."

"Okay, let me talk to Ryder. I'll be right back." He strode across the room, and I admired the way his suit fit him. He was so freakin' hot.

"They're so pretty in suits," Tessa whispered to me, grinning.

"They're so pretty. Period."

We laughed.

17

Vaughn

We wound up at a sports bar about twenty minutes from the arena called Cappy's. It was big with wall-to-wall TVs, lots of seating both in the restaurant and at the bar, and Juliet said the drinks were excellent. It was also low-key, and they served a full menu until midnight. That pretty much covered all the bases for us, and we settled into several tables pushed together.

The place wasn't very busy, which worked well for such a large group, and the waitress immediately took our drink orders. I hadn't brought a date to a team outing like this in probably five years, so this was novel for me, and I loved that Juliet seemed to fit right in with the other ladies. Even Coach Petrov and his wife had come with us tonight, so that was fun too.

"You two must have crazy stories from when you were in the Sidewinders," Peyton said to Coach Petrov and Zakk. "Tessa said she's not allowed to tell us. We have to ask you personally."

Coach chuckled. "Well, there are some crazy stories, for sure."

"Coach, is it true you got shot at your wedding?" Cam looked at him curiously.

Coach nodded. "I did."

"You got shot?" Peyton stared at him. "I had no idea. I was talking about road trip shenanigans, pranks, that kind of thing."

He waved a hand. "It's all good. That was a dark day." He slid his arm around the back of his wife's chair. "But it was in the news at the time, so it's not a secret. The sad truth is our goalie at the time was mentally ill and had a breakdown of sorts. One of my teammate's wives was also shot. We try not to think about that day."

"However," Zakk said, his eyes twinkling. "We do like to talk about the night you and Tessa met. And how I found her in my kitchen the following morning. Toli and I were roommates then."

Tessa groaned, though she had a smile on her face. "Oh my god, Zakk, shut up. I was so drunk that night…"

Toli laughed, leaning over to kiss the side of her face. "But if you hadn't gotten drunk, you wouldn't have had the nerve to proposition me, and then we wouldn't be here now."

"That's very true." They gazed at each other with what could only be described as adoration, and it was both sweet and weird to see my coach so in love with his wife.

Zakk went on to tell a hilarious story about Tessa getting drunk at a bar and propositioning Coach without realizing who he was or that she'd gone to college with two of his teammate's wives. By the end of it, we were all in stitches since Coach laid on his Russian accent and started telling parts of it in third person. Then Zakk told a story about how many times he asked Tiff to marry him before she said yes.

"Not true," she said, laughing and playfully swatting him. "I said I'd marry you; I just wouldn't tell you when."

"Uh huh." He pretended to give her the side-eye as we joined in their laughter.

We didn't leave until after one in the morning, and I hoped Juliet had a good time. She spent a lot of time chatting with Peyton, which I thought was great, and she talked about the evening all the way home.

"I didn't know what to expect," she told me as we pulled into my driveway. "But everyone was so nice."

"Did you think we'd all be assholes?" I asked, chuckling.

"You see the wives of pro athletes on TV and reality shows and stuff, and a lot of them seem…larger than life. Too much makeup, too much jewelry, too much everything. I don't know. I guess that's a terrible stereotype, but I was a little nervous I wouldn't fit in. I'm so plain."

I was just getting out of the car when she said that. I paused, staring at her over the top of the Corvette. "Did you just call yourself plain? Cause, baby, that's far from the truth."

It was dark in the garage, so I couldn't see if she was blushing, but the way she dipped her head told me she was. "I didn't mean I'm plain-looking, just that I'm simple. A little makeup, my hair is usually crazy in this humidity, and I never remember to put on jewelry."

"None of that matters. Not to me anyway." I went around the car to pull her against me. "I think you're perfect the way you are."

"You're very sweet."

"Sometimes." I smiled. "Let's go inside."

"Okay." She slid her hand into mine, and I hit the button to close the garage behind us.

"Your dad's not here, is he?" she asked, chuckling.

"He'd better not be." I looked down at her. "You thirsty or anything?"

"No." She met my gaze meaningfully, and I simply led her to the bedroom.

"You, uh, sure about this?" I asked. "We haven't known each other that long and—"

She cut me off by lifting to her toes and kissing me, just like she had that night on the beach. Except now we were alone. In my bedroom.

"Hang on," I whispered, gently pulling away. "I don't know where I put condoms. I've not brought anyone home since I've lived here."

She snickered. "Bathroom? Toiletry bag? Nightstand?"

"Definitely not the nightstand. Hold that thought." I turned and went into the bathroom. I had to turn on the damn light because I truly hadn't even thought about this. I had some in my travel bag, but that was in my locker at the arena.

Finally, I found them in a container in the linen closet. I grabbed a handful, turned out the lights and went back into the bedroom.

The sight waiting for me took my breath away. She'd undressed and was sprawled across my bed, wearing nothing but a soft smile.

"God, you're fucking gorgeous," I whispered, yanking off my own clothes in record time.

"Vaughn?" She sounded a little nervous.

"Yeah, babe?" I paused, looking down at her.

"I've never initiated sex before… Is it okay?"

"Okay? It's fucking awesome. I love a woman who knows what she wants."

"That's just it—I don't know what I want, but I want to try everything."

"I don't know if we have time for *everything* tonight, but we can do anything you want."

"I want to…touch you."

"Jules?" I suddenly had an odd thought. "You're not…a virgin, are you?"

"No, but…" She chewed her lip. "Carlo is kind of old-fashioned and—oh god, I'm sorry. We probably should have talked about this before."

"It's okay." I laid beside her so we were both on our sides, facing each other. "What you're trying to say is that you're not very experienced, and you want to try things you never did with your ex."

Relief washed over her face. "Yes. All we ever did was missionary, and I've gone down on him, but he's never gone down on me."

"Then he's too stupid to live and doesn't deserve you," I whispered. "Going down on a woman is my favorite thing. Wanna start with that?"

She shook her head. "I want you to kiss me first."

"Mmm. I love to kiss." I put out my left hand, since I was lying on my right side, and dug my fingers into the hair at the base of her skull as I pulled her toward me. Then I captured her lips in a soft, sensual kiss. A virginal non-virgin sounded so much sexier than I'd thought it would. I wouldn't have to deal with the nerves and pain that tended to go with a woman's first time, but I'd be able to show her how good sex could be. Too bad her idiot of an ex hadn't known what he had.

Her mouth was delicious, and I deepened the kiss, swirling my tongue around hers as I let my hand drift down her back. Her skin was silky, and so damn smooth. I trailed my fingers along the curve of her ass, wondering what the depth of her inexperience was. It didn't matter to me—I knew I could make it good—but I wanted to let her guide what we did tonight. If she had fantasies, I was all about making them a reality.

I broke the kiss and nibbled my way down her neck, cupping one of her breasts with my hand while I feasted on the other with my mouth. Her chest arched into my face, and I sucked her nipple deep into my mouth, waiting to see how rough she liked it. A whimper escaped her as I pulled away.

"More?" I asked.

"More."

I moved to her other breast, starting out soft and then increasing pressure and biting down until she cried out.

"Too much?"

"Oh no. I want more." Her eyes met mine, and all I saw behind her glassy glaze was pure need.

God, had she ever really been fucked? Did she even know what she was asking for? I'd thought sweet, shy Juliet would want romance and tenderness, and that I'd have to work up to rough and dirty. But that didn't seem to be the case at all.

"On your back," I told her in a gruff voice. I slid off the bed and pulled her down to the edge, so her sweet spot was right where I wanted it. I nipped her thighs, trailing my tongue along the crease until I nuzzled her sex. She shivered against me, and I lightly brushed my tongue along her slit. I had no idea what she liked, but she'd show me with her body. I pushed her thighs further apart and flattened my tongue on my second pass. Her hips shot up and she moved closer.

"Oh my god, Vaughn…"

With my hands on the backs of her knees to keep her legs back, I stabbed my tongue into her and feasted on her like a sensual delicacy. She was so sweet, and every swipe of my tongue drew the sexiest little sounds from her. Her fingers were in my hair, and she would pull harder every time I did something she liked. Which was a lot, but I knew she was close to the edge and since we had all night, I was going to get her there quickly. Because the second time she came would be a whole other ballgame.

I caressed and stroked her folds, letting her thighs settle on my shoulders so I could use my hands in addition to my tongue. I slid a finger into her, and she was drenched, but she clamped around me like a vise, her breath getting choppy. She groaned when I closed my lips around her clit and simultaneously slid a second finger inside of her. Her body jerked and her cry filled the room as she exploded around my face. I kept my mouth on her as the waves of her orgasm kept her fluttering against me, until she finally sank into the bed, breathing hard.

I crawled up over her and landed beside her, both of us on our backs breathing hard.

"Holy shit," she whispered. "How did you…wow."

I reached for her hand. "Did you like that?"

"Uh, yeah."

"Then you're really going to like what I do next." I rolled on top of her and kissed her.

18

"I can't wait to feel you inside of me," I breathed against his mouth.

"First things first, though." He adjusted his body so his groin was pressed against mine, his erection hard against my thigh. "Tell me what didn't satisfy you about sex before now."

"I could only come by myself."

"That was your first orgasm induced by a man?"

I nodded.

Our eyes locked, and I stared up into his gorgeous brown ones, somewhat mesmerized. He was so beautiful to look at, all angled lines and full lips. I couldn't even think about his hard, toned body right now, I was too busy getting aroused again.

"Next time, we're going to go slow and easy, and I'm going to show you how much fun missionary can be..." His voice was husky, and there was no mistaking the raw desire in his eyes. "But tonight, I'm going to show you how good it feels to fuck."

My breath caught in my throat, his naughty words sending my arousal into overdrive.

He sat up on his knees, using his hand to stroke himself, and I stared at his thick, hard erection. It was beautiful, so much bigger than I was used to, and I clenched just thinking about it. He reached over me to put a couple of pillows under my ass and then ran his fingers along the slit he'd just licked into oblivion.

"Wrap your legs around me," he whispered, edging closer.

My legs shook a little as I complied. He rolled the condom down his cock and then brushed the tip right where I wanted it.

"Ohhh…" My voice was raspy, filled with need. My eyes widened as he eased inside of me. His eyes didn't leave mine as he pushed in deeper, advancing a little at a time until the stretch started to burn. "Oh my god…"

"Easy." He angled his hips and went deeper and harder, until it was so uncomfortable it started to feel good. I was so full, so hot, so needy I whimpered.

His body was snug against mine, and he held still, his eyes still focused on mine. When he drew back slightly, I couldn't help but cry out, anxious for more, anxious to hold on to this amazing connection.

"Please," I whispered.

"Please what?"

"Please…*more.*"

"That's my girl." He slammed back into me so hard my eyes rolled back in my head and every nerve ending in my body came alive. His hips flexed into mine and satisfaction raced through my veins. I needed this, him, all of it, more of it, now. Nothing had prepared me for sensations like these, and as he started to drive into me, I lost all sense of reality. There was nothing but this, us, and I needed it like I needed to breathe. Except I couldn't. I was so caught up in him my lungs didn't seem to work, my heart was pumping too fast, and a primal need I didn't know existed was boiling up inside of me.

I reached up, blindly grasping his forearms as I arched up and into him. He grunted as he picked up speed and held on to my hips. The slapping of our bodies was loud but my screams were louder, and the moment he pressed a finger against my clit I went right over the edge. I bucked against him as he plunged into me over and over. At some point, he was so deep inside of me I could have sworn I felt his cock pulsing through his release.

And then it was over.

He collapsed on top of me, and my arms went around him shakily.

"Please don't move," I whispered.

"I'm not going anywhere."

I tried to gather my thoughts, but they were a jumbled mess of overwhelming sensations. I'd read about sex that was so good it changed your life, but I'd never experienced anything even close to this. Part of me wanted him to do it again while another wasn't sure what had just happened.

"You okay?" he whispered, pressing light kisses along the line of my jaw and the side of my face.

"I'm wonderful."

"Now what do you think about sex?"

"I think I want more."

"I have to get a little sleep, but stay with me tomorrow night and we'll do a lot more. I'll be done with practice by noon, one at the latest, and we can spend as much time in bed as you want."

"I have to go into the pizzeria, but I can get out of there by five."

"Do you work seven days a week?"

"Sometimes."

"Do you have to?"

Our eyes met and I swallowed. "No, I guess not. I just usually do."

"I want you here with me when I'm here, because I'm gone a lot."

"I want to be here with you too."

"Hang on a second. Be right back." He disappeared into the bathroom, and I heard the toilet flush and then the water running.

Then he was back in bed, tugging me on top of him.

"I leave on a road trip the day after tomorrow," he said, his hands skimming down my back. "But I'll be home Wednesday. I can pick you up on my way home from the airport."

I slowly shook my head. "I think it's probably better if I drive over on my own. That way you don't have to cart me around, and we can be together until one of us has to leave for work."

He chuckled. "Sounds good to me."

"Tonight has been amazing," I said softly. "I'm sorry I didn't talk to you ahead of time about the sex stuff, but I didn't know what to say. I wasn't sure if telling you my ex had never satisfied me in bed was a bitchy thing to do, or if it made me sound needy or something. I guess it was a little embarrassing too."

"No." He lifted a hand and gently stroked the side of my face. "There's nothing wrong with telling me what was wrong in your past sexual relationships so we can make them better this time."

"Just one relationship," I said. "I've only ever been with Carlo until now."

"You were each other's firsts and you never moved past missionary?"

"We didn't even do it until we were nineteen. He'd originally wanted to wait for marriage, but I told him that was ridiculous. And later, when we'd been doing it for a while, and I tried to explain that I needed him to touch me more, or kiss me more, or whatever, he would shut down and say he knew what he was doing, to just lay there and enjoy it."

"Well, he didn't know shit." Vaughn shrugged. "But he's not your problem anymore."

"Nope." I closed my eyes as he leaned up to kiss me.

"Is it always that intense?" I asked softly. "I mean… is it always like that when you know what you're doing?"

He looked thoughtful. "Sometimes? But not always. Sometimes the chemistry just isn't there. And other times we'll want something more sedate, romantic. Tonight was pretty fucking intense, but every time is different."

"Every time was always the same for me. Before, I mean."

"Not anymore." His hands slid up my torso, stopping at my breasts, where he began circling my nipples with his fingers. "Like this next time, I'm going to take it easy on you. I'm going to play with these perfect breasts of yours until you're so wet and ready for my cock it'll just slide right in. And when I squeeze them"—he pinched both nipples hard enough to make me gasp—"you're going to clench around me just like that."

"H-how did you know?" I whispered, though it was a little hard to concentrate because I was turned on again.

He gave me a lazy, sexy smile. "In fact, I can probably make you come just by playing with your nipples…Wanna find out?" He squeezed again, and I moaned.

"Y-yes."

"Just like that, baby. Put my cock between your folds and rock yourself home."

I nearly came again, right on the spot, but it felt too good to rush.

He was already hard, and feeling him between my legs, right where I wanted him but not inside me was a different kind of excitement. His hands were hot against my skin, and my nipples were hard little peaks as he toyed with him. Somehow, my body knew what to do, and I writhed above him, my hips gyrating in time to what he was doing with his fingers.

The space between my legs was slippery, and I ached to have him inside me again, but I was too close to the edge. *Again.* His fingers strummed my breasts like they were musical instruments with me making sounds I'd never made before.

This time my orgasm built up slowly, boiling in my belly, and then exploding out as I rode him. He came at the same time, and I watched in fascination as his come spurted out over his abdomen in thin little lines.

And it was one of the sexiest things I'd ever seen.

"You are so god damn hot." He pulled me down to kiss me, his semen spreading between us. "I'm going to fuck you again."

. . .

W e had so much sex that night I was sore the next morning. My nether regions ached with a beautiful reminder of the most amazing night of my life, and I was smiling as I let myself into the house.

"Well. Look who it is." Mom came out of the kitchen with her hands on her hips and a scowl on her face, immediately ruining my mood.

"I told you I might be out late."

"You went out with the hockey player again."

"His name is Vaughn." I met her gaze.

"Why, Juliet? Why would you ruin your life like this?"

"How am I ruining my life? Dating a nice man who makes me laugh and is sweet and kind doesn't hurt me in any way."

"And Carlo? What about how this hurts him?"

"I'm sorry about that, but I told him it was over. I don't want to marry him. I know—"

"You know nothing," she snapped. "You're throwing away your future—and for what? Some playboy professional athlete who will use you until he's bored and then find someone else."

"This has nothing to do with Vaughn," I cried. "This is about how unhappy Carlo and I were together. Not just me, both of us. Now that we're older we don't have anything in common. He's selfish and a freakin' prude. I'm not going to spend the rest of my life with someone who bores me to death. I'm just not."

She glared at me. "So, what? You'll go from man to man until someone exciting finally wants to marry you?"

"That's what Mario's done and yet, three divorces later, he's still your favorite."

"I don't have favorites." Her eyes blazed but color had crept onto her cheeks.

"Don't you? *Three* divorces and you've never said a word to him. I try to end an engagement that's destined to fail *before* we actually get married, and you're acting like I'm bringing on the apocalypse or something."

"He's a man."

My mother and I had always butted heads, but we were a close-knit, loving family. Most of the time. Sometimes we argued or yelled, but five minutes later we usually forgot about it and moved on. This was different, and I just stared at her.

"I'm sorry you feel that way. I have to get ready for work."

"Your father would be ashamed," she called after me.

I stopped and slowly turned around. "*Dad* would be ashamed of me? Or you are but don't want to say it? Because *Dad* wanted me to be happy. *Dad* was always telling me to follow my dreams of opening a bakery or to take classes part-time since I still wanted to go to college. Dad wouldn't have wanted me to marry a man I wasn't in love with. It makes me really sad that you do."

I turned and ran up the stairs, hoping I'd hold off the tears until I was in the shower. My mother was always a little tough on us kids, especially me, but the conversation we'd just had really hurt my feelings. Even if Vaughn never called again, I still wasn't going back to Carlo, and I didn't know how to make everyone understand that.

19

I'd been around the block enough times to know that good sex wasn't indicative of a good relationship, but it had been years since I'd had sex this good. Leaving Juliet to go on this road trip had been hard, especially knowing how bad things were between her and her mom. She'd told me what had happened after she got home from our date and, just like when she'd been in the hospital, I felt responsible for the bad things in her life. If I hadn't hit her with that puck, she'd still be engaged, getting along with her family, and not struggling to figure out what to do next in life.

But she wasn't happy, I reminded myself.

At least, that's what she told me, but it was hard to know for sure. Deep down, I was worried about how attached we'd gotten to each other in such a short time. I thought about her any time I wasn't on the ice, and we texted back and forth constantly, but it had occurred to me that this might just be her knee-jerk reaction to a serious head injury. It made perfect sense that in the aftermath of an accident that technically could have killed her, she was doubting everything about her life.

The problem with that was that she could wake up one day and realize she missed her old life. Worse than that, I also couldn't help but wonder if this was the excuse she needed to sow some wild oats before getting married. She'd never been with anyone but Carlo, and after a concussion and a bout of amnesia, there was a good chance she just wanted to see what else was out in the world. I felt a little guilty just thinking those things about her, but it also felt a little naïve not to at least consider it.

"We're going out tonight," Cam said to me on the bus to the venue before the game.

"What?" I turned.

"Jude has been talking about some strip club in town that's off the charts hot."

"I thought you had a girlfriend?" I asked, frowning.

He shrugged. "She said we're on a break. That being apart is too much of a distraction right now. So I'm free to do what I want."

"How much of a break?"

"No idea. She was kind of distracted, and then she started to cry and…" He made a face. "I hate when she cries. So I just agreed and told her everything would be okay. Now I'm kind of pissed at myself for letting her off the hook so easily after three years together, but whatever. I can't control what she does."

"I don't know if I can go to a strip club," I blurted out, squeezing my eyes shut the moment the words came out of my mouth. What the fuck had I just said?

Cam was smiling when I opened my eyes, though. "You really like her."

"I do. What the hell is wrong with me? It's been, like, three weeks."

"So? You don't have to formalize your relationship status to simply not want to be with anyone else. Until Sam and I had the talk about taking a break, I genuinely didn't want to cheat. There's nothing emasculating about being in love and treating the woman you're with right. Cheating doesn't make you a man. Hell, in my opinion, cheating makes you less of one. It's easy to fuck the first available woman. It's a lot harder to stay faithful when you're surrounded by temptation. And, on top of that, not wanting to sleep with other women even though you're not serious yet or whatever, just makes it that much better when you get home. Because technically it wouldn't be cheating if you haven't had a conversation about being exclusive, but that doesn't make it right."

I stared at him for a second. This was probably the most he'd ever said to me at one time since we'd met, and he had a point. Cheating wasn't something admirable, and while I wouldn't be cheating, it still didn't feel right to sit at a strip club drooling over naked women who weren't Juliet.

I nodded. "Agreed. I've never cheated on anyone I was in a relationship with, but this thing with Juliet is so new."

"Are you guys seriously talking about relationships when we're going to a strip club tonight?" Palmer asked, leaning over. "Jesus, is there anyone on this team who wants to live it up and party?"

"Dude." I gave him a look. "I've been living it up and partying since you were in elementary school. Talk to me in a decade."

Everyone around us snorted with laughter, including Palmer.

"How old are you, again?" he quipped. "Forty?"

"Hey! Easy with that number," Coach Petrov called out from the front of the bus. "Forty isn't old."

Palmer just grinned as the bus came to a stop, and we started filing off. Truthfully, Palmer was a good kid. Talented as hell, he worked as hard as anyone on the team, and despite being a little immature, he always had our backs on the ice. You couldn't ask for more from a teammate, so I cut him a little slack when it came to things like women and partying. Hell, he wasn't even old enough to drink yet, which I rubbed in his face now and then when he got annoying.

My phone buzzed as we walked into the arena, and I smiled at the text from Juliet.

JULIET: Play good tonight. I'll be cheering you on from Lauderdale!

VAUGHN: I'll do my best. You working?

JULIET: Actually, I'm not. I'm at my friend Chloe's place, hanging out and catching up.

VAUGHN: But you're still going to watch the game, right?

JULIET: Duh! I'm converting her into a fan. I have to bring her to a game.

VAUGHN: Let me know and I'll get her a ticket.

JULIET: I'll see if the boys are willing to give one of theirs up, but if not, that would be awesome. Text me when you get back to the hotel?

VAUGHN: Will do.

I put my phone in my pocket and headed into the dressing room to change. I was glad Juliet was taking a little time for herself and not working all the time, but I also worried about how that would impact her relationship with her family. Despite everything going on, they had always been close, and this situation hurt her more than she wanted to admit.

For the first time in my life I wished I had the kind of relationship with my dad where I could talk to him about stuff like this. My mom had been great with advice during puberty and my teen years. Even as I got into my twenties, Mom had always been there for me and almost always knew what to say. Now that she was gone, I didn't have anyone in my life that served as a mentor or parental figure.

I did have my father, though, and things were civil between us these days.

We still hadn't really talked, not about the stuff I wanted to talk about, and the only way for us to go any further in the relationship would be if I laid it all on the table for him.

When I got back to Lauderdale, that was exactly what I was going to do.

<hr>

My mother had always told me that it was better I didn't know the details of my dad's life. In her letter, she'd admitted she thought I was better off thinking he was a deadbeat than knowing the truth, but I knew more than she realized. Little kids listened to and heard everything, especially the stuff you didn't want them to, and though I hadn't understood it then, I sure as hell did now. I still didn't understand much about their relationship, but I had a lot of my own memories that were so confusing.

Dad driving up on his Harley and me tearing out of the house to greet him.

Dad showing up right before Christmas with a huge stack of Christmas presents.

Dad unexpectedly coming to one of my T-ball games and cheering louder than anyone else.

When I was around thirteen, he'd essentially disappeared. Mom had eventually told me he'd been in prison, but those years had been brutal with me thinking he'd just abandoned us and listening to Mom cry herself to sleep. And I needed answers. Even if they weren't what I wanted to hear. How else could Dad and I ever truly be a family?

We were meeting for lunch today, and I'd thought about what to say during the entire road trip. Ironically, I still didn't know exactly, but I figured it was time to get as much into the open as possible.

"Hey, son." Dad sank down across from me at the Mexican restaurant I'd chosen.

"Hi, Dad."

"What's good?" he asked, picking up the menu.

"Everything," I replied.

A waitress came and took our orders and then he looked at me. "Something on your mind?"

"Everything."

He nodded. "Somehow, I had a feeling this was coming."

"Tell me the truth about your relationship with Mom. The good, the bad, and the ugly."

For the first time that I could remember, Dad looked uncomfortable. He was a big, tough guy, covered in tattoos with a beard, long hair, and a scar across his cheek that told of the kind of life he'd had. Yet, he looked sad and couldn't quite meet my eye.

"I don't want you to think less of her," he said after a moment.

"I'll never think less of her," I said, and meant it. "She did everything for me. She was there for every scraped knee, every homework assignment and science fair project, every hockey game. Nothing you say will change how I feel about Mom."

He nodded. "So, let me preface this by saying I'll never pretend to be some kind of good guy, but there are different levels to bad guys. Like, I'm not a good guy, but I'm not evil. I'll never touch a woman against her will or hurt a little kid or an animal. I've never hurt someone who didn't deserve it. But your grandfather—Demi's dad—he was fucking evil."

That made sense because my mother had said similar things about her father when I asked about her family.

"So when Demi and I fell in love, he thought it was great. Everyone assumed I would join the club when I turned eighteen. My father was VP, and her dad was his Sergeant-at-arms—I know you don't understand the inner workings of the club but all you need to know is those were positions of power."

"All right."

"So Demi and me, we grew up watching the club and seeing the danger, the death, the drug deals, and even at sixteen and seventeen, we kind of knew we didn't want that life. Senior year we decided we were going to leave as soon as we graduated. Your mom had a full ride to UC Riverside, and I was going to take out student loans to go to mechanic school. I always tinkered with engines and shit, and it wasn't a bad thing to get some formal training." He paused, scratching his beard. "In retrospect, we were stupid. What we should have done was eloped and disappeared, but we thought we knew everything. So we had the wedding and told everyone our plans."

Even I knew that couldn't be good.

"My dad wasn't thrilled, but he understood because my older brother was shot and killed by a rival club when he was twenty-two. He didn't want to lose me too, but Demi's dad? He lost his shit. I can't prove it, but that night when the guys were ambushed on that drug run? That was bullshit. They sent me on a doomed mission to deliver drugs to a set-up."

"What?" I was confused. "Why?"

He sighed. "It's complicated. Suffice it to say, we were being set up. Your mom's dad figured it out but didn't tell anyone. He waited until the others had left and then sent me to go warn them."

"Why didn't he go?"

Dad met my gaze. "You tell me."

"Didn't you ask?"

"No one questioned Big Vic. You just didn't. And my dad was one of the guys who was on the run, so I went. I got caught, I got busted, and then the club basically blackmailed me. Either I agreed to join the brotherhood, or I was on my own. I was a kid. I didn't have any money or a lawyer or anything. So I did what I had to do, still planning to get the hell out of dodge the minute I was free. But leaving the club is a heck of a lot harder than joining." He was quiet as the waitress brought our food.

"So what happened?" I asked, taking a bite of my enchilada.

"I told them I'd pay back every dime they'd paid for the lawyer and every-thing they'd done to get me off with probation, but then I was out. Demi and I were going away to school." He stopped and took a sip of his soda, staring off at nothing, his jaw working. "One day while I was at the club, your grandfa-ther beat the shit out of your mom. Put her in the hospital. When I got there, he smiled and told me he'd kill his own daughter before he let us leave."

"Jesus fucking Christ."

"That was when we knew I was never getting out. I sent your mom to college down in Riverside, and I stayed up in Oakland with the club. I told her we should get divorced, that it would be safer for her, but she refused. So we agreed no kids. We didn't want to bring any more kids into that life. But she got pregnant her junior year, and once she knew you were growing inside of her, nothing could keep her from having you."

"Did you want me?"

Dad finally met my eyes. "More than fucking anything."

I got a huge lump in my throat.

"Anyway, we didn't know what to do, but I started making like we were having problems, like I wasn't happy. We needed an excuse why she wasn't coming home for visits anymore. You were a year old when she graduated and at that point, we knew we had to do something. So we decided to get divorced. I set you guys up in New Hampshire, and she got her teaching certificate and a job. My hope was to get out so I could join you, but that never happened."

"And you two just did a secret, long-distance thing?"

"That's what *she* wanted," he replied quietly. "I told her she could move on, that I understood how hard this was on her, but she wouldn't. So I sent money, I bought that house you grew up in, I paid for all your hockey equip-ment, and most everything else you needed while she raised you. I came around a lot when you were a kid because I loved you. But I started backing off when you got older because I knew there would be questions we couldn't answer."

I had a million *more* questions, but I had to digest all of this first. "Mom sacrificed everything for me," I said sadly.

"You mom and I sacrificed everything, together."

"Why didn't her dad go after her, though? He just let her go?"

"He thought we were divorced, and he didn't know there was kid. At that point, she had no value to him because he couldn't use her to manipulate me if I didn't love her, which is what we wanted everyone to believe. So you can hate me for my choices, but do not, ever, negate my sacrifice. I loved you and your mom more than my own life. Now I'm trying to fulfill her dying wish."

"Which was?"

"Exactly what your mom said in the letter: get out of the club and have a relationship with you."

20

JULIET

Vaughn had picked me up when my phone rang. We were on our way to a Halloween party hosted by one of his teammates, so I would have ignored it, but seeing the name of the dress shop where I was supposed to get my wedding dress gave me pause.

"Sorry, let me take this," I told him. "Hello?"

"Hello, Juliet Cicero?"

"Yes?"

"This is Pamela from Martinique's Dresses. The wedding is only two months away, and with the change in dress we need to have you come in for a fitting as soon as possible."

"I'm sorry…what? What dress change? I was very specific when I called. I don't need a dress anymore because the wedding has been cancelled. What change are you talking about?"

There was a beat of silence. "I spoke with your mother personally, just last week. She told me you and your fiancé had a disagreement, and one of the things you fought about was the wedding. Now that you'd made up you wanted a different dress…I don't understand."

I bit my lip to keep from screaming in frustration. "I'm sorry, Pamela. If at all possible, can you put a note in my file that the wedding is cancelled? And it doesn't matter who calls—unless I personally come into the store that's not changing."

"But we ordered you a second dress."

"I'm sure you can sell it," I replied, feeling a little testy. "And if not, you should reach out to my mother. I'm not the one who told you to order another dress."

"I… I'm going to have to speak to my manager about this."

"By all means. Have a good evening." I disconnected and closed my eyes, trying to breathe through the pounding in my chest. My mother was driving me bat-shit crazy, and I didn't know what to do.

"What happened?" Vaughn asked, reaching for my hand.

"My mother is what happened." I shook my head. "I can't believe she went behind my back, after I called to cancel the dress, and not only un-cancelled it, but ordered another dress. Oh hell, I bet she ordered the dress with the flowers…" My voice trailed off. I probably shouldn't be talking to him about the dress I'd planned to wear to my marriage to someone else.

"Dress with the flowers?"

I sighed. "I loved this one dress. It was sexy, but elegant, and had a long train with lavender roses and Swarovski crystals sewn into it. Mom thought it was too risqué, so she went ahead and ordered the one she liked instead of the one I wanted. I'm willing to bet, with everything that happened, she figured she'd score points with me by ordering the dress I really wanted."

"Are you sure you want me hanging around at the pizzeria? It doesn't sound like your mom is even a little bit over your break-up with Carlo."

"I told her you'd be coming around and she said it was fine."

"Isn't it bad when a woman says something is fine?"

"It's bad when it's your wife or girlfriend. It's different when it's your mom."

"I don't know. When my mom used to say 'fine' I always got in trouble later."

I chuckled. "Well, I've been in trouble for weeks, so nothing will change for me. And whenever it gets really bad, I go stay with Chloe for a day or two. I was at her place almost the whole time you were on the road."

"Have you talked to Carlo at all?"

"No. Why?"

"Because maybe you need to."

"I need to talk to Carlo? Why on earth would you even suggest that?"

"Because if my fiancée had gotten a concussion so severe it led to amnesia, and she promptly broke up with me, I'd be wondering if something *else* was going on. Like if this was temporary insanity or something. You know?"

"Is that what you think?" I looked over at him in confusion.

"No, but that is absolutely what *he's* thinking. So until *he* believes it's over, how will everyone else?"

"Why is that my problem?" I asked. "I've told everyone who would listen that things weren't good before the accident. I'd been unhappy, and so had he. We'd been fighting nonstop about everything from the wedding details to where we wanted to live after we got married. To the point we'd discussed getting counseling. Well, I discussed it, and he pouted, but regardless, things were bad. The only thing that changed after the accident was my refusal to put up with it anymore. I don't want to settle. Why doesn't anyone understand?"

"Hey, I'm sorry." He squeezed my hand. "I do understand. Really. It's just hard for me to watch you go through this because I can see how much it hurts you when your family does the things they've been doing. And maybe talking to Carlo will help."

"Maybe." I stared off at nothing.

"Are you mad?"

"I'm *fine*." I emphasized the word fine and then fought to keep a straight face.

"Babe?" Vaughn was looking at me worriedly, and I finally burst out laughing.

"I'm kidding. No, I'm not mad, and maybe talking to him will help, but I don't want to think about that tonight. I just want to have fun. I haven't been to a Halloween party in years."

"What did you make?" he asked, referring to the cupcake carrier I had on my lap.

"Cupcakes," I said. "Very special cupcakes."

"How special?"

"White chocolate cupcakes with white chocolate liqueur infused buttercream frosting dyed with the team colors."

"For real? I think I just drooled a little."

I smiled. "I love baking, especially cupcakes. I have a whole file of recipes I make on special occasions. The brandy and eggnog cupcakes I make for the holidays are the best thing you'll ever put in your mouth."

"Well, I don't know about that." He grinned over at me. "But they might come in second."

"Don't tease me," I murmured. "It's been four days since we've had sex, you know."

"I am well-aware. Don't worry, baby, I'll take care of you tonight."

"I know, but it's so many hours from now."

"We can turn around and just go home," he teased.

"Normally, I'd say yes, but I spent a long time on this costume." I was Little Red Riding Hood, and he was the big bad wolf. It had taken me forty minutes to do the makeup on his face, not to mention another half hour to do my own. We'd had fun shopping for our costumes, but I'd told him I didn't want him to wear a mask that would cover his face, so I'd done his makeup instead. It looked pretty good, too, if I did say so myself.

We got to Zakk and Tiff's house just after eight and cars were already lining the street. Most of the team was coming, so there were going to be a lot of people. I was a little nervous about such a big gathering, but I liked everyone I'd met so far and was looking forward to seeing some of them again.

We walked inside with Vaughn carrying the cupcakes—I'd made sixty of them—and Tiff greeted us at the door.

"Hi! Happy Halloween."

"Happy Halloween." I hugged her. "We brought special cupcakes."

"Oooh, let's get them to the kitchen." We followed her through a two-story foyer and down a hall to a massive kitchen. Vaughn put them down, and I took off the top of the first carrier.

"Oh my god, they're so pretty!" Tiff squealed with excitement. "Babe!" She called to her husband, and Zakk came around the corner. "Check these out."

He peered down and grinned. "Wow. Those are our colors, and you got the hockey sticks just right. Did you make those?" He stared at me.

"I did." I nodded.

"Thank you so much," Tiff gushed. "They look too pretty to eat."

"The frosting is infused with white chocolate liqueur," I told her.

"Oh, fuck it." Tiff picked one up and took a bite, sighing happily as she chewed.

"Hey!" Zakk frowned at her, and she let him take a bite.

"What about me?" Vaughn asked.

I laughed and picked one up. "Here. Try it."

He took a bite and then moaned. "Oh my god. You made these? Sweet Jesus, they're amazing."

"Thanks, guys." Their compliments warmed me from the inside out. I'd been making cupcakes for friends and family for years, and while everyone loved them, they'd all scoffed at the idea of me selling them at the pizzeria. Carlo didn't even like cupcakes, so I'd stopped making them for a while, but I'd felt like it today, and now I was glad I did.

The three of them finished the two cupcakes before Tiff covered the container again. "I'm going to hide these until later. They'll be gone in no time flat if people find them." She put them in a cupboard and closed it. "Don't let me forget to bring them out. Now, what would you guys like to drink?"

Tiff tugged me in one direction toward a cauldron of fancy punch she thought I would like, while Zakk and Vaughn went out to the patio where a bunch of guys were doing shots.

"Have you met Noelle Knight?" Tiff asked me. "She's married to the team owner, Remy."

"I've met Remy. Hi." I smiled at the attractive blond.

"Noelle, this is Juliet. She's the one Vaughn hit with the puck on opening night."

"Oh!" Noelle's eyes widened. "Hi. How are you feeling? I heard you had amnesia."

"I did, but my memory came back and there don't appear to be any lingering effects from the concussion. The cut healed pretty well, so I think I'm good."

"Are you Little Red Riding Hood?" Tessa asked, joining us.

"Yes. And Vaughn is—"

"The Big Bad Wolf!" Noelle, Tessa, and Tiff finished in unison.

We chatted as Tiff got me a glass of the very potent punch in the cauldron. Peyton came by to say hello, along with a few others I hadn't met before, and out of nowhere the "Monster Mash" came through the speakers.

"I love this song," Tiff giggled. "And I'm going to make my husband dance with me."

"May I have this dance?" Toli, dressed as a knight of some kind, extended his hand to Tessa, who accepted it happily.

I was just looking around for Vaughn when he appeared, sliding an arm around my waist.

"Hello, little girl… you look good enough to eat."

I wiggled my eyebrows. "I'll bet."

"Should we dance?"

"I'd love to."

We drank and danced for the next couple of hours, pausing to eat a little in between, and talk with his teammates and their significant others. We'd just finished slow dancing when Tiff stood on a chair and yelled to get everyone's attention.

"Everyone outside! Ladies, it's time for blow jobs!"

I glanced at Vaughn. "I'm afraid to ask."

He laughed. "I don't know either, but I think I'm looking forward to it."

We headed out to the back patio where Tiff was putting out what looked like a row of fancy shots. Vaughn started to chuckle, and I nudged him.

"What is it?" I asked.

"You'll see." He slid an arm around my shoulders as we gathered around.

"Okay, this is a throwback to the eighties," Tiff said, "but I've personally always been a fan. Now, as you can see…" She lifted one of the shot glasses and showed it to everyone. "This is a shot. It's called a Blow Job, and it's made with Kahlua, Bailey's, and whipped cream. And I'm going to show you the proper way to drink one." She put the shot back on the table and turned to her husband. "Will you do the honors?"

"I will." He moved behind her and pulled her hair back.

I had no idea what she was about to do, but she put her hands behind her back, leaned down, wrapped her mouth around the shot, and then stood up straight, drinking the whole thing. She grabbed the shot glass and licked her lips, as we all whooped with delight. There were remnants of whipped cream on her lips, and she licked them off.

"So." She turned and grinned. "I want to know who's next?"

One of the other wives immediately stepped up and another round of cheers went up as she swallowed and wiped her mouth with the back of her hand, laughing as her husband whispered in her ear.

"I'll do it." I didn't know what prompted me to speak up, but I'd never done anything like this before, and I really wanted to. I felt Vaughn moving behind me as I stepped up to the table. My hair was up in a demure little bun since I was Red Riding Hood, but I was glad to have him beside me because I was inexplicably nervous. It was all in fun with a naughty edge to it, and I wondered why I'd never heard of this shot before.

I leaned over, opening my mouth as wide as I could—which was harder than it looked—and finally got my lips clamped around the glass. Then I lifted up and my eyes watered a little as the concoction slid down my throat. I'd done it, though, and I grinned at Vaughn as I pulled the shot glass out of my mouth. Everyone was cheering, and I did a little bow, making them cheer louder.

"That was so fucking hot," Vaughn breathed in my ear as we moved to the back of the group so others could take their turn.

"Yeah?" I met his gaze, licking my lips. "We, uh, haven't done that yet."

"You want to?" His eyes glittered with heat that made my insides liquify.

"Mm, yes."

He grabbed my hand and pulled me into the house, through the main room and to a room in the back.

"Is this a guest room?" I asked, looking around as he shut the door and locked it.

"Yup." He raked his eyes over me. "And the big bad wolf is hard as granite."

21

VAUGHN

I'd almost lost my mind when she'd wrapped her mouth around that shot glass. I'd seen stuff like that at strip clubs and stuff but having all the wives and girlfriends doing it at a team party was off the charts fun. Especially when Juliet had done it. And now I groaned as she dropped to her knees in front of me, unbuckling my pants. With her hair up in that prim little bun and the red cape flowing around her shoulders, this was one of the sexiest things I'd seen her do.

Her eyes traveled up to mine for a moment, and I wasn't sure what I saw in hers, but then her mouth was on me, and I sucked in a breath. Her mouth was hot against my skin and one of her hands traveled down to cup my balls as she licked her way along the underside of my cock. She wrapped a hand around me and sucked deep, making my breath hitch, and the fingers of one hand dug into her hair. I was probably going to fuck up her bun, but I didn't care.

She backed off, using the tip of her tongue to circle my slit, one of her hands squeezing my balls hard enough to make me moan. Jesus, this was my favorite kind of torture, and she totally had my number. Her mouth was hot and sexy, alternating between gentle nibbles and hard sucking until I couldn't help but to start pumping in and out of her mouth. I held her head by gripping that bun, and I fucked her mouth the way I hoped to be fucking her pussy when we got home.

Pleasure raced down my spine and exploded out of my cock as I came hard. She swallowed and coughed, and I realized I was halfway down her throat.

"Sorry." I let go of her hair. "You okay?"

"Yes." She smiled up at me as I reached down to help her up.

"That was awesome."

"I thought so too."

"But I messed up your hair."

"That's okay. Little Red Riding Hood has just been ravaged by the wolf and doesn't care who knows it."

"Oh, baby, this is nothing compared to what I'm going to do to you when we get home."

I slid my hand into hers as we walked back into the hallway just in time to see Palmer's date going down on him.

"Jesus, Palmer—get a room," I told him as we passed by.

"Yeah, yeah."

"Are team parties always like this?" Juliet whispered as we went back toward the main room.

"Not usually, but sometimes. Depends on who's hosting, who's in attendance, stuff like that. I think we tend to let loose a little more when we're at home, so to speak, than when we're on the road."

"I thought you guys partied hard on the road?" she asked.

"Not really. There's always someone who's the party animal, and the single guys definitely party more than the guys with wives or girlfriends, but being on the road is exhausting. We need our sleep and to stay focused. I'm far more likely to party at home than on the road, though I don't do a lot of partying during the season in general."

"I've never been much of a partier," she said quietly. "Carlo didn't like to go out, so we didn't. Now I feel like I've missed out."

"We can go out whenever I don't have hockey going on."

"If we're still dating in the off-season, we can get our party on then."

Knowing most of the team would be out partying the night before, Coach had given us today off. We had a couple of home games coming up and then we were back on the road next week, but I had never been so happy to have a morning off. Rolling over, I nuzzled Juliet's bare shoulder, and she murmured something sleepily. Waking up to her naked body beside me in my bed was the kind of thing I could get used to.

Before I could decide if I wanted to wake her up or not, my phone buzzed and there was a text from my dad that made me groan.

DAD: I've got donuts and bagels. Thought I'd come over for breakfast if you're around?

VAUGHN: Juliet is here.

DAD: That's all right with me. Unless you don't want me around her?

I hesitated. I still wasn't sure if I wanted him around me, much less Juliet, but they'd gotten along well the last time he'd shown up.

"Hey." I kissed her shoulder. "Dad wants to come over for breakfast. Are you cool with that, or should I tell him another time?"

She rolled over and rubbed her eyes. "I don't mind."

God, she was beautiful here in my bed, her soft, round breasts jutting up and tempting me. I leaned down lightly sucked one of her nipples between my lips, gratified to hear her moan softly.

"Vaughn…your dad," she whispered.

"I know." I let out a sigh as I rested my chin on her chest. "You sure you don't mind?"

"I'm sure."

I kissed her and then texted my dad back.

T wenty minutes later, I was in the kitchen making coffee with Dad when Juliet came padding in after taking a quick shower.

"Good morning." She smiled at Dad. "How are you, Buzz?"

He smiled back. "Doin' pretty good. You two have fun last night? Saw some pictures on the team's social media. I like those costumes."

"It was a good time," she said, leaning against the counter. "What did you do last night?"

He shrugged. "Hung out in my motel room and watched TV."

"What are your plans, Dad?" I asked him as we settled at the kitchen island. "You can't keep staying at a motel."

"I've been searching for a garage that might be for sale," he said, taking a sip of coffee. "But so far I haven't found anything that works for both my needs and my budget."

"Are you a mechanic?" Juliet asked him.

"Yeah. But it takes a lot of money to start from scratch, and I feel like I'm too old to work for someone else."

"Maybe that's the best way," I suggested. "Get a foot in the door and meet the locals. That way, as soon as something comes available, you might hear about it first."

"Still takes a lot of money, you know? And the longer it takes me to get settled, the more money I'm blowing living in hotels and eating out and shit."

I frowned, taking a bite of my bagel, and trying to read between the lines. Was he hinting that he wanted to move in with me? Because that wasn't happening. I not only wasn't ready to be around him twenty-four-seven, I also needed my privacy. Especially now that I hoped Juliet would be sleeping over more often.

"You'd probably be better off renting a room somewhere," Juliet said. "It'll be cheaper than a motel room in the long run."

"I guess I haven't decided for sure whether or not I'm going to stay." Dad looked at me for a few seconds and then focused on his coffee cup again.

Christ. It was too early for this, but I needed to know the answer to the question I was about to ask. "Then what's going to tip the scales?"

He met my eyes and, as always, his were somewhat shrouded.

"You."

I sighed. "Dad, you can't make these decisions based on me because I could get traded tomorrow. I mean, I just got here, so probably not, but in a couple of years? There's no reason to believe I'll finish my career here."

"I know that, but at the end of the day, I don't have anyone else."

"Your brothers from the ga—club?"

"Once I make the decision to get out, those relationships mostly go away. That's how it works."

"Are you saying you have to choose between me and them?" I asked in surprise.

Juliet got to her feet. "I have to start getting ready for work." She squeezed my shoulder as she left the room, and I stared after her for a second before turning back to Dad.

"Look, I don't want to pressure you," Dad said.

"That's kind of what this is," I told him. "And I simply can't promise you I'm going to be here in five years."

"I know that, son. But I can't follow you around either. I have to settle somewhere if I leave the club."

"There's that word—if. Are you leaving or not?"

"There's no point in leaving if I'm not going to be in your life. Why else would I walk away from the only life I've ever known?"

I sighed and blew out a breath. "Dad, we've started to make our peace, but we have a long way to go, and my hockey schedule keeps me too busy to be around regularly."

"I'm not trying to push anything, but I have to make some decisions. And all of them are expensive."

"Dad, it would be great if you were close by, and if you want to retire to Florida, that's great. Just don't do it solely for me because I don't know where I'll end up."

Neither of us spoke for a few minutes before Juliet came back in the room.

"You need to get going?" I asked her.

"I do."

"All right, let me get my wallet, and we'll go. Dad, you gonna hang around? I'm off today, so I can come back after I drop Jules off."

"Sounds good."

"You can, uh, hang out here until I get back."

"Thanks, but I have a few things to do."

I grabbed my wallet and keys from the bedroom and went into the garage with Juliet and Dad behind me, since he was leaving too.

"You look kind of stressed," Juliet said to me once we were on the road.

"I think he's hinting he wants to move in and that's…well, it's not happening."

"From the pieces I heard, I think he wants you to ask him to stay," she said softly.

My grip tightened on the steering wheel, and I clenched my jaw. "I don't know him," I said after a moment. "And worse than that, despite my mother's letter asking me to trust him, I don't." I'd told her about the letter.

"Those are both things that take time."

"I know. Dammit, I know."

22

With Vaughn on the road, I got caught up on things at work. As usual, part of me felt guilty for taking so much time off these days because I made a good salary, but I'd warned everyone I wasn't going to work fifty- and sixty-hour weeks anymore. It wasn't fair, and I wasn't going to do it. That was all there was to it. Except the guilt part. That was harder to come to terms with.

My mother was as frosty as a blizzard toward me these days, and I didn't know what to say to her anymore. I knew she only wanted what was best for me, but I had to figure that stuff out on my own. I was an adult, and if she could trust me to run a restaurant that made a million dollars a year, she could trust me to know whom I did and didn't want to marry. Or date.

Today I wasn't going in until lunchtime because I had something special to do. Tiff had reached out to me and asked me to bake three dozen special cupcakes for her twin sons' birthday party this weekend, and I was doing a practice run today to see how they came out. They wanted chocolate fudge cupcakes with white chocolate frosting decorated with hockey sticks and little candy pucks that Tiff had found and provided. Since I'd never made anything like that before, I was going to try a small batch today.

Everything about baking cupcakes relaxed me. I'd forgotten how much I enjoyed it because I hadn't been doing much of it in the last year, but after baking the ones for Halloween I was back in the groove.

I'd just put them in the oven when my mother came into the kitchen, frowning. "What are you doing?" she asked.

"Baking."

"Why? Aren't you going to work?"

"I'll be there by lunch. I have to work late tonight to do payroll so I'm going in later."

Mom looked at me for a minute, and then absently started putting the dirty bowls and measuring cups in the dishwasher. "You're different lately," she said after a moment.

"I'm not," I responded. "I'm just more vocal about things that bother me."

She nodded. "Which is different. Not like you used to be."

"We all change as we grow up, mature. I'm sure you're not the same as you were in your twenties." I started getting out the ingredients to make the frosting.

"No, but I don't think I changed so much between eighteen and twenty-five." She leaned against the counter and searched my face. "What is it you're looking for, Juliet? Is it money? Success? Something…in the bedroom?"

My cheeks burned as images of the things Vaughn did to me came to mind, but no matter how good it was, that wasn't what was going on with me at all. "Mom, it's hard to explain. The thing is, I don't know exactly what I'm looking for. I want to try some things instead of just doing the same thing I've been doing since I was a little girl. I want to meet new people and travel and maybe go back to school. I'm only twenty-five and there's a whole world out there I know very little about. What's wrong with living a little before I settle down?"

"Nothing. But why do you have to do all this exploring with other men? If you told Carlo you wanted to travel, and maybe take some classes at the community college—"

"But that's just it," I protested. "*He* doesn't want me to do those things. He wants to get married and start having babies. Not only am I not ready for that, like I keep telling you, Carlo isn't the right man for me. He's a sweet guy, and I still love him, but I'm not *in love* with him."

"This doesn't make sense," Mom said, a hint of impatience in her voice. "What's the difference?"

"I love my brothers," I said gently. "But I'm not *in love* with them. Carlo is like another big brother now."

"And what about the boys? Your brothers and Carlo are best friends. How will they be able to spend time together if you break up?"

I sighed. "I don't know. But I'm pretty sure that's not a good enough reason to marry someone."

"And my relationship with Leonora—how will I look at her? We're already family, Juliet. You're not just ending a relationship; you're eliminating part of our family."

"I'm sorry. It's still not a good enough reason to marry him."

"You know." Mom turned and started making coffee. "Your father and I went through a phase where things were… boring in the bedroom."

I clapped my hand over my mouth to keep from saying something inappropriate because I absolutely didn't want to hear this.

"So we talked, and then we spiced it up." She got cream out of the fridge. "And then things were really, really good. Like the best of my whole life. You and Carlo need to have this conversation. Your father had never been with anyone but me, and he didn't know better, but as we got older, we discovered things together. That was a different time, though, so—"

"The eighties and nineties?" I asked, hoping to get her away from this particular train of thought. "Everyone was screwing everyone. Come on, you can't tell me you guys didn't have friends to talk about that stuff?"

She turned to look at me over her shoulder. "Your grandparents were strict. We were devout Catholics. We waited until our wedding night. It didn't matter what everyone else was doing, we did what we wanted, what we felt was right for us."

"I understand that, and it's the same for me. I want to do what I think is right. And sadly, I don't think Carlo is right for me. Believe me, don't you think my life would be so much easier if I just married him?"

"Yes," she said quietly, putting a damp hand on the side of my face. "Yes, I do. And you should think about why that is." She turned and left the room.

I got to the pizzeria just after twelve and immediately started helping with the lunch crowd. We were busier than usual today, and it had been a while since I'd gotten tips, so I jumped in to take care of a few tables. Normally I ran the register, made sure there was clean silverware, and seated people as they came in. Today I was doing everything, so I was startled when Mom came over to me.

"Juliet, there's a gentleman asking to sit in your section. Are you okay with putting a single customer at a four-top?"

"Of course." I turned and nearly gaped.

Buzz was standing at the entrance, and he nodded in my direction.

"Holy shit," I muttered.

"Who is he?" Mom asked. "He's very handsome, but too old for you, no?"

I laughed. I couldn't help it.

"Mom! That's Vaughn's dad."

"Vaughn?" She looked confused for a moment and then arched her brows. "You've met his father?"

"I have." I smiled and walked over to Buzz. "Hi, Buzz! What a nice surprise. I hope you're hungry?"

"I sure am." He smiled over my shoulder, and I realized Mom had followed me.

"Uh, Mom, this is Bu—er, Adam. Adam Elliott. Buzz, my mother, Maria Cicero."

"Your mother!" He held out a hand and then gripped hers for an extended moment. "I'm sorry, but you look far too young to have a kid Juliet's age."

"Oh!" My mother actually blushed, something I hadn't seen her do in years. "Such a charmer. You know my oldest child is actually thirty-five."

"Thirty-five!" Buzz laughed as Mom led him to a table, the two of them chattering away like old friends.

What was happening here?

I trailed behind with a menu and tried not to laugh as he showed a keen interest in both her and the pizzeria.

"I do love good Italian food," he said, putting his napkin on his lap.

"Doesn't everyone?" Mom countered. "I think you should try the calzone. You like calzone?"

"Sure."

"What do you like in it?"

"Surprise me." He winked. "I'll eat just about anything but those little fish."

"Anchovies?" She wrinkled her nose in distaste. "Not in calzone. Give me a few minutes. And I'll bring some garlic knots. They're the best in South Florida. Probably in all of Florida—Juliet, find out what he wants to drink."

Mom disappeared into the kitchen, and I looked down at Buzz suspiciously.

"What was all that?" I demanded.

He chuckled. "Vaughn's told me a little of what's been going on with you and your mom, so it can't hurt if your boyfriend's dad flirts a little, makes her laugh, and maybe smooths things over just a bit?"

He had a point, but I'd never seen anyone flirt with my mother. Ever. Other than my dad, of course, but that had been different.

"I don't know if I like it," I deadpanned.

"You'll get used to it." He blinked innocently.

"What do you want to drink?" I asked, shaking my head. "Unsweetened tea, water, a soft drink?"

"How about some unsweet tea? Lots of ice, please."

"Be right back." I went to the drink station and filled a glass for him, making sure there was plenty of ice. This was a surprise, but Mom was at his table when I got there with his tea, and they were talking like old friends.

"Did you know Adam is from California?" Mom asked me.

"I did." I put his drink down. "Are you handling his order, Mom? I have another table."

"Yes, yes, go." She shooed me away, and I glanced over my shoulder as I went to greet my next table.

I'd just taken their order when Chloe came in, waving to me.

"Hey!" I smiled. "What are you doing here?"

"I never see you anymore, so I figured I'd come stalk you at work."

"Girl, I don't have an empty table." I motioned with my hand. "We're packed today."

"I'll wait." Her blue eyes twinkled playfully.

"Guess who's here?" I whispered, leaning forward.

"Who?" she whispered back.

"Vaughn's dad. And my mom has been talking to him nonstop."

"About what?"

"Who the hell knows? Parent things?"

We both snickered.

"Is he by himself?"

"Yeah. Why?"

"So seat me with him."

"What?"

"I need a place to sit, and I might as well meet Vaughn's dad since you don't seem interested in introducing me to Vaughn."

I rolled my eyes. "Dude. You're always gone these days, and he's always on the road. There hasn't been a chance."

"Yeah, yeah." She started walking toward Adam's table.

"Chloe!" I hurried after her.

"Hey, Ma." She hugged my mom as she dropped into the chair across from Adam. "Hi. I'm Chloe Haverty, Juliet's best friend. You must be Adam."

"I am." He smiled and shook her hand. "Have a seat, Chloe Haverty, Juliet's best friend."

She laughed, and I went to get her an iced tea, since I knew that's what she would want.

"Buzz is very nice," Mom said after she'd brought him his calzone, and he gushed over it for at least five minutes.

"He is."

"He and Vaughn are not close." It was a statement, not a question, and I turned to her curiously.

"No, they're not."

"That makes me sad. It's sad when a parent can't be close to their child. I don't know what I would do without all of you."

"Sometimes adults make bad decisions," I said lightly. "Like Buzz divorcing his wife and leaving her and his young son."

"Sometimes adults make hard decisions," she countered.

I wondered if we were still talking about Vaughn and his father.

"Sometimes," I said at last. "But all decisions have consequences. He alienated his son, no matter what his intentions were, and now it's going to be a long road for him to rebuild that relationship."

Mom gazed over at where Buzz and Chloe were laughing.

"There's a kindness inside of him. A bright light struggling to emerge. I can't explain it. I hope Vaughn gives him a chance."

"Vaughn is giving him a chance, but this kind of thing takes time. And anyway, why do you care?"

"As a mother, it hurts my heart to see another parent struggling to connect with their child. I know how it feels."

Yup. Here it came. She was about to pour on the guilt.

"I have to check my tables."

"Juliet." She put a gentle hand on my arm.

"Yes?"

"Sometimes you have to trust that we know what's best for you. Even though you're an adult, we've been around the block a few times. I just don't want you to throw away your future for a fling."

"Where is this coming from, Mom?" I asked in frustration. "I thought you liked Buzz?"

"I do. And I'd probably like Vaughn as well. That doesn't mean he's right for you."

"He's not right for me because you didn't choose him?"

She sighed. "You need to think, Juliet. Vaughn is going to be gone all the time. What do you think he's doing when he's traveling? And what happens when he gets traded?"

"I don't have time for this, Mom." I stalked over to one of my tables, trying not to think about the things she'd said.

Vaughn and I were still new, but I had to trust him, or we didn't have any kind of future together. The possibility of a trade made me uncomfortable, though. Could I pick up and leave my family, my friends, and my job? Although it was way too soon to worry about stuff like that, I did have to keep it in the back of my mind because it was Vaughn's reality. And it would become mine too if we continued seeing each other.

23

VAUGHN

November was busy, filled with a lot of travel and back-to-back games leading up to Thanksgiving. Whenever I was home, I was with Juliet as much as possible, and we'd gotten extremely close in a very short amount of time. My father's words 'when you know, you know' had stuck with me and with each passing day, I felt like this thing between Juliet and me was getting serious.

She'd invited Dad and me to her house for Thanksgiving, and though she'd warned me that we'd probably get a mixed reaction from her family, I was going to go anyway. Dad said Juliet's mom was a hoot, and that didn't seem to jive with anything Juliet had told me, but I figured I'd reserve judgement until I got to know her.

I picked up wine and flowers, and Dad rode to the house with me.

"You look nervous," he commented as I parked in the driveway.

"Well, yeah. Her family hates me."

"Her family hates the idea that she's grown up and making her own decisions. It has nothing to do with you personally."

"It amounts to the same thing, though. They're making it hard on her, and I'm going to have to be on my best behavior today so I don't make it worse for her."

"What are you going to say if they ask your intentions?"

I grimaced. "It's been a little less than two months. My intentions are to continue to date her and let things progress naturally."

He clapped me on the shoulder. "Then I guess you're all set."

I shook my head, watching him head to the front door without hesitation. I'd never seen him dressed up before, and though Juliet had promised it was casual, Dad had shown up in gray dress pants, a black button-down shirt that covered almost all his tattoos, a nice belt, and black dress shoes. He'd trimmed his beard and put his hair back in a ponytail. He looked civilized, and it occurred to me things had shifted between us.

We spent a decent amount of time together, usually when Juliet was at work, but he came with us when she and I did things sometimes too. We'd all gone to see a movie last week, and he'd come along when we'd gone bowling with some of my teammates the other day. All in all, I was getting used to having him around.

"Happy Thanksgiving." Juliet opened the door looking stunning in a form-fitting red dress that hugged her curves and fell to just above her knees. She had on high-heeled red sandals, and she'd straightened her hair so that it was sleek and smooth.

"Happy Thanksgiving." I leaned down and kissed her cheek. She smiled up at me before turning to Dad.

"Hello, Buzz."

"Hey, darlin'. Happy Thanksgiving." He hugged her, and we followed her inside.

"Buzz!" Maria acted like she and Dad were old friends as they hugged. She accepted the flowers he handed her with a grin and then turned to me, hand extended. "Hello, Vaughn. Nice to see you again."

"Hello, Mrs. Cicero. Thank you for letting us join your family on Thanksgiving."

"Of course. That's what Thanksgiving is, right?" She took the bottle of wine and motioned for us to join everyone in the family room.

Holy shit. Juliet's family was huge. There were kids and adults in every chair, on the floor, standing, walking, talking, and running around.

"There are far too many people to introduce you to everyone," Juliet said, taking my arm. "But everyone, this is Vaughn Elliott and his father, Adam."

"Are you the hockey player?" A little boy of about three came running up to me.

"I am."

"Ice skates hurt my feet," he announced.

I smiled. "Sometimes they hurt mine too, but you get used to it."

"Hey, Vaughn. I'm Tony. We met at the hospital." Juliet's brother came over and shook my hand. "This is my son, Albert."

"Good to see you again."

"You guys are picking up steam," he said. "You're, what? Nine and one in the last ten games?"

"Ten and one, after Tuesday night."

"It's been really fun watching you guys play. Never thought I'd see a pro hockey team in Lauderdale."

"Me either."

We laughed.

"Vaughn, do you want something to drink?" Juliet asked me. "Beer? Wine? Water?"

"A beer would be great. Anything in a bottle."

"I'll be right back." She briefly met my gaze, and I wasn't sure what I saw in hers, but it probably mirrored my own nervousness.

"So, uh, you and Jules gettin' serious?" Tony asked, stuffing his hands in his pockets.

"Seems like it," I said. "But you should probably ask her."

"She hasn't been the same since the accident, you know? We're all worried about her."

"She seems fine," I said carefully.

"You don't understand," he said, shaking his head. "She used to be quiet. Focused on work and family and her fiancé. Now she's not focused on anything."

"I'm not sure what you want me to say," I said.

"Here you go." Juliet handed me a beer. "Come on, I want to introduce you to some of the people you haven't met yet."

She slid her fingers into mine and tugged me toward the kitchen.

"Where's Dad?" I asked, looking around.

"With my mom. In the kitchen." We walked into a large, spacious kitchen filled with women. And Dad.

He was leaning against a counter with a glass of wine in his hand, laughing at something someone I didn't recognize was telling him.

"Desi, Diana, Michelle—this is Vaughn," Juliet said. "Vaughn, Desi is Tony's wife, Diana is Robbie's wife, and Michelle is Sal's fiancée."

"Nice to meet you." I nodded politely.

Juliet motioned to an older woman standing next to Maria. "That's Aunt Minnie, and the one mashing the potatoes is Aunt Francis."

There were a thousand more names and faces—I wasn't going to remember many of them—so it was chaotic and loud. I'd never seen a family this big, but it would have been cool had it not been for the odd looks I was getting from pretty much everyone. Ironically, they all acted like my dad was already part of the family, which made no sense at all.

"Stick close to Peter," Juliet whispered to me at one point. "He knows to keep the others from being jerks."

"Don't worry. I'll be fine." I kissed her cheek and moved into the living room since it seemed that the kitchen was the ladies' domain. There was football on, of course, and there was a lot of yelling and cheering so I didn't attract any attention at first.

Juliet's oldest brother, whose name I thought was Mario, did glance at me a few times, but I just tried to keep it friendly. I'd never been in a position like this before, and it was awkward as fuck. I wasn't sure if I was supposed to be friendly, aloof, or something else. I knew most of the family wanted Juliet to get back with her ex, so I wasn't exactly welcome, but at the same time I really liked her. She seemed to be equally crazy about me, so it didn't make sense that they would continue to make it so hard on her.

"Hey. I'm Peter." The brother Juliet had told me would be the friendliest came and stood beside me since there was nowhere to sit.

"Nice to meet you. I think we met briefly at the hospital."

"Yeah. You have a team?" he asked, motioning to the TV.

"Yeah, but neither of these two."

He chuckled. "Yeah, I'm a Giants fan."

"Patriots."

He made a face. "Jesus, dude, can you *not* say that in this house? You're already on thin ice."

"I can totally be a Giants fan today," I said with a grin. "But I grew up in New Hampshire, so I come by my team honestly."

"Yeah, yeah."

We chatted about football and hockey for a while, and I liked him. He was smart and funny, a lot like Juliet, and wasn't busting my balls for no reason.

"I just want to say, I think you're a stand-up guy," Peter said quietly. "Coming here today knowing that most of the family doesn't approve of you and Jules."

I didn't know how to respond to that so I waited for him to continue.

"I think they'll come around, but it's going to take a while, you know? Everyone has been on edge since Dad died, and we all look out for her since she's the only girl, but she's twenty-five. I think she can take care of herself."

"For sure." I nodded. "But I appreciate the support. I really care about Juliet. I hope you know that. I have no intention of hurting her."

"I hope not. Because I'm pretty chill, and I'm also kind of scared of you, but I will have to at least *try* to kick your ass if you make her cry."

I chuckled, holding up my hands. "Nothing to be scared of. I'm not going to make her cry."

"Thank god. I'd hate it if you beat my ass while I was trying to defend my sister's honor." He cracked up and so did I.

I was feeling better about all of this, knowing that at least one of her brothers was okay with our relationship. According to my dad, her mom was coming around, so maybe things were going to be okay after all. I was planning to ask her to come on an upcoming road trip with me, but I'd been reluctant, knowing how guilty her family was making her feel.

"Hey, uh, Vaughn, you wanna come outside for a few?" Mario asked me when the game went to half-time.

"Uh, sure." I glanced at Peter. "Am I about to get that ass-beating you were just talking about?"

"I don't think so." Peter looked worried, though, which made me worry.

I followed Mario, Tony, and Sal outside with Peter trailing behind us.

This was weird and I took a quick look around, wondering what the hell was going on.

"So, uh, we know you care about Jules," Tony said. "But the thing is, we're also kind of worried about you."

"About me?" I squinted in the bright sun. "Why would you be worried about me?"

"Because she's coming back to me." A voice I didn't recognize spoke from behind me, and I slowly turned.

Carlo.

Oh, for the love of everything holy.

I managed not to sigh, but I could already tell this was going to turn into a shit show.

"Look, that's between you and her," I said. "I don't have any beef with you, but until Juliet tells me different, my understanding is that you two are broken up."

"We're on a break," he replied evenly. "She hit her head and has been going through some stuff since her dad died, so she's not herself. But it's not over-over."

I sighed, trying to keep my voice level even though I was pissed. "I don't know what you want from me. That's not what Juliet says, and frankly, I'm more inclined to believe the lady than her jealous ex."

"I'm trying to explain," Carlo said, talking slowly as if I was stupid or something.

"Try harder," I muttered, meeting his gaze.

"Listen. I'm asking you, man-to-man, to step out of the equation and let me and my fiancée work this out between us."

24

I walked into the living room to see how Vaughn was doing and noticed he and my brothers were gone.

Jesus fucking Christ.

I'd thought Peter would be on top of this, and there was no way it was a coincidence that all five of my brothers and Vaughn were the only ones missing.

"Where are they?" I demanded of Uncle Lenny.

He motioned toward the front of the house with his head, and I ran to the front door, throwing it open.

"Vaughn?!" I spotted him in the yard surrounded by my brothers and Carlo.

Fucking Carlo.

"Go inside, Jules." Mario said. "We're handling this our way."

"You're not handling shit," I snapped, hurrying over to Vaughn. "What the hell is wrong with all of you? Do you really think this is how you might possibly get Carlo and me back together? Even if that was possible, which it's not, this is the worst possible thing you could do." I stared at Carlo. "And you…seriously?"

"We love each other," he said. "I'm not letting you go just because you're going through a bad time."

"No," I agreed pleasantly. "You're not letting me go because I've been through a rough time. You're going to let me go because I don't love you that way anymore."

"You don't mean that."

"I do. I absolutely do. Carlo, go home. Please."

"But—"

"We have nothing to say to each other, and if we do, it won't be with my brothers as an audience.

Carlo stared at me, his dark eyes filled with hurt and questions I'd already answered, but as much as I felt for him, I blamed my brothers for this.

"Let's go get your dad," I said to Vaughn. "Then we're leaving."

I grabbed his hand and tugged him back inside, starting to shake now that it was over.

"You okay?" he asked softly.

"No. Not even a little. I'm so sorry."

"It's all right."

"Come on." I went upstairs to my room, pulling him along with me even though I knew everyone was probably watching.

I shut my bedroom door behind us and sank onto the bed. "Oh my god. I am so, so sorry. I can't begin to apologize."

"It's okay."

"No. It isn't." I lifted my gaze to his. "Can I stay with you for a few days?"

"Sure, but don't you think that's just going to add fuel to the fire?"

"Probably, but I don't care anymore. I'm so humiliated right now, and the worst thing is, I feel bad for Carlo because I know my brothers talked him into this. What did he say to you?"

Vaughn paused. "He, uh, asked me, man-to-man, to leave you alone so you two could work things out."

I grunted under my breath. "That's not like Carlo. He's always been very respectful of me, so he would never confront you like that, knowing it would embarrass me without the guys encouraging it. So not only did he do something he didn't want to do, he got humiliated in the process because I shot him down again." I got up and pulled an overnight bag out of my closet. I tossed in panties, shorts, T-shirts, and a pair of capris. I went into the bathroom and grabbed my toiletry bag, tossing some essentials in it even though I was still shaking.

"Hey." Vaughn came up behind me, wrapping his arms around my waist. "Stop and breathe for a minute, okay? I can see how upset you are."

"I just need to get out of here. Please. Can we just go?"

"Of course we can, but you should at least explain it to your mother."

"I will." I leaned back against him, hating what a mess my family was making of everything. It was becoming abundantly clear that I had to make some hard decisions, ones that would hurt feelings and potentially change my relationship with my family forever. But what my brothers had done today wasn't okay.

There was a soft knock on the door and Peter came in. "Jules?"

"I'm here." I walked out of the bathroom with Vaughn behind me.

"I didn't know," he said. "I never would have let them do that, especially not on Thanksgiving. They didn't tell me because they knew I'd tell you."

"I know. It's okay."

"It's actually not." Peter shook his head and then looked at Vaughn. "I'm sorry, man. That was totally uncool of them to ambush you that way."

"It's all right," Vaughn said. "I can take care of myself. I just wish they didn't constantly do shit to upset Juliet."

"I know." Peter sighed. "Well, I don't know if it helps, but I just want you to know that if there had been a fight, I would've had your back."

Vaughn grinned and held out his fist for Peter to bump. "Would that be before or after I kicked your ass about that whole other situation?"

Peter burst out laughing. "Probably after."

"Other situation?" I asked, narrowing my eyes suspiciously.

"It's a joke," Vaughn said. "I'll tell you later."

"Does Mom know what happened?" I asked Peter.

"She didn't, but she probably does now."

"Let's just go," I told Vaughn.

"You're not going to talk to your mom?"

"I can't right now. I'm too mad. I'm probably going to—"

"Juliet?" Mom came into my room, a scowl on her face. "I'm sorry, love. Your brothers, they are…" Her voice trailed off.

"Don't pretend you weren't in on it," I grumbled. "You don't like Vaughn any more than they do."

"This is not true!" She shook her head vehemently. "I don't like that you've broken up with Carlo, I admit this, but it has nothing to do with Vaughn as a person. I like him very much, and his father is delightful. And even if I didn't like him, he is a guest in our home today. It's a holiday. I would *never* embarrass someone, a guest, in our home. You know better than that."

As angry as I was, she was right. We had a thing about how we treated guests. If she'd truly wanted to embarrass Vaughn, she wouldn't have allowed him to come at all. Not to mention inviting his father as well.

"Everything okay?" Buzz peeked his head in the door.

"We're leaving," I told him.

"What happened?" He looked concerned, his eyes immediately traveling to his son.

"My sons, they don't have the brains they were born with sometimes," Mom said, shaking her head. "I'm sorry, Buzz. I had no idea they would do something stupid. And I apologize to you as well, Vaughn."

Vaughn nodded. "Thank you. I appreciate that."

I headed for the hall and Mom gripped my arm. "What will you eat?"

I smiled. "I'm sure we can intrude on Chloe's family."

"I'm sorry, sweetheart." She reached out and hugged me.

"I love you, Mom."

<hr>

Buzz was following us in Vaughn's Corvette since that was how they'd gotten to my house, but Vaughn and I were in my Charger, with him driving. We were quiet for a few minutes when we left the house. My brothers, except for Peter, had been moping in the living room and random aunts and uncles kept asking what was going on. It was a huge clusterfuck, and I was embarrassed, frustrated, and hungry.

"Are there restaurants open today?" Vaughn asked, all but reading my mind.

"Yeah, this is South Florida. Everything is open. We could also head over to my friend Chloe's house."

"Or we could go to Coach Petrov's," Vaughn said. "He invited anyone on the team who had nowhere to go. I'm sure he wouldn't mind."

I was about to protest when I realized he probably wanted to be somewhere that was familiar, where he wouldn't have to worry about explaining himself or our relationship or anything else.

"Sure." I nodded, reaching for his hand. "I'm sorry, babe."

"It's not your fault."

"Did they threaten you?" I asked.

He chuckled. "No. Well, Peter did, but that was before."

"*Peter* threatened you?" I stared at him.

"He was joking. He actually said he was afraid of me, but if I made you cry, he'd have no choice but to attempt to kick my ass to defend your honor."

I laughed. That sounded like Peter. "Peter and I are closer than the others because we're the youngest. There's only eighteen months between us so we kind of grew up together."

"Makes sense."

"Can we just enjoy Thanksgiving? And I promise, I'm going to have a long talk with everyone on Saturday when I get to work."

"I thought you had to work tomorrow?" he asked, frowning.

"I did, but now I'm not going in. I have some Christmas shopping to do. You in?"

"Shopping on Black Friday?" He grimaced. "Do I have to?"

"Nah. I'll go with Chloe."

"Whew." He pulled up to the guard gate of the same development Zakk and Tiff lived in and told the guard where we were going.

We pulled up to Toli and Tessa's house, and he leaned over and lightly kissed me. "Your family is making things hard on us, but mostly on you."

"I know. I'm sorry."

"I need you to be honest with me, Juliet."

"About what?"

"This. Us. I'm falling for you, and I need to know that you're not going back to him. I would completely understand if you did, but—"

"No. Wait. There are no buts here. I'm not going back to Carlo. Not today, not tomorrow, not ever. The feelings between us are like family, a brother… not a lover." I put my hand on the side of his face. "And I'm falling for you too. But I'm not going back, even if you tell me you don't want to see me anymore. I swear it on my dad's grave."

He captured my mouth in a kiss that curled my toes, his tongue plunging in and out like it did when we were in bed, and he was doing amazing things to my body.

We jumped when someone tapped on the window, and Vaughn glanced up at his dad impatiently.

"We're coming," he said. "Hang on."

"Are we good?" I whispered.

"We are very, very good. Ready to have some fun?"

"Absolutely."

Ten minutes later, we had drinks and Buzz was sitting outside with Vaughn and a bunch of his teammates, listening to them telling stories. I stood in the family room, gazing out to where Vaughn was, but not really seeing much of anything. The day's events ran through my head over and over, and I felt the beginnings of a headache starting. I hadn't had one in a couple of weeks, and I hoped it wouldn't get any worse.

"Hey. Are you okay?" Peyton put a gentle hand on my arm.

"It's been a very, very stressful day."

"With your family?" I nodded, horrified that tears filled my eyes.

"Oh, no, none of that." Peyton quickly hugged me. "What can I do? Do you need to talk or another drink? How can I help?"

"I could really use some Advil or something," I whispered. "I've got a headache and I really, really don't want anyone to see me crying."

"Too late." Tessa was on my other side. "Come on." She and Peyton flanked me, guiding me up the stairs and into what I assumed was the master bedroom. "You sit there," she told me, pointing to a chair by the window. "I'll see what's in the medicine cabinet."

I sank into a chair and Peyton handed me a tissue, sitting on a second chair. "You want to talk about it?"

"My family." I shook my head and dabbed at my eyes. "I'm so angry right now."

"Okay, tell us everything." Tessa handed me a couple of Advil and a bottle of water I hadn't noticed her carrying.

"Thank you." I downed the Advil and took a long drink. Then I told them everything that had been going on the last eight weeks or so.

"Oh, wow." Tessa gently rubbed my shoulder. "That's a lot."

"And they're not bad people," I whispered, resting my chin in my hand. "They love me. They just don't understand."

"Sometimes you have to show them," Peyton said. "Don't ask, don't even tell them what you're doing—just do whatever it is you want to do."

"I don't even know at this point. I want to go out with Vaughn and maybe fall in love and bake cupcakes and maybe take a college class. More than anything… I want the time to figure out what I want. Does that make sense?"

"Of course it does."

"Why does it make sense to you, people who barely know me, but not to the people who supposedly love me the most?"

"Because they still see you as a little girl," Tessa said softly. "We see you as a grown woman. We don't know the little girl you were. We just know you now."

"Juliet?" Vaughn's voice came from the hallway.

"In here," Tessa called out, smiling at him as he came in.

"Am I interrupting?" he asked slowly. "I was worried when I didn't see you anywhere."

"Just taking a few minutes to decompress," I whispered. "It's been a long day."

"I think we'll leave you two to talk," Tessa said, grabbing Peyton's arm. "But no sex on my bed. There's a guest room downstairs if you absolutely can't help yourselves."

She and Peyton laughed as they walked out.

Then Vaughn dropped to his knees in front of me. "What happened, babe? I thought you were okay?"

"I want to be okay," I whispered. "I'm fighting so hard to be okay, but it's so fucking much. I'm tired and stressed and once we got here my head started to hurt. I'm sorry. I didn't mean to worry you."

"I'm fine, but I am worried about you." He reached out and touched my face. "I hate seeing you like this."

"I'll be okay. I took something for my head. I'll be all right in a few minutes. Why don't you go back down to your friends and—"

"Juliet."

"What?" I was startled at the seriousness in his voice.

"I want you to move in with me."

25

I hadn't been planning to ask her to move in with me, but the words slipped out, something that happened a lot with her. It was fast, I knew that, but I hated being away from her. I also hated knowing that whenever she was at home she was potentially barraged with negativity about our relationship. I'd known her exactly seven weeks today, but I'd known I was falling for her the night we got caught in the thunderstorm. Now I wanted us to be together so we could figure this relationship stuff out without the constant lack of enthusiasm from everyone she knew.

"Vaughn?" She looked as startled as I felt. "It's only been—"

"I *know*. I know it's soon, but it feels like we have so much going against us, I'd like a chance for us to be a couple and really get to know each other. It seems like living together might be the only way to give us a real chance. What do you think?"

"I don't..." She took a breath. "I'm not sure I'm ready for a step this big."

My heart sank. "Why? This, whatever it is we've found together, is different. Special. *You're* special."

"Yes," she whispered, nodding. "It is. Which is why I don't want to screw it up by going too fast. I want to be with you, but I think we should start with sleepovers and stuff. I broke off my engagement not even two months ago. I don't know how I feel about moving in with someone this quickly. Please don't be mad."

I wasn't mad. Disappointed, yes, but not mad. Everything she said made sense. I was moving way too fast and couldn't seem to help it. Geez, she was the greatest women I'd ever met, and I was going to fuck it up.

"Are you mad?" she whispered when I didn't respond right away.

"No. I get it. It just feels like living together is the only way we'll ever be able to spend quality time together."

"I'll sleep over whenever we can," she said. "We can work up to living together. I'd just like to go a little slower in that department."

"Okay." I kissed her forehead. "How's your head?"

"The headache is starting to go away. It probably doesn't help that all I've had today is a cup of coffee."

"Come on." I tugged her to her feet. "Let's find you some food."

"Vaughn." She paused, squeezing my hand.

"Yeah, babe?"

"You have to know things might get worse before they get better."

"It's okay. We'll figure it out."

"Thank you for being patient with me." She squeezed my hand. "This thing between us is very special so I don't want to screw it up."

"Agreed."

"That was a real quickie," Coach said as we got to the family room. "I figured you'd last ten minutes."

"Ten minutes?" Zakk burst out laughing. "I was thinking more like five."

"Three," Ryder called out.

I held up my middle finger. "We were talking, you Neanderthals."

Laughter filled the room as we talked and joked. As disappointed as I was that Juliet didn't want to move in, her reasoning made sense. She was probably worried about her family's reaction to something like that as well, and despite how much I'd hoped she would say yes, I was also a little relieved she'd said no. Which made no sense.

"When's the next party?" Ryder asked, grinning. "We need one where we have more of those blow—"

"Children in the room!" Coach playfully smacked him in the back of the head, cutting him off before he could finish saying blow job.

"Sorry, Coach." Ryder glanced over to where Peyton was holding Stella. "I forget since she's not at the repeating stage yet."

"Oh, she is," Coach said, chuckling. "You just won't know it until she actually says fuck or something else equally inappropriate."

"My little angel is *never* saying words like that," Ryder deadpanned.

Everyone burst out laughing.

"Yeah, she will. And more." Dad shook his head. "Kids are full of surprises. I only had a boy, but lots of my buddies have girls, and I think I'll go so far as to say the girls were a hell of a lot more work than the boys."

I almost said something about how he hadn't been around enough to know but stopped myself before it came out.

This whole father-son relationship was still a work in progress, and I had a long way to go toward forgiveness. But I was getting there, and that was what was important. I probably needed to take things as slow with Juliet as I was taking them with my dad.

***

"You have anything you want to do today?" I asked her the following day when she got home from shopping with Chloe. We were sprawled on the leather couch in the living room, her feet on my lap.

"No." She looked over at me. "I just want to be. To sit in the quiet and be with you. We've never watched a movie together or gone to bed at a normal hour or just hung out. And that's what I want."

"Okay." I held out my arms, and she moved, adjusting her position so she could nestle into my chest.

"Have you ever lived with anyone before?" she asked after a moment.

"Officially? No. I've had girlfriends who slept over a lot, like on weekends and stuff, but they always had their own place. And that's been a while. Hockey keeps me busy. Casual dating is hard. It's kind of all or nothing with my schedule."

"You can't call being engaged a casual relationship," she said slowly. "But that's what it felt like with Carlo. Like we saw each other on Saturday nights, and usually on Sundays since we were both off, but mostly it was texts and phone calls and checking in. There hadn't been any depth to our relationship in years. I can't believe I agreed to marry him."

"Doesn't seem like he believes you've changed your mind."

"I know. I think that's why I'm hesitant to move in yet. I always do what I'm told, I'm usually the peacemaker, and I've always been the mostly obedient daughter. Since the accident I've felt like someone else, but I'm not sure who, and I don't think it's fair to take things to the next level with you with all this indecision in my life. I truly don't know who I am anymore."

"You're still young," I told her. "You don't have to know who you are yet."

"I thought I knew," she admitted. "But now I realize I don't have a clue. And it's kind of scary."

"Why?"

"You're twenty-six and know exactly who you are, what you're doing, and what your life will be like for the next, say, ten years. Sure, shit happens, you could get hurt, whatever, but that's true of almost everyone so it doesn't count. Me, I have no career, no plans, no nothing now that I'm not getting married. And it's fucking weird."

"What do you want to do?"

"I want to take some college classes, see what there is to see. I feel like I'm going to do something in the food industry because it's what I know and love. I don't love being forced to work in my family's pizzeria as a glorified manager, but I love baking and creating sweets that people are excited to eat."

"Like those cupcakes you've been making."

"Exactly."

"A bakery?"

She shook her head. "No. I don't want to have to get up at three in the morning to start putting bread or whatever in the oven and be the same kind of slave in a totally different scenario."

"So catering?"

"I've been thinking about more of a specialty business. Like cookies, cupcakes, and confections of some kind—I'm still thinking about it all—that are customized for each order. So I wouldn't want a store front, but an online business and website where people can order whatever I decide to specialize in, and I'd deliver it. Fresh and on a one-on-one basis."

"Sounds to me like you do have a plan," I said lightly.

"Is that a plan?" She wrinkled her nose as she looked up at me. "It feels like a pipe dream."

"Why?"

"How can I make a living, like support myself, doing cupcakes and cookies to order? I can only bake so many at a time. And while I can charge up to five bucks per cupcake and maybe three or four per custom cookie, that's a lot of cookies and cupcakes to pay the bills."

"Then this is the perfect time for you to grow your business," I said. "Start it up and see how it goes. Test your theories about how much you can make, how much you can reasonably bake in a day, stuff like that. You still have your job at the pizzeria, you live at home rent-free, and you can always come here and use my kitchen if you need extra space to work."

She smiled up at me. "That's really sweet. Thank you."

"Let's come up with a name."

"A name?" She looked confused.

"For your new business. You have to treat it like it's the real thing or why bother?"

"Juliet's Confections." She made a face. "Ugh. No."

"Sweets by Juliet."

"Sweeter than Juliet." She snickered.

We batted names back and forth until we got hungry and decided to table the name talk for a while.

Her phone had buzzed a few times, and she finally picked it up while I ordered takeout for dinner.

She looked annoyed as she read whatever it was, sighing heavily.

"Everything okay?" I asked after I ordered Chinese food for us.

"It's Chloe. Apparently, she just got a call from the dress shop to go have her dress altered. I've told them at least three times that there's no wedding. Why the fuck aren't they listening?"

"You might want to put it in writing," I said. "Maybe type up an email or something and request confirmation that it was received?"

"This is probably about money," she muttered. "I'm sure everyone is freaking out about how much everything cost. I knew there would be some penalties from the caterer and such, but now it's looking like I might have to suck up the cost of the wedding dress and bridesmaid dresses. Shit, I have to call Chloe back. How long until dinner gets here?"

"Twenty minutes."

"I'll be done by then." She picked up her phone and walked out of the room, leaving me staring after her.

Every time the wedding came up, I got a weird feeling in the pit of my stomach that I couldn't explain, and it was starting to annoy me. It was compounded by the fact that she didn't want to move in with me. Intellectually, I knew that was probably the best decision right now, but emotionally I was a little hurt and a lot conflicted. I just wasn't sure what to do about it.

2 6

I got to the pizzeria early on Monday, hoping to hole up in my office and catch up on everything from the weekend so I could get out of here after lunch. I also wanted to avoid my brothers because I was still pissed about what they'd done on Thanksgiving. We had to work together peacefully, but I didn't have to talk to them. I definitely wasn't ready to forgive them. I still loved them, of course, but what they'd done really hurt.

I'd just turned on my computer when there was a soft knock on the door and Mom stuck her head in.

"Mom." I was surprised because she rarely came in before nine.

"Good morning." She smiled. "How was your weekend?"

"Relaxing. How was yours?"

"Stressful." She cocked her head. "Do you have a minute?"

I sighed. "For what? I don't have any more family drama in me, Mom."

"I know. This isn't that." She motioned to someone in the hall, and to my surprise, my brothers filed into the office, including Sal and Robbie.

Oh boy. So much for avoiding my brothers.

"We're sorry," Mario said, speaking first. "What we did on Thanksgiving is inexcusable. We just wanted to make sure you and Carlo had a chance to figure things out before you moved on with someone else."

"But, uh," Tony spoke up. "We should have gone about it in a different way."

"And we weren't threatening Vaughn or anything," Sal added. "We just wanted to talk outside, away from the rest of the family and in retrospect, he probably felt ganged up on. Even though I'm sure he can take care of himself. But that wasn't what we were doing."

"Carlo loves you," Robbie said. "And he's been really torn up about the breakup. We wanted to help."

"But you're a grown-ass woman who can make decisions about her love life without us," Peter added dryly. "Also, I don't have anything to apologize for because I wasn't part of that whole thing. Obviously, I'm the black sheep of the family since the boys didn't think they could trust me."

"You would've told her," Mario grunted.

"And if I had, all of this would have been avoided, and you guys wouldn't be here groveling." Peter shrugged. "If you'd trusted me, things would have gone so much better."

Tony sighed.

Sal started tapping his foot.

Robbie stared at the floor.

Mom looked at me expectantly.

"I'm not ready to forgive you yet," I said finally. "I appreciate the apologies, but essentially you're only here because Mom made you. I understand you've known Carlo most of your lives, and he's like a brother, but I'm *actually* your sister. At some point, you're going to have to choose because I am never going back to Carlo. It's a thousand percent over. I don't know how else to tell you or show you, but you can't side against me in this. You just can't. Because if you do, we're never going to be the same family we were."

"Ridiculous," Mom said, frowning. "We are always family. This will pass. The boys understand they went too far. You won't do it again, right?"

"You were all in," Mario said to her. "Don't play innocent."

"I have never denied I want Carlo and Juliet back together. But I knew nothing about a confrontation on a holiday, at our home, with both Vaughn and his father present. Never in a million years. My participation has been in private with me trying to get her to see reason. Not by humiliating her, Vaughn, and Carlo, all in one swoop."

Everyone was silent, and I didn't know what to say. On one hand, I appreciated that my mom was at least being classy and honest about her intentions. But she was still Team Carlo, and that hurt my feelings all over again.

"We all have work to do," I said after a moment. "Thank you for apologizing and opening up a dialogue. For now, we all need time to think, and I have food orders to place."

"I have to go to work," Peter said. "See you later, sis. Bye, Ma." He kissed Mom's cheek and headed out.

"Me too." Sal was right behind him, but Mario, Tony, and Robbie lingered.

"See you later, Sis." Robbie's voice was soft, apologetic, but the others didn't say anything at all as they left my office.

"They're really awful sometimes," I said when my mom was the only person left. "Why aren't they at least a little bit like Dad? He was never mean-spirited. Ever. And it feels like they're getting meaner as they get older."

Mom sighed. "Things would be so different if your father were still here."

"But he's not. And they should be stepping up to be the patriarchs of the family. Instead, they're just dismissive and self-absorbed. As if because I'm a girl I don't matter. It really pisses me off."

"I know, my love." She perched on the edge of my desk. "You remind me of your grandmother. Your father's mother. She was traditional, old-fashioned, and very, very Italian. Yet, she spoke her mind when it mattered. She didn't allow anyone to disrespect her or anyone she cared about, not even those people she cared about. I wish you had known her."

"Me too," I said softly.

"You carry parts of her within you, and you'll do well to remember there's a place for tradition, respect, and independence, all in one."

"But respect is earned."

Our eyes met and she nodded. "And forgiveness?"

"Oh, I'll forgive them. Just not yet. I'd like to see them sweat a while."

Mom shook her head, biting back a smile. "As they should. But Juliet?"

"Yes?"

"I wish you would tell me what you're thinking. What you really want. Is it Vaughn?"

"Yes. I think so. But not everything is about him."

"No?"

"I want to do more than be married and have babies. I want that too—like you said, some combination of tradition and independence—but I need to find myself along the way. Don't you see? Carlo wouldn't allow it. None of you would. But since the accident, it's like I can't help it. I have to figure out who and what I'm meant to do."

"So, what? College?"

"Maybe. But also…" I poured out my ideas to her, talking about cooking and cupcakes and other confections. I'd never dared tell her these things, because I'd known she would shoot them down, but today she listened. She moved from the edge of my desk to dragging a chair next to me to digging out a pad and making notes.

"I don't know if the money makes sense," I said when I was finished.

"I think it does. Let me see." She pulled out her phone and opened the calculator, typing in numbers. "Let's assume you have fifty orders per month. One order is a minimum of twenty-four cupcakes, at four dollars and fifty cents a piece. That's one hundred and eight dollars. Your supplies probably cost ten dollars? Fifty times ninety-eight times twelve makes nearly sixty thousand dollars per year. That's not terrible money."

"No." I stared at her calculations. "But that's assuming I have a place to bake with state-of-the-art supplies."

"Those are one-time purchases."

"We also have to deduct gas for deliveries, and a little wear and tear on my car."

"Those are tax deductible."

We stared at each other.

"It could work," I said, chewing the inside of my cheek.

"You'll also need packaging with branding, but if you buy in bulk, the prices won't be bad, and you don't have to have it all right away."

"A website, business cards…" I was making notes on the pad.

"And if the wives of Vaughn's teammates start talking about your stuff, I think this business could take off quickly."

A jolt of excitement shot through me for the first time in a long time. It could work. I really, really wanted to do this. I'd been thinking about it for a few years, but my dad died and then Carlo and I got engaged, so I hadn't had the time or energy to start a new business. Now I did.

"Tiff was super excited about the cupcakes I made for the boys," I said. "And I think the minimum of two dozen cupcakes is a good idea. I think a minimum of a dozen for custom cookies, though."

"Sugar or shortbread or something else?"

"I don't know. I have to play with them, see what sticks. I'm sure Tiff and Tessa and the others will be happy to sample them and give me their thoughts."

"In the meantime, you'll still do payroll, yes?" Her eyes glittered with amusement.

"I'll always do payroll," I whispered. "This is my home. Even when I'm gone and married with a family of my own, this place is part of me. It's just not all of me."

"Ah, my beautiful girl." She cocked her head. "Is he good to you, Juliet? Is Vaughn truly the man you want him to be? The man you want in your life?"

"He's wonderful, Mom. Kind and soft-spoken and patient. He's sexy and easy-going, but also protective and caring. I like him a lot, Mom. I might even love him."

"Ah." A faint smile crossed her face. "You never had this look in your eyes with Carlo."

"Not since high school."

"Vaughn is…different. Not like us. But also very much in need of a family."

"How do you know that?" I asked in surprise.

"What? You think Buzz just flirts with me? We talk. Our children are involved. Even though I didn't think Vaughn was the right man for you, *you* thought so, and I had to be cognizant of that. Buzz told me about his wife, Vaughn's mother, and how difficult it was to lose her. And how much he regrets not being part of Vaughn's life."

"Hey, Mom?"

"Hmm?"

"How come you've changed your mind about Vaughn and me?"

"Because I have no choice. You're a grown woman. I can be difficult and make you feel guilty and treat Vaughn badly, but what will this accomplish? I'll lose you. And that's never going to happen. Your brothers will come around too, but Vaughn will have to prove himself to them. It will just take longer."

Tears filled my eyes. "I love you, Mom."

"I love you too. Now get to work. We have a restaurant to run."

I smiled and turned back to my computer.

27

The team headed north right after Thanksgiving, hitting Washington D.C. and Philadelphia before we got to New York City. We'd gotten in late last night and had practiced this morning, but now we were back at the hotel waiting for Coach to come down and tell us the plan. He was always planning stuff for us to do, which wasn't what I'd done on other teams, and tonight we were all going to dinner and to see the tree light up in Rockefeller Center. Coach's wife and kids had even flown out for the event, along with Zakk's wife and kids, and I realized I'd finally hit a point in my life where I wanted that too.

Maybe not kids. Not yet. But the wife? I hadn't given it a lot of thought until Juliet, and now I just wanted to know that she felt the same way about me as I felt about her. We hadn't used the L word yet because it had only been two fucking months, but I was so ready I felt a little stupid. Especially in light of everything going on with her.

The never-ending cancelled-wedding-that-wasn't-completely-cancelled had started to bug me. Obviously, she wasn't lying about it in the sense that she was hiding something, but I couldn't help but wonder if she was lying to herself. Did she still love Carlo and was just mad at him or sowing oats like an extended bachelorette party? I felt like an asshole for even thinking these things, but when she'd said no to moving in, I couldn't help but think that was a failed test of sorts.

I hadn't planned it that way, but in retrospect, maybe I had. Maybe I was testing her to see if she was really into me, or if this situation with Carlo was a lot more complicated than either of us imagined.

"This is bullshit," Jude muttered as we hung out in the lobby, still waiting for Coach.

I turned to him in surprise because he was rarely grumpy. "Wow. Someone's in a pissy mood."

"Ah, this bonding shit is a waste of time." He slunk down in his chair a little more.

"It's an expansion team," I pointed out needlessly. "And we have to trust Coach to do what he thinks is best for us."

"Like I said, it's bullshit. And now his family is here, along with Zakk's, and I think Ryder's fiancée flew in this morning too. So it's not really a team thing anymore."

"Sounds to me like you want a girlfriend," I teased, trying to make him lighten up.

He gave me a look. "Like I say every time it comes up, I'm not averse to relationships, I just haven't met anyone I'd want to get that serious with."

"You haven't met her *yet*. I'm sure she's out there."

He rolled his eyes. "And anyway, it's not that I mind being single, it's that I have to come to these events. I mean, I hate Christmas. I just want to play hockey and get the hell out of dodge."

"You hate Christmas?" I made a face.

"It's stupid."

"You wanna talk about it?" I asked.

"Nothing to talk about. I hate Christmas. That's all."

"Wait a minute." I eyed him. "That's when you were supposed to marry your ex, right? On Christmas Eve?"

Jude grunted. "Where'd you hear that?"

"I think Ryder said something at Thanksgiving."

"Whatever." Jude shrugged. "I was glad we broke up when we did instead of finding out it was a mistake after we were already married."

"How did you know?" I asked quietly. "Like, what were the warning signs?"

He looked like he was going to protest but then looked away. "It was a lot of stuff, I guess. The big thing was that she didn't want to be married to a professional athlete who essentially had no choice in where he went. Like when

I was going to Alaska, she absolutely didn't want to be that far away from her friends and family. But before that, there were signs. She was always busy. Not too busy for me, but busy in general. She was involved in church stuff, charity stuff, planning her sister's wedding, working late at her job. Her life was super full without me, and I don't think she wanted to just uproot it. We didn't have that kind of bond where we loved each other to the point of making huge sacrifices. In her case, moving would have been a bigger sacrifice than she was willing to make for me." He paused. "Something going on with Juliet?"

"I asked her to move in, and she said no."

"How come?"

"She said it was too soon."

"Is it?"

"I don't know. Is two months too soon when you feel something is special?"

"From what I've seen and heard, she's from a big Italian family and living together might not be a thing they approve of."

"They don't approve of me at all."

"And maybe that's why she wants to go slow, to give them time to get used to the idea."

I hadn't thought of that, but it still bugged me.

"All right, boys. Who's ready for some fun?" Coach came into the lobby rubbing his hands together.

"Not me," Jude muttered under his breath.

"I heard that." Coach eyed him. "Stop being a grinch. Let's go!"

We actually had a great time that night. We went to an amazing steakhouse and watching Coach's and Zakk's kids enjoy the lighting of the tree was fun. For the hundredth time I wished Juliet was here with me, and I took a moment to text her as we walked around and took pictures. I sent her a short video of the tree just as the lights were turned on for the first time.

VAUGHN: Too bad you couldn't come with me.

JULIET: It's beautiful! Maybe next time you play in NYC I can tag along.

VAUGHN: That would be fun. Whatcha doin'?

JULIET: I'm baking chocolate-covered strawberry cupcakes.

VAUGHN: That sounds interesting.

JULIET: Noelle wanted something over-the-top for Valentine's Day so I'm experimenting.

VAUGHN: You already got orders for February?

JULIET: Yup. Tiff has me doing strawberry cupcakes with the frosting swirl made to look like the bottom part of a dress for her daughter's birthday in January—three dozen of them—and Remy wants me to make a two hundred red and green holiday-themed cupcakes for the staff at the arena for Christmas.

VAUGHN: Holy shit. That's amazing.

JULIET: I'm going to be crazy busy in the next few weeks because this is still really new, and I have to practice some of them first.

VAUGHN: That's going to cut into your profits, though, isn't it?

JULIET: Yes, but it's giving me the opportunity to create photos and content for the website I'm going to have designed. In the long run, it'll be worthwhile because people can look at what I've done for others and just order those. In the meantime, customers at the pizzeria are getting to sample stuff for free, which makes them tip well and come in more often.

VAUGHN: I hope there's going to be a little time for me in the midst of all this.

JULIET: Well, when you're home I could do some of the baking at your place. That way we'll be together while I work. There's lots of down time while the cupcakes are cooling and stuff like that. You can sample stuff too.

VAUGHN: I want to lick frosting off your pussy.

JULIET: Sugar isn't good for vaginas—it can cause yeast infections. But you could smear it on my boobs and then lick it off...

VAUGHN: That works for me.

JULIET: It definitely works for me. By the way, I saw your dad today.

VAUGHN: He come into the restaurant?

JULIET: He and my mom had lunch. Like, she actually sat down and ate a meal with him. I waited on them. It caused quite a stir among the regulars, wondering who Mom is dating.

VAUGHN: Oh fuck. My dad can't date your mom!

JULIET: I mean, technically he can, since none of us are related by blood, but I don't think that's what's going on. Mom has said she'll never get married again, and that they're just friends. She was quick to point out that men and women can be friends without anything else going on.

VAUGHN: You want me to talk to him?

JULIET: No! She would kill me. Don't you dare. Just when she's starting to chill out about everything.

VAUGHN: OK.

JULIET: OK, I have to go frost these cupcakes. I'll send you pictures when they're done, and you can tell me what you think.

VAUGHN: I'll call you later.

JULIET: I can't wait for you to get home.
VAUGHN: Six more days.
JULIET: And that's six too many...

I felt better about things as I put my phone away. If her mom was making friends with my dad, maybe the rest of the family would follow suit and I wouldn't have this damn knot in my stomach all the time. Maybe this was why I'd avoided relationships.

Love was a big distraction, and if I was honest I'd been distracted a lot lately. I wasn't playing bad, but I wasn't lighting it up on the ice every night either. Some of the younger guys were skating circles around me, which meant I needed to stop thinking about my personal life and get back into my game. That was easier said than done, but between my father's reappearance and spending far too much time thinking about Juliet, I was coasting through the season. For five million a year, the Knights deserved more from me. But after being alone for so long, I deserved more from life too.

With a sigh, I decided not to think about anything else tonight and just enjoy where I was and what I was doing. Everything else would either fall into place or it wouldn't.

28

JULIET

Vaughn was getting home later this afternoon, so I'd packed a bag and a bunch of my baking supplies before heading over to his place. I stopped at the grocery store first and stocked up on basics like sugar, flour, vanilla, and shortening, figuring it couldn't hurt to have what I needed at his place. My fledgling business was already taking off thanks to the ladies I'd met from the Knights, and word spread through the wives like wildfire. In fact, Tiff was hosting a "sample" party on Thursday night. It would be a chance for everyone to meet me, get a taste of what I was offering, and I could give out business cards.

A friend from high school was a graphic artist, and she'd designed them for me. They'd be ready tomorrow, and I was as excited as I'd been about anything. I hadn't realized how much I wanted to do something like this until the day my mom and I had talked it all out. Once the details were in front of me, and I got a feel for the money I could make, I'd gotten fired up. I wouldn't make that much right away, but it wouldn't take long if word-of-mouth kept going the way it had in the last week.

I pulled up to Vaughn's house and grabbed a handful of grocery bags. I walked up to the garage and punched in the code, bending down to scoot under it as it lifted. I faltered once I got inside, noting that the door that led from the garage to the kitchen was open, and Vaughn never did that because of lizards. They always got into the garage, and if you left the door open for any length of time, they'd get into the house.

It occurred to me Buzz might be here, but his truck hadn't been outside, and I hesitated as I stepped inside.

"Hello? Buzz?"

There was nothing but silence, and I fumbled for the light switch.

The sight in front of me made me take a step back in shock.

Plates and glasses were smashed on the floor, the refrigerator was open, its contents strewn across the floor, and someone had dumped out the garbage bin.

He'd been robbed.

Or at least the house had been ransacked and suddenly fear shot through me.

I dropped my groceries and ran back to my car, fumbling to get the door open and get my phone out of my purse. I called Vaughn, but his phone went right to voice mail, and I remembered he was on a plane.

I didn't know whether to call the police or try to reach his father or something else. I didn't live here, so I wasn't even sure what to say to police when they asked what I was doing here.

Without hesitation, I pulled Remy's business card out of my purse and dialed his direct line.

"Remy Knight." His deep voice nearly made me cry with relief.

"R-remy, this is, uh, Juliet. Cicero." Why was my voice shaking?

"Juliet? What's wrong? Are you okay?"

"I'm, I just got to Vaughn's house…something is wrong, and he's on a plane. I don't know what to do."

"Give me the address."

"I…" I didn't know the address, but I knew the street name. I walked outside and looked at the numbers by the front door. "Um, 3341… Bronson Road. It's in Coral Springs."

"I'm on my way. Don't do anything until I get there. And don't go back inside."

"I won't." I disconnected and then quickly called my mom. If anyone knew what to do in a crisis, it was her.

Remy pulled up in a sleek, black Lamborghini about eight minutes later. He hurried over to me, his dark eyes narrowed with concern.

"You okay?"

"Yes. I've been out here."

"I'm going to go take a look around." He went inside and a few minutes later Buzz's truck pulled up—with both Buzz and my mother in it.

"Juliet!" Mom came running toward me. "What's happening?"

"I don't know. Mr. Knight, the owner of the Knights, went inside."

"I'm going in too," Buzz said.

"Wait," I called. "Mr. Knight doesn't know you. Let me warn him." I ran to the kitchen door, feeling a lot braver with Buzz and Mr. Knight here. "Remy? Vaughn's dad is here."

"The place was definitely broken into." Remy came back to the garage. "But they're long gone."

"This isn't good," Buzz muttered.

"I'm calling the police," Remy said, pulling out his phone.

"Why didn't you call me?" Buzz asked me.

"I don't have your number," I whispered.

"Your mom does."

"I wasn't sure what to do. I knew something was wrong as soon as I walked into the kitchen, but then it occurred to me someone might still be there, so I ran outside. Then I felt stupid, like what if I was imagining it... I figured Mr. Knight would know what to do. And if we had to call the police, I wasn't sure what to say since I don't live here."

"It's all right, love." Mom put her arm around me. "Buzz was at the restaurant when you called, so I told him what was going on. We came as fast as we could." She glanced at him. "I do believe you broke some speeding laws."

Buzz smiled. "Maybe."

The police showed up a few minutes later and they asked me a lot of questions I didn't have answers to.

No, I don't know if anything is missing.

No, I don't have a key.

Yes, I have the garage door code.

I was incredibly grateful to have Remy there because the police were relentless.

"The team's flight just landed," Remy said to me after a few hours. "I spoke to Coach Petrov because I didn't want Vaughn to panic but—"

"Too late," I said, holding up my phone and showing him Vaughn's name flashing on the screen. "I'm okay," I said as I answered.

"What's going on?" Vaughn asked.

"Just come home, okay? I'm here with your dad and my mom and Remy."

"You're all at my house?"

"The house was broken into, but no one was hurt, everything is okay."

"I'm coming." He disconnected.

"He's upset," I told Remy.

"I'll stick around."

Two hours later, we sat around a table at the pizzeria and Mom went into the back to order food for all of us. It had been a long, harrowing afternoon and the police had told Vaughn not to sleep at his house tonight. They'd allowed him to take some clothes, and Remy had offered to let him stay at his house, but Vaughn had said he'd get a hotel room. Remy had gone home, and now we were trying to regroup.

"I don't get it," Vaughn said. "That's a really safe neighborhood. Everyone there has kids, and the moms are always snooping into everyone's business…I don't understand how this happened, or why they didn't take anything."

"Nothing at all?" I asked.

He shook his head. "They broke stuff, knifed my couch, dumped garbage everywhere, but didn't actually take anything. My Rolex is still in the drawer in the walk-in closet, both TVs are worth several thousand a piece, and there are some gold cuff links on my dresser that are worth a lot. All they did was ransack the place." He glanced at his dad. "Almost like it was personal."

"Okay, dinner's coming soon." Mom sank down next to Buzz. "Vaughn, you and your dad should stay with us tonight. Frankly, my nerves are a little shot, and it would be nice to have a man in the house. Peter's out of town on business, and we have plenty of room now that most of the kids have moved out."

"Is that the house you raised the family in?" Buzz asked her.

She nodded. "Yes. We bought it for a steal back in the nineties and renovated it about five years ago. It's a lot of house for me to keep up with these days, but thankfully I can afford help."

"I'll be happy to sleep on the couch if you feel better with a man in the house," Buzz said, nodding.

Vaughn frowned but then looked over at me. "You want me to stay over?"

"Of course." I reached under the table for his hand, and when his warm fingers linked with mine I felt safe for the first time all day.

"I'm really sorry you had to be the one to find the place like that," he whispered to me as Buzz and my mom chatted.

"It was a little scary, but I called Remy who came right away."

"That was nice of him," he said.

"He thinks maybe it was a disgruntled fan who somehow got your address?"

He shook his head. "I don't buy it. We're having a good season, and I've been playing well. Not my best season ever, but I'm putting up decent points, so why come after me?"

"I don't know."

"Fuck. I don't have time for this shit." He ran a hand through his already unruly hair, and I scooted closer to him.

"I can go over tomorrow and work on cleaning up. In fact, if you want to pay for it, I know several of the wait staff here who are always looking for easy money."

"I can find a service," he began.

"A service will charge a fortune, and they might talk once they get your name. No one here will say anything. And I'd be there to oversee it."

"I don't deserve you. Thank you." He leaned over to kiss me, and I sighed against his mouth.

I'd so been looking forward to getting naked tonight, but there was no way we were doing anything like that at my mom's house. Especially not with her in the next room. Well, the master suite was downstairs, and the rest of the bedrooms were upstairs, but it didn't matter.

I texted a few trusted employees, and once I explained the situation, the two who weren't working day shift tomorrow said they would help.

"I'll be there to help too," Buzz said. "Not just because you'll need the free labor, but just in case anyone is thinking about casing the joint."

"I can come for a while," Mom said. "And Desi and Michelle too."

"Really, you guys, I don't mind paying someone," Vaughn protested.

"That's not how it works in our family," I said gently. "We're there for each other. Even when we're arguing or butting heads. Family trumps everything."

"The police dusted for fingerprints," I told my mother. "We'll probably need that heavy-duty cleaner you use for the bathrooms."

She nodded. "Good idea."

"It's going to be okay," I whispered to Vaughn. "Don't stress, okay?"

"Someone just trashed my house. I'm more than stressed. I'm pissed and a little bit scared too. Not because I can't take care of myself, but because I don't know what's going on, or if this was personal. If it was a random crime, well, I've learned my lesson, and I'm going to get a top-of-the-line security system this week. But if not, then that makes me nervous. Not just for me, but for you. I don't want you at the house by yourself until I get the alarm put in, okay?"

"Don't worry. I'm not going anywhere near it alone until then."

29

M y heart hadn't stopped pounding roughly against my ribcage since Coach had told me something had happened at my house.

"No one was hurt," he'd told me. "But your home was broken into."

Knowing Juliet had found it sent me into panic overdrive, and I'd probably broken more than one traffic law getting home from the airport. And even though everything was okay now, I was pissed. Deep down, I felt this had something to do with my dad. I hadn't had even a second alone with him yet, but once I did, we were going to talk. He knew what I was thinking because he hadn't made eye contact with me once.

I finally had my chance in the morning when we were heading out to our vehicles. I had to get to practice, and he'd said he was going to his motel to change so he could help with the clean-up operation, but I paused next to his truck.

"Did that bullshit at my house have anything to do with you, Dad?" I wasn't going to beat around the bush.

Dad blew out a breath. "I don't know. I've made some inquiries."

"Why would it?"

He didn't respond and I slapped my hand down on the hood of his truck. "Dammit, Dad, tell me the fucking truth! I'm not a kid anymore. If your history with the club is blowing back on me, I need to know."

"I already told you—I don't know. I'm trying to find out."

"Jesus fucking Christ. I thought you were out."

"I'm trying to get out. It's not like working at the widget factory where I can just put in my two weeks' notice, and that's the end of it. I'm responsible for shit, and without me some of it doesn't get done, which affects the club's bottom line. And there are only two things that piss them off: Money and loyalty."

"Are you saying you need to pay them off to get out?"

"It's not black and white like that." He finally looked at me. "Listen. Son. I'm trying, okay? I just—"

"You just what?" I was suddenly done with how he talked in circles and made excuses. "Are you out or not?"

He didn't answer for what felt like a really long time. "No."

"And you came down here trying to be part of my life? Juliet's? Her fucking mom? What is this lunch date bullshit anyway? Are you fucking her mom?"

"Watch your mouth." His eyes turned black. "Don't talk about her like that."

"Dad!" I threw up my hands. "What the hell is wrong with you? You can't just date my girlfriend's mother! Mom gave up everything to protect me, and now you just come barreling into my life like a fucking hurricane. What are you trying to do to me?"

"Your mom isn't the only one who sacrificed," he growled. "I was without her just like she was without me. And frankly, I'm not the only one who left her. You started playing hockey, and that was it. Your mom was a fucking afterthought."

"I was always there for her," I snapped. "But I had to work, have a career. That's what kids do—they grow up and move away. But I was always a phone call away."

"Yeah? Were you the one holding her when she died? Or was that me?"

I stared at him. "You were with her?"

"Fuck yeah, I was with her. I loved your mom, and I love you. But you don't understand what we come from. Where I *still* come from. You think your mom walked away from what we had because she wanted to be a single mom and live on her own in New fucking Hampshire?"

"No, I don't, but that's what I don't understand. If she sacrificed so much to protect me, why are you even here? Why would you put me in the line of fire after all the years you guys tried to avoid that?"

"Because she asked me to," he snapped. "On her deathbed, she told me it was time. Even if it cost me everything, I needed to rebuild my relationship with you. And I'm trying, dammit, but everything comes at a cost."

"So this is about money? What happened at my house was a warning because they want whatever drug or gun money you get for them? How much, Dad? How much do they want to cut you loose?"

We stared each other down before he shrugged. "Doesn't matter. Cause I'm goin' back."

"You're going back to California?"

"Yup. Leaving tomorrow. I already told the boys back home. That should keep you safe, assuming they figured out who you are."

"So that's it? You just come to town, upend my whole fucking life, and then take off like you were never here?"

"I don't know what you want me to do. Your mom and I did what we did to hide your existence. Now that she's dead, I figured they wouldn't pay attention, but maybe I underestimated everything. And the only way to find out is to go back, keep an eye on things."

"That's just great, Dad. Just fucking great. You practically beg me to give you a chance, and the minute I do you pull the rug out from under me. Just like when I was a kid." I yanked out my keys, opened the door to my Corvette and turned on the ignition. I had practice in twenty minutes and didn't have time to argue with him.

When I got to my house after practice, there were at least ten cars in the driveway and parked on the street. One of them was my dad's truck, and I steeled myself. I wasn't going to fight with him or ask him to stay. I was done with that shit. I'd cried all the tears I would ever cry over that bastard when I was a kid, and my mom had cried enough for both of us. If he was going to just walk away again, I wasn't going to stop him.

I didn't know much about his world, but I knew enough to know I didn't want to be part of it. Especially not if it was going to impact me and the people I cared about. As much as I'd started to get used to having Dad around, I couldn't put Juliet, my neighbors, or even my teammates at risk. It just pissed me off that he'd come down here at all before completely pulling the plug on his affiliation with the club.

I walked inside and was surprised to see the place almost clean. All the shards of glass and china had been cleaned up, garbage thrown away, and everything that had been broken was gone. Maria was vacuuming, someone I didn't recognize was wiping down the kitchen counters, and Dad was just coming around the corner with three big bags of garbage.

"Hey, son. We're just about done here." His eyes met mine with a silent question, but I wasn't going to answer it. Not now anyway.

"Everyone's done an incredible job. I'm really grateful."

"It was our pleasure." Maria smiled at me. "Just make sure you pay the girls—they need the money."

"Of course." I'd stopped at the bank and gotten out cash since I figured they would want it but wasn't sure what Juliet had worked out with them.

"We cleaned up everything, but I don't think there's anything we can do to save your couch," Juliet said sadly, looking over at it.

"That's all right," I told her. "I'm probably going to buy something when my lease here is up, so I'll buy new stuff then."

I paid the two waitresses from the restaurant, but Juliet and her mother refused to take anything, and though Desi had been here earlier, she was already gone. Dad was avoiding eye contact again, and I forced myself to ignore him because I couldn't allow him to mess with my head. Not after how hard it had been to let him get close to me in the first place.

"I'm going to the restaurant," Maria said. She touched Dad's arm. "See you later, yes?"

"I'll be by later this afternoon," he told her.

I waited until Maria had left and then turned to him. "Have you told her you're leaving yet?"

"I will when I see her."

"You're leaving?" Juliet came up behind us, her eyes wide with confusion. "Where are you going?"

"Back to California. I think it's best that way." Dad nodded.

"I don't understand." Juliet looked at me. "I thought…" Her voice trailed off when both Dad and I were silent. "Well, I mean, we'll be sorry to see you go."

"Yeah, me too. I just don't know if this year-round beach weather is for me. I'm from Northern California, you know? We don't do heat and humidity. Anyway, I've got some errands to run, but I'll see you later." Dad grabbed his keys and left the house.

"What's going on?" Juliet asked me once he was gone.

"I don't fucking know. I'm guessing he thinks the break-in has something to do with his past."

"So he's trying to protect you."

"I'm a little tired of my parents making all these decision under the guise of protecting me," I muttered. "What about what I want? Fuck. The last two days have sucked."

"I'm sorry, babe." I moved closer to him. "Would a blow job help?"

I smiled, sliding an arm around her waist. "It might, but the security company is on their way to install the new alarm."

"Damn." I kissed him. "Well, I have to go up to the pizzeria for a few hours anyway. I'll see you later?"

"You want to go to dinner?"

"Sure. Maybe pick me up at the pizzeria, and we can go from there?"

"All right. I'll text you in a few hours." I walked her out to her car and watched her drive away.

Then I went back inside and looked around, taking in the enormity of what had happened. It felt like a violation of everything I held dear. Not just my home, but the chance that Juliet could have potentially walked in on the vandals. Would they have hurt her? Was this really about my dad's club or had it been random? My mother had once told me my father was the toughest, strongest, most resilient man she'd ever known. The only thing that had ever made him cry was the birth of his son.

And yet he was leaving that son. *Again.* As if the relationship we'd been building the last couple of months didn't matter. As if I didn't matter.

I hated how pathetic that sounded, even in my own head, but Dad leaving hurt so much it pissed me off. If the club was going to make his life difficult by coming after me, I wasn't afraid. We could fight them off together. Yet, instead of asking what I thought, or giving me a say in the matter, he was just going to cut and run.

It had felt like I was all alone in the world when my mom died; Dad going back to California after the last two months felt like he was rubbing salt in the wound.

30

Buzz came into the pizzeria around four o'clock. He sat at a table by the window and waved to me. I called to my mother as I waved back. She came bustling out and sank into the chair across from him. I was at the register, running a credit card for a customer, but I glanced over at my mom and Buzz a few times. She'd reached across the table and put one of her hands over his, and while the gesture spoke of intimacy, I didn't think it was sexual in nature. Buzz looked upset and the look on Mom's face was the same one she used when she was comforting one of us kids.

"Do you want anything?" I asked Buzz.

He shook his head. "Nah, I just came to talk to you mom and say goodbye."

"It's like you two are besties or something," I teased.

Buzz's eyes crinkled as he smiled. "Been a long time since I had a BFF."

"I don't think I've ever had one," Mom said. "We didn't use that term in my day."

"Are you coming back?" I asked Buzz pointedly.

He sighed. "I wish I knew."

"I'm not sure Vaughn is going to forgive you if you just walk away," I said softly. "He tries to pretend he doesn't need you in his life, but I think he does."

"I know he does," Buzz muttered. "But just like when he was a kid, I don't have a choice. I have to protect him, no matter what either of us want."

"Maybe it's time to stand up for what you want," Mom said gently. "Maybe it's time to say goodbye to your old life, no matter the cost."

"The cost can't be Vaughn," Buzz said. "Anything else is fair game, but if they go after him…" His voice trailed off. "Well, that's not a risk I'm willing to take."

"If you need anything, you'll call, yes?" Mom asked him.

"Of course. And same goes for you."

I was about to tell him I was going to miss him when a familiar car pulled into the parking lot.

Shit.

Why was Leonora here?

"Mom…" My voice was a harsh whisper. "Tell me you didn't invite her!"

"Invite who?" She turned in confusion.

"You didn't know Leonora was coming by?"

"What? No!" She got up, looking around.

"Hello, hello!" Leonora came bustling in like she owned the place. "I have a surprise for you guys."

Mom and Leonora hugged while I stared at what looked like a garment bag.

A big, white garment bag.

The kind often used for a wedding dress.

"Oh, crap." Buzz looked as horrified as I felt.

"Juliet." Leonora crooked a finger at me. "Come. Let me show you something."

"I'm working." I looked at my mother pointedly.

"Nora, we're busy," Mom said patiently. "Why don't you sit down and have a glass of wine? We can catch up and you can talk to Juliet later."

"All right." Leonora gave me a look but settled at a booth near the kitchen.

I went into the back and started gathering my things. Vaughn was meeting me here in about fifteen minutes, and we were supposed to go to a Mexican restaurant I loved down by the beach. I was going to hide back here until he was supposed to arrive, and then I would slip out the back and meet him outside. I didn't have the time or energy for Leonora's games, especially not after the last twenty-four hours.

I changed clothes, touched up my makeup and slid my feet into cute sandals. It was four forty now, and Vaughn had said he'd be here at a quarter to five. My phone buzzed, and I looked down.

MOM: Vaughn just pulled up!

I grabbed my purse and went out the back door. I hurried to the front of the building just as Vaughn was getting out of his car.

"Hey." He looked at me in confusion. "Where did you just come from?"

"The back. Leonora showed up unannounced and—"

"Jesus fucking Christ! Does this Carlo stuff ever end?" I'd never seen Vaughn look so annoyed about my situation, and I wasn't sure it was out of jealousy.

"Apparently not."

"Do I need to have a talk with him? Because this is getting old, Jules."

"I know. I'm sorry. I wanted to avoid another scene because—"

"Well, I need to go inside because I see my dad's truck, and I want to talk to him." Vaughn looked even more irritated now.

"I…" I blew out a breath. "I guess we can go back in if you want, but—."

"Good." He cut me off before I could mention the dress and stalked toward the entrance with me hurrying to catch up to him.

"Vaughn, slow down, please."

"Sorry." He turned to me. "I'm having a bad day."

"I understand." I slid my hand into his, and he opened the door, letting me walk in ahead of him.

We walked right over to where Buzz was sitting, and Vaughn sank down across from him.

"Dad."

"I was going to stop by later, son," Buzz said.

"I know, but I have something I want to get off my chest, and I need to do it."

"I'll let you two have some privacy," I said.

"Just a few minutes, Jules." Vaughn squeezed my hand, and I nodded.

I went to the drink station and poured myself some water, taking a long drink. What a crazy couple of days this had been. Maybe I'd been stupid not to move in with Vaughn. I was crazy about him and hadn't wanted to rush things, but I realized just how much he grounded me. My life was always busy and loud and chaotic, but never more so than since my accident. Vaughn was the one thing in my life that made sense, and it had been stupid to try to slow things down. And I was going to tell him so as soon as we left for our date tonight.

I was heading for my office, to wait for Vaughn in peace, when Leonora got up. "Juliet!"

I paused and turned to her. "Leonora, please don't make this any more difficult than it's already been."

"Nora, enough." Mom came over to us. "We can't force them to get back together."

"I know, but this is different. I have a surprise for her." Leonora was holding the damn garment bag and wiggled it.

"Please tell me you didn't buy me another dress," I groaned.

"The dress you wanted," she said, her eyes twinkling. "With the flowers and the crystals."

Oh, for fuck's sake.

I swung my gaze to my mother, who looked a little shell-shocked as she approached us. "Leonora, this isn't the time or the place for—"

"This is exactly the time and the place." Leonora glanced at Vaughn, whom I noticed was gazing over at us with that same look of annoyance he'd had since he arrived. "In fact, it's beyond time to stop this nonsense and finalize wedding plans."

"Nora, I think you've miscalculated." Mom reached for the garment bag, but Leonora appeared to be on a mission, holding on to it for dear life.

"You are the one who's miscalculated, dear Maria." She smiled triumphantly as she unzipped the garment bag and started pulling out the dress.

"Nora!" Mom was shaking her head.

"Just look at it," Nora cajoled, looking at me. "It's so pretty. Imagine how you'll feel wearing it."

"Of course it's pretty," I muttered. "I picked it. But I'm not getting married."

"Nora, knock it off." Mom snatched the dress and garment bag out of her hands. "I swear, the bunch of you have lost your minds!"

"This will get her excited," Nora protested, wilting a little bit. "Think of yourself walking down the aisle, Juliet."

"Jesus fucking Christ." I heard Vaughn's soft growl and nearly groaned to find him eyeing both me and the dress Mom was holding. Before I could think of what to do, he got up and walked out of the restaurant.

"Vaughn!" I called his name, but he kept going.

"Goddammit." I turned and ran after Vaughn, ignoring everything else. "Vaughn, wait."

"I can't do this, Jules." He stopped walking, his hands on his hips, but he didn't turn around.

"I'm sorry about this, but I don't know how else to tell them it's over between me and Carlo."

"Maybe that's because it's not. Not really."

"What?" I walked up to him and forced him to look at me. "What are you talking about?"

"You keep saying it, but in my experience actions speak louder than words, and your actions say you're half in and half out. You obviously never got around to emailing the dress shop, I know you're still getting calls about the bridesmaid dresses and the cake. Your brothers won't let up, your ex shows up every five minutes, and frankly, your mom told my dad that this is something you do. Get a wild hair, go full steam into something you want to try, and then decide you made a mistake. Am I your latest impulsive mistake?"

I stared at him. "My mom... You can't believe that's what this is."

"I don't know what to believe, Jules. I asked you to move in with me so we could spend time figuring out where we're going with this, and you said you weren't ready. That tells me a lot."

"I wanted to be sure we weren't rushing things," I protested, tears stinging my eyes.

Vaughn didn't say anything at first. "Well, whatever your rationale, I can't do this anymore. My dad is leaving, you're all wrapped in drama, my house got trashed, and we have no idea why. I don't have the energy for this. You have to sort out your relationship with Carlo, and I have to focus on hockey. I'm sorry, Juliet. Take care."

He turned and walked toward his car.

"Vaughn." I whispered his name as tears slipped down my cheeks.

He paused but didn't turn around.

Then he got in his Corvette and drove away.

31

The worst part of breaking things off with Juliet was that it didn't hurt. I felt a million other things—like anger and frustration and even a touch of self-pity—but not hurt. In fact, I was battling so many emotions, it was hard to deal with any of them. Before all hell had broken loose with Juliet at the pizzeria, I'd sat down with my dad and told him I wasn't afraid of the repercussions, and that he should stay if he wanted to. And the sanctimonious bastard had refused.

As much as it pained me to admit it, that had hurt more than I'd imagined it would. I knew the reasons why intellectually, but somewhere deep down, the little boy in me missed his dad. It made me feel like a pussy, but there was a loneliness in me I hadn't recognized until Dad and Juliet had pretty much simultaneously come into my life. And now they were both gone.

I was a mess, and it was impacting the one part of my life I rarely allowed anything to touch—hockey. I hadn't scored a goal or even managed an assist in the two weeks since everything had gone down. I was sluggish on the ice because I wasn't sleeping for shit, and my focus was nonexistent. My teammates had all noticed, and a few had reached out, asking what was wrong. But being a loner was second nature, and I had no interest in talking about my dad or Juliet.

"Are you going to be grumpy for the rest of eternity?" Palmer asked on the flight back from a quick trip to Dallas just before Christmas.

"None of your business," I muttered, putting on my headphones.

Jude nudged me with his elbow. "What crawled up your ass? Seriously, dude, you're a real downer these days."

"Sorry I'm not bringing sunshine to your life."

"You and Juliet on the outs?"

I shrugged. "It was no big thing. She's got other priorities."

"She dumped you?"

"No, she didn't dump me." I scowled. "Leave it alone, man."

"You dumped her?"

"Why do you care?"

"Because you've been a real shit the last couple of weeks, and I'm trying to be a friend. But if you'd rather I was an introverted prick like you, fine. No skin off my teeth." He put on his own headphones and opened his laptop.

Great.

Now I was not only in a bad mood, one of my teammates was mad at me too.

I wasn't sure how my life had taken a turn like this.

Three months ago I'd been enjoying training camp, excited about this new team and new city, and ready to start the season. Now it was two days before Christmas, and I had nowhere to go and nothing to do. Well, that wasn't entirely accurate. Lots of the guys were having get-togethers, and all of them had invited me to join them, but I wasn't in a very festive mood.

I hadn't heard from my dad at all, which wasn't surprising, but I'd thought he would at least let me know what he'd found out about the break-in at my house, especially if it hadn't had anything to do with him. Bad things happened, and I had a badass alarm system now, so it would've been nice for him to keep me in the loop.

That was who he was, though, and I should have known better than to get attached to him. I'd kept my distance right up until I hadn't, and then I'd suddenly taken for granted he would swing by the house or meet me for lunch. He'd ingratiated himself into Juliet's family's good graces too, or at least her mother's, and it made no sense that he would work so hard to build our relationship only to leave again.

"Vaughn." Coach stopped me as I grabbed my suitcase. "You have a minute?"

"Sure." I followed him out to the parking lot.

"You okay?" He searched my face curiously. "And don't say you're fine because there's no doubt in anyone's mind you're not. Also, my wife told me you and Juliet broke up, so I wanted to reach out, let you know I'm here if you need to get anything off your chest."

I looked at him and managed a slight shake of my head. "I don't know, man. I got hit with a double whammy—my dad leaving town and me breaking things off with Jules at the same time. I'm trying to find my footing, but after losing my mom a couple of years ago, it's hard to…" I swallowed.

"Hard to?"

"Hard to admit I'm completely alone in the world." There. I'd said it. Now even my coach would know what a fucking loser I was.

"You're not alone," he said, frowning. "Maybe we haven't known each other long, but my door is always open. I know you have friends on the team —Jude and Ryder and even Palmer. Though he probably needs a big brother more than a friend."

I managed to smile, because Palmer absolutely needed a father or big brother or something. He was a hot mess.

"Thanks, Coach. I appreciate you. I do. And everyone here is great. But it takes time to form friendships, and right now I hate everybody and everything."

"This breakup with Juliet—it's permanent? You don't care about her?"

I sighed. "No, I do. It's just her family, her ex, her wedding…"

"Her wedding?" Toli frowned. "Who is she marrying?"

"Her ex."

"When?"

"New Year's Day. I think."

"You think?"

"Look, it's a long story, and I'm tired."

He looked at me for a moment and then squinted a little. "You think she's been dating you all this time just to turn around and marry some other guy in like three weeks?"

"I don't know," I admitted. "But there have been a lot of mixed signals, and her ex is always around and… it's a lot, Coach. It's just been a fucking lot."

"So what are you going to do about it?"

"What do you mean?"

"Do you love her? And don't give me some tough-guy bullshit answer. Yes or no."

"Yes."

"Then, I repeat, what are you going to do about it?"

"I…don't know?" I wasn't sure what he was getting at.

He shook his head. "You're not going to fight for what's yours?"

"I don't think she's mine."

"Then go find out."

"How? She keeps saying she's not going to marry him, but then the wedding vendors keep calling about all the stuff that's still booked, and I don't know what the fuck is going on."

"Then perhaps, you wait until January second, and you go find out. You should have your answer by then, no?"

I just stared at him. "Yeah, I guess."

"See you later, Vaughn." He clapped me on the back, and I turned and headed for home.

I got home and dumped my mail on the counter. I needed to drop my suits off at the dry cleaner in the morning so they'd be ready before our next road trip, and I had to order some groceries for the next ten days or so since we were home until January second.

I got undressed, took a shower, and settled on the couch with my mail. Most of it was junk, there were a couple of bills, and some flyers. Nothing that mattered. Hell, right about now nothing mattered. I hated everything. I'd never missed my mom as much as I did at the moment, and I dug out the letter Dad had given me a month or two ago.

Had it only been a couple of months that he'd been back in my life? It felt like a lot longer. I would never have predicted that I'd start to miss his presence, our breakfast conversations, his showing me all the different types of tea he liked to drink. I'd had no idea how much I would miss having a dad once I had him back in my life.

I pressed my fingers against my eyes and tried to hold back tears. I really fucking hated to cry, but they snuck up on me as I re-read Mom's letter. I'd had no idea she'd known about the cancer years before she actually passed and that hurt because I could have, and should have, made more time for her. Hockey had been busy, but I'd spent my off-seasons partying with friends instead of hanging out with her in New Hampshire. She'd told me to go, to live my life, that she was fine. And I'd believed her.

God, I was such a fucking idiot.

I'd forgotten about the money she'd mentioned in the letter and had never asked my father about it. I'd thought we had time.

I really needed to talk to him but wasn't sure how to make him understand

I needed my dad more than I was afraid of his past. He supposedly had money, I had a shit-ton of my own since I'd had a money manager handling it for me since the day I'd joined the league, and we could figure out a way for him to move down here. He just had to be willing to risk it. And just like when I was a kid, that part of it was simply out of my control.

32

Haiti was hot. Like, hotter than a cast iron skillet on the asphalt in the middle of summer hot. But as I wiped the sweat dripping off my brow with a bandana, I was incredibly content.

Coming to Haiti for two weeks had been an impulsive and completely last-minute thing, but after what happened with Vaughn at the pizzeria, I'd needed to get the hell out of dodge. Chloe mentioned that she was going on some hurricane relief mission with that same non-profit she'd worked with before, and the next thing I knew I'd signed on to go too.

We'd left the week before Christmas and had been here two weeks. Today was supposed to have been my wedding day, but I'd never felt less bride-like than I did right now. I wore cut off shorts and a bikini top, my hair in a braid down my back. We'd been building shelters and medical stations for the people who'd been ravaged by a hurricane just last month, and while I was physically exhausted, I was more relaxed than I'd been since the accident.

Here in Haiti, no one knew me or my family or Carlo. No one cared about my wedding or who I was dating or anything else. They cared about tooth-brushes and sunscreen and food. They cared about picking up the broken pieces of their lives since a natural disaster had left many homeless with nothing but the clothes on their backs. And it felt good to be part of something bigger than my normal life.

"You should reapply your sunscreen," Chloe told me as we took a quick lunch break under a couple of trees.

"I will."

We chewed our peanut butter sandwiches in silence for a while. She was in the medical tent treating cases of sunburn and minor wounds while I was working on setting up the new food pantry.

"I would kill for a cold shower," Chloe muttered.

"I would kill for any shower."

"When we get done for the day, let's go for a swim," she suggested. "We've been working twelve-hour days since we got here, and a sunset swim would be fun since we're leaving tomorrow."

"Sounds great. The water should be refreshing if nothing else."

"That's for sure."

We ate in amicable silence, a faint breeze making it a tiny bit more bearable to be outside.

"How are you doing?" she asked after a moment. "For real."

"I'm pretty great right this minute," I said softly. "Coming here is exactly what I needed to clear my head. Seeing the devastation here has been eye-opening, and it feels good to do something for these people."

"Why do you think I love it so much?"

We smiled at each other.

"So what have you discovered now that you've cleared your head?" she asked.

I laughed. "If you mean, do I think I want to marry Carlo, the answer is still a resounding no."

"Actually, I wasn't talking about him at all." She wrinkled her nose. "I was thinking more about Vaughn, your cupcake business, everything with your family…"

"Well, the cupcake business is happening. I made a thousand dollars the week before we left, and I could've made a lot more if I hadn't been here leading up to New Year's. I have that birthday party coming up almost as soon as I get back, and last I checked, I had a dozen orders for Valentine's Day. So things are picking up, thanks to the women I met from the Knights."

"They've been really good to you."

"They have. And I've gotten pretty close to Peyton and Tiff."

"They weren't deterred by the fact that you and Vaughn aren't together anymore?"

"Nope. They all said it's his loss."

"They sound great. I can't wait to meet them." She paused. "Are you still going to go to Knights games?"

"I don't know." I chewed my sandwich and took a long drink of water, trying to think of what else to say since the breakup with Vaughn still hurt a lot. "I'm doing okay, but I miss him, and I think it'll be hard to see him on the ice every night knowing he didn't have enough faith in me to stick by me while I sorted out that situation with Carlo."

"What Leonora did that day was a fucking disaster," Chloe said, making a face. "I'm so glad your mom isn't speaking to her."

"Yeah, too little, too late. If she'd stepped up right away, Vaughn might not have lost it."

"Vaughn was also dealing with that situation with his dad, you know?" Her eyes met mine. "Maybe he needs time to deal with all of that before he can open himself up to something with you."

"He'd already started something with me. Then he just did an about face, and it hurts."

"I'm sorry, girlfriend. It just seems like there's more to it than him not loving you. At least that's what it sounds like to me."

"Well, whatever it was, it's a bummer because I love him." I stared out at the tent city I'd helped create. "I didn't mean to fall for him, but from the first time I laid eyes on him when he showed up at the hospital there was something special about him. I felt it right away and he said he did too. And you know what's most frustrating of all? He asked me to move in with him, and I said no because I wanted to make sure I was emotionally ready to take things to the next level, after the amnesia, ending the engagement, all of that. I wanted to be sure I was giving us the best chance possible at making this work. Instead, when we were breaking up, he held it against me."

"I know he hurt you, but from what you've told me, it sounds like he was hurting too."

I sighed. I didn't want to think about Vaughn's pain because it was hard enough to deal with my own. The scene at the restaurant that day had gotten ugly after Vaughn left. I'd been hurt and furious, so when I'd gone back inside, I'd lost it. I'd screamed at Nora to get out, and then I'd taken the wedding dress bag and stuffed the whole thing in the dumpster out back. There had been tears and harsh words, and then I'd quit my job.

Sort of.

I was part owner, so it was hard to quit something I owned, but in retrospect, I'd been a little hysterical that day. And it was the first time in years Tony had stood up for me. He'd come out of the back right in the middle of my tirade and had kicked out Leonora, telling her to back the fuck off. It had been a long time since I'd felt like my big brother cared about me, but he'd come through in a big way.

"What are you going to do when you get back?" Chloe asked.

"I'm going to cut my hours at the pizzeria in half," I told her. "Along with my salary. I'll still run the business side of things, like payroll and ordering supplies and stuff, but I'm not working out front anymore. Definitely not working weekends. Fuck that. I'm going to expand the business from just cupcakes to cupcakes and custom cookies, and that's going to take time."

"What about Vaughn?"

"There is no Vaughn," I said sadly. "He's the one that broke it off, Chloe. Not me."

"You don't think he might come around now that he's had time to cool off?"

"I don't know, and right now I don't care." I got to my feet. "I have pantry shelves to stock and little kids waiting for popsicles to freeze so they have a treat this afternoon. The last thing I want to think about is my broken heart or the guy who broke it."

"Well, then, you do you, girlfriend."

"What about you?" I countered. "Are we ever going to talk about this medical school situation?"

She rolled her eyes. "Not if I can help it."

"Chloe, you'd just started your residency when you just bailed to join this non-profit. On top of that, you're still not sure you want to be a doctor—how can you avoid talking about it?"

"By taking time off to go on missions and leaving my mark on the world in a different way."

"But you're so close…don't you want those letters after your name?"

"What? MD? Why? I mean, calling me Dr. Haverty is nice, but it doesn't change who I am or the things I want to accomplish."

"I thought you wanted to be a pediatrician."

"I don't know what I want to do right now," she said quietly. "But the good news is that I don't have to make any big decisions until July. That's when my residency will start again."

"Sticking your head in the sand won't make the decisions any easier."

"No, but absolutely nothing is going to change or be decided while we're here in Haiti, and this is probably the one and only time I'll ever be on a mission with you, so let's not ruin it? Deal?"

"Fine." I chuckled.

She smiled at me, dusted off her scrubs, and walked toward the medical tent as I went in the opposite direction.

One of the nice things about having a bestie was that we each understood when to push something and when to leave it alone. Right now, we both had things we needed to leave alone. At least until we got back to Lauderdale.

33

I woke up on the second day of January with a knot in my stomach.

I'd thought of very little but Juliet the last few days. I'd driven past the pizzeria at least half a dozen times, but her car was never out front, and I didn't have the balls to walk in and ask where she was. I'd thought about calling or texting, but I wasn't sure what to say. Coach had been right that the truth, or at least the biggest part of it, would come out on New Year's Day. Either she was marrying Carlo, or she wasn't.

One way or the other, I had to get some closure because being without her sucked. I hadn't thought she'd broken my heart because I'd been too distracted with all the bullshit about my dad to really let it sink in that I'd ended it between us. Now that we'd been apart for several weeks, I missed her every minute of every day. The thought of her marrying Carlo made me crazy.

I had to get through practice first, and then I was going to go to the pizzeria and flat-out ask someone. Even one of the waitresses would know, and I had to get answers. The simplest thing would be for me to ask her, but I couldn't bring myself to do it.

Of course, I had no plan for what I would do if she hadn't gotten married because that meant I'd been a total asshole to her, so I was beyond distracted. Luckily, Coach kept practice short, and I practically raced through my shower.

I pulled on jeans and a T-shirt and grabbed my bag, nearly knocking into Jude in my haste to get going.

"Sorry," I said to him.

"Where are you going all fired up like this?"

I hesitated. I really needed a wingman today, but I'd been such a dick to him lately, I wasn't sure he'd be willing. "I, um, you busy today?"

He gave me a look. "Not particularly. Why?"

"Can you take a ride with me?"

"Sure. Where we goin'?"

"Can you just come along without asking a lot of questions?"

"Are we going to do something illegal?"

"No."

"Okay, then. I'm in. Let me get my shit."

We'd just gotten into the hallway when Coach came around the corner and motioned to me.

"What's up, Coach? I'm kind of in a hurry."

"Yeah, I know." He leaned against the wall and eyed me. "Today is January second."

"I'll wait for you outside," Jude said.

"No, it's okay. I don't think this is hockey related."

"No." Coach hesitated. "So I'm breaking a huge code of honor between married couples, but I'm doing it because I know how heavy this is weighing on you."

"Does Tessa know something about the wedding?" I asked, my voice a little rough.

"There was no wedding," Coach said, shaking his head. "There was never going to be a wedding. Not since the day you hit her with that slap shot. In fact, Juliet is in Haiti right now."

"Haiti?" I stared at him in confusion.

"I don't know the details." He made a face. "Something about hurricane relief? She and her friend, the doctor?"

"Chloe," I supplied, as if that gave us information we needed.

"Yes. Juliet and Chloe are in Haiti helping people who lost everything after the hurricane. They're coming back tonight."

"Wait a minute," Jude stage whispered. "Is that what we were going to do? Go watch your ex get married or something? Dude, you're a dumbass. I could've told you she wasn't marrying him. She might not be into *you*—I don't know—but she definitely wasn't into him."

I gave him a look, and he raised his hands in mock surrender. "Sorry."

"Now, if I were you," Coach continued casually. "I would go up to her family's restaurant for lunch. If you're smooth, which you obviously aren't but maybe Jude can help you, you can find out what flight she's on and pick her up from the airport. Then you can grovel and explain how stupid you are. Maybe she'll forgive you, and then you'll stop being such a pain in my ass."

"All of our asses," Jude said, nodding.

I stared at him. "Really? You think that would work?"

Coach looked at Jude. "You have more game with women than this guy? He needs a wingman."

"Yeah, I got this. Let's go." Jude nudged me.

"Where we goin'?" Palmer asked, falling into step beside us.

"Nowhere," I grunted.

"Lunch," Jude said at the same time.

"Take him along," Coach called after us. "He could use some lessons too."

"Lessons in what?" Palmer asked amiably.

"You're driving," I told him since I knew he had a big SUV that all of us could fit in.

"Cool. My SUV is awesome." Palmer really was a good kid.

In the end, by the time we got going, six of us headed off to Cicero's for lunch. Ryder came along because Peyton and the baby were in Buffalo visiting family. Felix came with us because he didn't have anything to do, and Cam joined in because he happened to overhear us in the parking lot. I wasn't sure if having five wingmen was a good thing, but we'd just pulled up, so I didn't have much of a choice.

"You guys need to play it cool," I said as we headed for the entrance. "Juliet's brothers work in the back, sometimes her sisters-in-law help waiting tables, and her mom is always there during the day. Please don't embarrass me because this is important." I cleared my throat. "She's important. After this is all over, you can give me all the shit you want, but not today. Not when I've got to figure out how to get her to forgive me."

"We've got your back, or we wouldn't be here," Ryder said. "But giving you shit later on is going to be epic."

"I'm hungry," Palmer said. "Can we just go inside?"

We walked in and the hostess looked up with a smile, obviously recognizing me from the times I'd come in to pick up Juliet. "Hey, Vaughn. Six of you today?"

"Yeah. Thanks, Shelley."

She sat us in the back and brought us menus.

"Is the calzone good?" Palmer asked me.

"Everything I've had here is good," I told him.

"Of course it is." Maria's voice was distinct, and I slowly turned to say hello.

"Hi, Mrs. Cicero."

"Vaughn." She fixed me with the type of glare only a mom could give, and I wilted a little.

She was pissed, which probably didn't bode well for me.

"Can we get a pitcher of soda?" Ryder asked when the silence between me and Juliet's mom got awkward. "Six glasses. And I want deep dish pizza. With pepperoni."

Everyone immediately jumped in, placing their orders even though we'd barely had time to look at the menu.

"Calzone," I said absently. "With bacon and pepperoni."

Mrs. Cicero nodded and turned her back on us.

"Yikes, you're in big trouble," Palmer stage whispered. "What did you do to her?"

"That's Juliet's mom." I'd filled him in on the basics on the drive over.

"Oops." He grimaced. "My balls shriveled right up when she gave you that look."

"Tell me about it." I stared at her retreating back, suddenly regretting my decision to come here.

"Look, just man up," Jude said under his breath. "Go over there and ask her if she has a few minutes. Do it."

"Yes." Felix nodded. "That's the way to go."

"She can't hurt you too bad in public," Palmer added.

The other guys all gave him a look and he slunk down in his chair.

"Okay, I have to do this." I took a breath. "Why does it feel like I'm walking to the guillotine or something?"

"Moms have that effect," Ryder said. "But you got this. Go find out what you need to know."

I stood up and approached Juliet's mom, wondering how the hell I was going to make this right. Even though I could have, and should have, reached out directly to Juliet, deep down I felt like I had to make the first move with her mother. Juliet had gone through a lot of changes since I'd first met her, but she had a special relationship with her family, no matter how much they pissed her off sometimes.

"Mrs. Cicero, do you have a minute?"

"It's lunchtime," she said. "I'm busy."

"Have you talked to my dad?" I blurted out.

She nodded. "Yes."

"Is he, uh, doing okay?"

She turned slowly. "You haven't spoken to him?"

"He hasn't reached out at all. I'm a little worried, but more pissed that he just walked away. Again."

"He has a lot on his plate," she said in a much gentler tone. "He'll get in touch. Don't give up on him."

I snorted. "I gave up on him a long time ago. I was just starting to trust him again and then…" I sighed. "It's been a rough few weeks."

"Not just for you." Her gaze sharpened, and I realized she wasn't going to make this easy on me.

"I wanted to ask about Juliet," I said finally. "How she is. When she's getting back."

"I spoke to her last night, and she's fine. She arrives tonight."

"I screwed up," I said finally. "The whole thing with my dad hit me hard, and I took it out on her. But I love her, Mrs. Cicero. And I'll do anything to make it right."

"Why are you telling me? I'm not the one you need to apologize to."

"Because your approval is important to her. She's strong enough and independent enough to do whatever she wants, but she still needs to know you love and support her."

"She already knows this. Even when we're angry or actively arguing, she knows I love and support her. It's unconditional."

"I'd like to pick her up at the airport," I said finally. "I need to talk to her, explain what was going on that day. How fu—er, messed up I was when my dad said he was leaving."

"Your father is also too stubborn for his own good," she said lightly. "But give me your number, and I'll text you the flight information."

I frowned. "That's it? You're not going to make me beg or grovel or anything?"

She chuckled. "That's Juliet's job. Me, I just have to sit back and watch. Figuratively speaking, of course."

"That might be the scariest thing anyone's ever said to me."

"Love is scary. Relationships are scary. Marriage is terrifying. You'll see."

I pulled out my phone. "Tell me your number, and I'll text you. Then you'll have mine."

She recited the digits, and I typed them in. Then I texted her.

"I'll text you as soon as I finish putting in this order. Now go back to the table. Your friends are going to hurt themselves trying to eavesdrop."

34

JULIET

The flight from Haiti landed in Fort Lauderdale a little after ten. There had been a weather delay so our eight thirty arrival turned into ten fifteen, and I was exhausted. My time in Haiti had been amazing, the best thing I could have done after the breakup with Vaughn, but reality was setting in, and I just wanted a hot shower and a good night's sleep. Tomorrow I had to get back to my regular life, and without Vaughn it had lost a bit of its luster. I'd checked my website on the flight since there had been Wi-Fi, and there were ten emails from potential customers wanting quotes and availability, so at least two weeks off the grid hadn't ruined my business.

"Peter's going to take me home, right?" Chloe asked.

"I'm sure he will. Unless you want to crash at my place?"

"No offense, girlfriend, but I want my own bed, my own shower…"

"Oh, I hear you." After clearing customs, we walked through the terminal without saying much. We headed for baggage claim, and I got out my phone, looking for a text from Peter since he was supposed to be picking us up.

"Nothing from Peter," I murmured. "I wonder if he's running late."

"Mm, I don't think so." Chloe's voice was filled with amusement.

"What? Why?" I looked at her in confusion.

Then I followed her gaze and froze.

Vaughn was standing near our baggage carousel with a huge bouquet of roses in his hands, looking right at me.

"Oh my god." I was frozen in place, unsure what to do or how to keep walking.

"Looks like someone came to apologize," she whispered. "Why are you just standing here?"

"I…" I swallowed hard and met Vaughn's gaze from across the room.

"Hi," he mouthed.

I took a tentative step forward.

"I'll go get our bags," Chloe said, finally moving past me.

I took some more steps and finally stopped a few feet away from Vaughn.

I couldn't believe he was here.

"What, uh, why are you here?" I blurted out.

"I owe you an apology." His dark eyes were filled with regret.

"Okay." I wasn't going to make this easy on him because I truly had never expected to see him again.

"The day I broke things off was a bad day," he said, taking a step closer to me and proffering the flowers.

I unconsciously reached for them and brought them to my nose, taking a deep whiff. "Thank you," I whispered.

"You're welcome." He came a little closer. "When my dad and I talked, I basically asked him to stay. I told him we'd find a way to cut his ties with the club, that I could protect myself, and I even offered to let him move in. And he basically said no. That he wasn't going to take the risk. I knew he was just trying to protect me, but I'm so tired of hearing that. My mom talked about it my whole life, he talked about it the whole time he was here, and it felt like something inside of me…broke." His voice cracked a little and most of my irritation melted away.

I was still mad about what he'd done to me but hearing him admit how much his father hurt him hurt me too. I'd lost my dad and would have given anything to have more time with him, so I felt his pain almost as if it were my own.

"I'm sorry about your dad," I said quietly. "That had to hurt."

"But I shouldn't have taken it out on you," he said quickly. "It was just too much all at once. Carlo's mom was being so bitchy and dramatic. They were parading around your wedding dress, as if it were a foregone conclusion that this wedding was happening, and I couldn't deal with it. I love you, Juliet. The thought of you marrying someone else ripped me up inside, so all I could think about was getting away. From the situation, from the pain, from *you*. And I'm really, really sorry."

Holy shit, he'd just said he loved me.

Was I hearing things?

"You love me?" I asked softly, and this time I was the one who inched closer to him, my eyes never leaving his.

"I do." He extended an arm, pulling me even closer. "I know I fucked up, but I'll do anything to make it up to you. To get a second chance."

"I told you repeatedly I was never going back to him," I said, trying to make sure he understood how much it hurt me that he hadn't trusted me. "If you don't have faith in me, and don't believe me when I tell you something, we can't be together."

"I do trust you. It was a momentary lapse of judgement. It was a rough day, but if you give me another chance I swear to you it'll never happen again. Not like that anyway."

I looked up at him and there was a promise in his eyes I'd never seen before. Not with him, and certainly not with Carlo, but it was a look that told me far more than his words did. It was the look of a man in love. I recognized it because it was almost the same look my father always had when he looked at my mother, and tears sprung to my eyes.

"Jules?" He was still looking at me intently, his eyes dark and warm and sweet.

"When we have rough days, we're supposed to weather them together," I whispered.

"I know." He gently pulled me against him. "I'm sorry. I love you."

"I love you too."

I watched his face as he leaned down and capture my mouth with his. It was sweet and sexy and just like the look in his eyes, it spoke of more than sex. This was a kiss filled with romance, tenderness, and forever. As his tongue sought out mine, my body gave in, and I melted against him, oblivious to the crowded airport.

"Okay, you two, I can't stand here with this luggage forever." Chloe's voice broke us apart, and we turned.

"Sorry." I smiled at her. "Chloe, this is Vaughn Elliott. Vaughn, this is my best friend, Chloe."

"Nice to finally meet you." Vaughn shook her hand. "I've heard a lot about you."

"Likewise." Her eyes twinkled, and we all laughed.

"So my understanding is I'm taking you home, Chloe?"

"If you don't mind? My bed is super lonely, and I need to go show it some attention."

He laughed. "Gotcha. Just give me directions. Let's get out of here." He grabbed both of our suitcases, and we headed out to the parking garage.

Much later, after I'd showered and we'd made love, I snuggled against Vaughn in his bed, warm and happy and sated. I'd texted my mom to let her know I wouldn't be home tonight, and now I was drowsy but too excited to sleep. Vaughn's big, warm hands were stroking my skin, making me shiver with pleasure, and I couldn't help but nestle deep against his chest, despite the myriad thoughts running through my head.

"You need to go again?" he asked after a moment. "I can feel you fidgeting like you can't relax."

"I'm just happy. And excited." I lifted my head to look at him. "I have so much going on, but I've had a thought."

"Oh?"

"I'm ready to move in."

"Really." He seemed amused by that.

"What's funny?" I asked.

"You. You're cute when you're excited. And I was ready for you to move in weeks ago. So just let me know when you want to go get your stuff."

"The only problem is the kitchen."

"The kitchen?"

"I need double ovens."

"Well, I have a solution. I heard from the police a few days ago. Turns out, there were a group of teens going around vandalizing houses in the neighborhood. They did two more before they got caught, so now we know it had nothing to do with my dad."

"That's wonderful, but how does that solve my kitchen issue?"

"I'm using it as an excuse to get out of my lease early. So we can start looking for a house now. As soon as we find one that fits all our needs, including your kitchen, I'll buy it and we'll move."

"Oh my god, that's awesome." I snuggled against his chest. "Until then, though, I'll probably have to do a lot of the baking at my mom's."

"That's okay, babe. Whatever you need to do, we'll make it work."

"And also… would you be willing to do some charity work over the summer, like I did in Haiti? Chloe is planning to do as much as she can until July when she starts her residency again, and I'd like to go with her a few times a year. It felt amazing to be able to help out like that."

"I'd love that," he said softly. "It has to be in the off-season, but I'll absolutely go with you when I can."

"One of a thousand reasons I love you."

"Just a thousand?"

I chuckled. "How many reasons are there that you love me?"

"At least a billion. Maybe more."

"I think you're exaggerating."

"You could be right." He tightened his arms around me. "But there are lots and lots of things about you that I love."

"Ditto." I settled against him again, finally starting to quiet my brain by focusing on him. His warmth. His steady heartbeat. His deep, quiet breathing. Holy shit, he'd fallen asleep. I smiled to myself, thinking this was exactly what I'd always envisioned for myself when it came to the man I loved.

And with his strong arms around me, I drifted off to sleep.

EPILOGUE

A MONTH LATER

J*uliet*

I'd been baking all day, and I quickly packed up the last of the cupcakes. I had ten dozen cupcakes to get out tomorrow. All but three dozen were decorated, but I could do those in the morning. I had to be at the Knights game in a little while, and cupcakes or no cupcakes, I'd have to be on my death bed before I'd miss a game.

Things with Vaughn and I were better than I'd ever imagined, and I'd officially moved in last weekend. I still spent tons of time at my mom's since I baked in her kitchen at least three days a week, and today had been busy. I'd been at it since eight o'clock this morning and still had more to do, but it would wait until morning. Vaughn was leaving on a road trip, so I would probably just sleep here at my mom's tonight so I could get up and get to it.

"Hey, are you ready?" Chloe came into the kitchen with her hands on her hips. She'd come over to help me this afternoon since we were going to the game together. This was the first time it had worked out with her schedule that she could go with me, and I was excited to introduce her to the wives and girlfriends I'd become friends with.

"Just about."

"Would you go touch up your makeup?" she demanded. "And there's powdered sugar on your clothes."

"I'm going to change real quick. Give me five minutes." I hurried upstairs to my old room to freshen up, change clothes, and try to tame my hair a little. Vaughn said he loved the wild waves and the way it was always out of control, but it drove me crazy. Most of the other wives and girlfriends had sleek, shiny hair, which seemed to be in style right now, but that was way too much work. I didn't have time for that kind of hair care, so I hoped Vaughn really did like it this way.

Chloe had her car keys in her hand, and we'd just walked outside when a familiar black pick-up pulled into the driveway.

"Holy shit," I murmured. "It's Buzz."

"Vaughn's dad?" she asked in confusion. "And is that your mom with him?"

"It appears to be." I ran forward to greet Buzz as he got out of his truck, hugging him tightly.

"Well, you're a sight for sore eyes." I told him. "Vaughn didn't mention you were coming back."

He met my gaze. "I, uh, haven't told him."

"Yes, yes." Mom looked impatient. "Juliet, can you call one of your friends from the team and get us passes or whatever they are, so we can go to the lounge after the game? Buzz didn't want to say anything to Vaughn until after the game, since he's been playing so well the last few weeks."

"Uh, yeah, sure." I pulled out my phone and texted Tessa, telling her what was going on.

"Are you going too?" I asked my mother.

"Of course." She looked offended that I would even consider anything else.

"Okay, give me a minute." I texted with Tessa while Mom introduced Buzz to Chloe and finally I nodded. "Okay, Tessa talked to Toli and there are tickets and passes waiting for you guys at Will Call."

"Perfect. Let's go." Mom looked excited.

"Mom, have you ever been to a hockey game?"

"Not a professional game, but it's time, no? My future son-in-law is a professional hockey player."

"Mom, we're not engaged," I said, shaking my head. "Don't do that."

"You're living together. You love each other. What else is there? Marriage is coming, mark my words. Now let's go!" She turned to get into Buzz's truck, but then looked back at me. "Is there a place at the arena I can buy a jersey?"

My mouth dropped open, but I snapped it shut again. "Yes. We can get you one."

"Good." She got in Buzz's truck, and I looked over at him.

"You know how to get there, or you want to follow us?"

"I'll follow you," he said.

"Okay." I smiled and got into Chloe's car.

"Tonight is going to be interesting," she said.

"You can say that again." I just hoped it would be interesting in a good way and not in a way that upset Vaughn. He'd reached out to his father several times, but Buzz hadn't responded except to say he was okay, and he'd be in touch. Then radio silence. I knew Vaughn had all but written him off, so this would be quite the surprise.

V*aughn*

I'd been having a hell of a season since Juliet and I got back together. I'd scored at least one goal a game, we'd won nine out of the last ten, and one of the sports stations had named me NHL player of the month. It was nice to be on top, and even nicer to have Juliet at my side.

Tonight was no exception, and we brutalized the team from San Jose with an 8-2 win. So I was in a great mood as I headed back toward the family lounge after the game. Jude fell into step beside me, giving me a little grin.

"Did you say Juliet was bringing her friend with her tonight? The blond you told me about?"

"Yup."

"Dude, you didn't say anything, did you? Like, I don't want it to be awkward if I don't think she's hot."

I rolled my eyes. "You think I'd even mention it to you if she wasn't hot?"

"Yeah, but hot is subjective. You might think she's hot, but maybe I won't."

"If you don't think she's hot, I'm literally going to ask her to go out with Palmer, just to show you what a douche you are."

Jude laughed. "Whatever, man."

We rounded the corner, and I saw Juliet right away, her dark eyes shining as she came toward me.

"Hi." She threw her arms around my neck, a little breathless as she kissed me.

"Hi." I slid an arm around her waist. "What's got you so excited?"

"There's a surprise for you in the lounge, and I just want you to keep an open mind, okay?"

I frowned. "Babe?"

"Promise?"

"I promise." I had no idea what she was talking about, but I took her hand as we walked into the lounge.

And I immediately froze because I saw my father right away.

He was taller than almost anyone else in the room, so he was hard to miss. Even though he'd cut his hair short and shaved his beard so it was cropped close to his skin. He looked like a different man in jeans and a Knights jersey, and I approached him slowly.

"Dad."

"Hey, Vaughn." He smiled. "Great game."

"Thanks. What are you doing here?"

"He needs to talk to you." Maria, as she'd told me to call her, spoke up from next to him.

"I figured. But I can't leave just yet," I told him.

"I know. I just, I was really excited to see you play."

"It's so fast," Maria said, fanning herself. "I was completely lost. How do you follow the puck? It's very confusing. Also, there were no fights. I thought fighting was part of hockey?"

"Mom." Juliet slid an arm around her mother's waist. "You can ask him all that next week at Sunday dinner. Tonight, he needs to talk to his father."

"Vaughn." Coach came up behind us, and I turned at the sound of his voice. "Buzz."

"Nice to see you again." My dad held out his hand and they shook.

The two men started talking hockey and I watched them curiously.

I was a little flustered, unsure why Dad was here or what we had to talk about. His change in appearance was confusing too. I didn't dare get my hopes up, but it felt like something big had changed, and I was anxious to find out what it was. Maria seemed to be bubbling with excitement, which was entertaining in itself, so I tried not to overthink things as I introduced my father to more of my teammates. What else could I do?

"Hey." Jude whispered in my ear. "Are you going to introduce me to Chloe or what?"

"I thought you were worried she wasn't hot?" I smirked at him because I'd known the moment I'd met her that any number of my teammates would find her attractive. She was tall and blond with striking features and gorgeous blue eyes. I was crazy in love with Juliet, but Chloe was one of those women who was hard to miss. I figured if she came to a few games, at least one of my teammates would try to get in her pants. Chloe had said she had no time or interest in a serious boyfriend, but that she wouldn't mind getting to know some of my friends.

As I'd predicted, she was currently surrounded by Palmer, Cam, and Felix.

"You're behind," I told Jude as we approached them.

"They save the best for last," he said, grinning.

I introduced everyone, but I kept looking around for my dad, as if he might disappear. He seemed content to hang out with Coach Petrov, Maria at his side, and it was oddly comfortable to have them both here tonight.

The team had to be at the airport at nine in the morning, and I still had to finish packing and get some rest, so I finally approached my dad to find out what his plans were.

"I'm leaving in the morning," I told him. "But I feel like we have a lot to talk about."

"I want to move to Fort Lauderdale," he said quietly. "If you'd rather I didn't, just say so. I've left the club, for good, and I'm free and clear from all of that."

"How did you get out?"

He shook his head as he glanced around. "Doesn't matter."

"Yeah, Dad, it does."

"The long and short of it is, I used the money your mom and I had put aside in case we ever needed to run. Essentially, I bought my freedom."

"How much money?"

He looked away. "A lot. Everything I had. I've got my truck and a few thousand in the bank and that's it. But I'm lucky all they wanted was money. Usually, it's not that simple. I did eight years in prison for the club, though, so they owe me, and I made sure they knew it."

"Money doesn't matter," I said slowly. "I have plenty. I just… I guess I want to know what you're going to do. Are you going to stay? Get a job? What?"

"I'm a felon, so finding a job will be hard, but Maria said she can hire me to bus tables and be a sort of maintenance man at the pizzeria. It's not a lot of money, but I don't need a lot."

"Again, money isn't the issue. You are. We are." I blew out a breath.

"Son, you're a grown man, so I don't know that you need a dad at this stage of your life but—"

"Of course I need a dad!" I hissed under my breath. "I've never had one so it's about time."

"If you need a dad, then that's what I'll be. I just want to be in your life. Whether it's as your dad, a distant relative, a friend. You're all I have left, son."

"I have Juliet and her family now, but it looks like they've adopted you as well." I gazed over to where Maria and Juliet were laughing at something Coach was telling them.

He smiled. "Me and Maria—it's not what you're thinking. It's really not. We're both lonely, but we know how weird it would be for you kids if we hooked up, so we agreed we can be friends. Someone to talk to and hang out with who understands what it's like to lose the love of your life far too young. That's all it is. And Juliet, she's a sweet, smart girl. Perfect for you. I'm excited to see you two get married and start a family." He paused. "I'm kind of hoping I can take on the role of grandpa at some point."

"That's a few years away, I think," I told him. "But I can work with this."

"I love you, son." Dad looked down, as if saying the words out loud embarrassed him. "All I want is to be in your life in some way. I know we still have a lot to work through, but I'm here for it if that's what you want."

I stared at him for a long time and as we stood there looking at each other, years of pain and longing seemed to slip away. I'd loved him. I'd hated him. I'd missed him. And now he was here. I didn't need a parent, but I absolutely needed my dad. Now more than ever, as I set out on this new level of relationship with Juliet.

"I do," I said finally. "I really do."

"Babe, it's almost midnight," Juliet said softly, coming over to join us. "You need to get some rest."

"I'm going to stay at Maria's for a few days," Dad said. "In the guest room."

"You should stay at Vaughn's house," Juliet told him. "I have a ton of baking to do, so I'm going to stay at my mom's while Vaughn's gone anyway."

"I don't want to put you out of your own house," he said quickly.

"No, it's not like that at all. I was staying at mom's this week regardless. I'm super busy between keeping up with orders, doing the actual baking and decorating, and then making deliveries. Believe me, I don't have time to breathe."

"You know," Vaughn said thoughtfully. "Maybe Dad could help you with deliveries."

"I could," Dad said enthusiastically. "It'll help me learn my way around better."

"Then it's settled," Maria said, nodding. "Now, Vaughn has to rest, Juliet and Vaughn need to say goodbye, and Chloe also has to get home. Shall we go?"

"We should," I said, taking Juliet's hand. "I'll take Juliet home. Dad, I'll see you when I get back?"

"You will."

For the first time in a long time, I reached out and hugged him.

He held on for all he was worth, and I had to work hard to force back all the emotions I was feeling. Then I looked over at Juliet and there were tears in her eyes as she watched us.

"I love you," she mouthed.

"I love you too."

Thank you for reading Slap Shot and diving into the world of the Lauderdale Knights! If you'd like more, get ready for Big Shot! More info on the next page.

BIG SHOT

Welcome to Fort Lauderdale—where the days are hot and the Knights are hotter.

Jude:

I've always said I would settle down when the time—and the woman—was right. So having a friends-with-benefits relationship fits right into my plans. Until it doesn't. The line between friendship and wanting more with the gorgeous doctor is blurring with each passing day. The more I get to know her, the harder it gets to stay away. I need to show Chloe there's more to us than just chemistry… but first I have to admit it to myself.

Chloe:

I thought I had my life all mapped out. College, medical school, and then a demanding career as a successful doctor. Now I'm having doubts about all of it, and the last thing I need is a professional athlete with abs for days to add to my distraction and derail my plans. Falling for a big shot hockey player like Jude would be a mistake. But everything is so good between us— there's no way I can just walk away.

Flip the page for buy links for this and all my other books!

ALSO BY KAT MIZERA

Las Vegas Sidewinders:

Dominic

Cody's Christmas Surprise

Drake

Karl

Anatoli

Zakk

Toli & Tessa

Brock

Vladimir

Royce

Nate

Sidewinders: Ever After

Jared

Dmitri's Christmas Angel

Ian

Dax *(A Royal Protectors/Sidewinders crossover novel)*

Suze's Diary (A Sidewinders Companion Novella)

Sidewinders: Generations:

Zaan

Tore

Anton

Van

Decker

Alaska Blizzard:

Defending Dani

Holding Hailey

Winning Whitney

Losing Laurel

Saving Sara

Chasing Charli

A Very Blizzard Christmas

Tending Tara

Calling Cassie

Playing Peyton

Catching Lana (An Alaska Blizzard Companion Novel)

St. Louis Mavericks (with Brenda Rothert)

Hard Fall

Hard Limit

Hard Pass

Hard Luck

Hard Hit

Lauderdale Knights:

Knight Before Christmas (A Garland Grove/Lauderdale Knights holiday novel)

Slap Shot

Big Shot

Long Shot

Hot Shot

Sure Shot

Rough Shot

Cheap Shot

Rock Hard:

Play

Pause

Rewind

Fast Forward

Rock Harder:

Rock Bottom

Rock God

Rock Steady

The Royal Trilogy:

Nowhere Left to Fall

Nowhere Left to Run

Nowhere Left to Hide

Royal Protectors:

Sandor

Cocky Protector (book 1.5, part of the Cocky Heroes Club series)

Xander

Axel

Dax (A Royal Protectors/Sidewinders crossover novel)

Inferno:

Salvation's Inferno

Temptation's Inferno

Redemption's Inferno

Tropical Inferno (formerly "Tropical Ice")

Romancing Europe:

Adonis in Athens

Smitten in Santorini

Lucky in Lugano

View Kat's entire collection of books at www.KatMizera.com

ABOUT THE AUTHOR

USA Today Bestselling author Kat Mizera was born in Miami Beach with a healthy dose of wanderlust. She's lived from coast to coast, and everywhere in between, but home is wherever her family is.

A devoted mom and wife to her wonderful and supportive husband (Kevin) and two amazing boys (Nick and Max), Kat loves to travel the globe with her adventurous, hockey loving family. Greece is at the top of that list. She hopes to one day retire there, spending her days writing books on the beach.

Kat is former freelance sports writer who now writes steamy hockey romance about her favorite fictional teams, the Las Vegas Sidewinders and the Alaska Blizzard. The library of novels she's penned also include sexy contemporary stories about baseball stars, alpha sex club owners, special forces heroes, rock stars and royalty. Regardless of genre, her books about bad boys with hearts of gold will steal your breath, rock your world and melt your heart.

WHERE TO FOLLOW KAT:

WEBSITE
FACEBOOK
TWITTER
INSTAGRAM
BOOKBUB
KAT'S PRIVATE FACEBOOK GROUP

9 781963 997026